Easy

tammara webber

Easy

BERKLEY

THE BERKLEY PUBLISHING GROUP
Published by the Penguin Group
Penguin Group (USA) Inc.
375 Hudson Street, New York, New York 10014, USA

Penguin Group (Canada), 90 Eglinton Avenue East, Suite 700, Toronto, Ontario M4P 2Y3, Canada (a division of Pearson Penguin Canada Inc.) * Penguin Books Ltd., 80 Strand, London WC2R 0RL, England * Penguin Group Ireland, 25 St. Stephen's Green, Dublin 2, Ireland (a division of Penguin Books Ltd.) * Penguin Group (Australia), 707 Collins Street, Melbourne, Victoria 3008, Australia (a division of Pearson Australia Group Pty. Ltd.) * Penguin Books India Pvt. Ltd., 11 Community Centre, Panchsheel Park, New Delhi—110 017, India * Penguin Group (NZ), 67 Apollo Drive, Rosedale, Auckland 0632, New Zealand (a division of Pearson New Zealand Ltd.) * Penguin Books, Rosebank Office Park, 181 Jan Smuts Avenue, Parktown North 2193, South Africa * Penguin China, B7 Jaiming Center, 27 East Third Ring Road North, Chaoyang District, Beijing 100020, China

Penguin Books Ltd., Registered Offices: 80 Strand, London WC2R 0RL, England

EASY

Cover design by Jeanine Henderson and Stephanie Mooney.
Interior text design by Jeanine Henderson.

PUBLISHING HISTORY
Berkley trade paperback edition October 2012
Berkley trade paperback ISBN: 978-0-425-26674-8

An application to register this book for cataloging has been submitted to the Library of Congress.
PRINTED IN THE UNITED STATES OF AMERICA

1 3 5 7 9 10 8 6 4 2

To Kim

Best friend

BFF

Confidante

Sister-I-never-had

None of these titles is adequate to describe what you mean to me

Thank you for all you are

Love you, always

Easy

chapter *One*

I had never noticed Lucas before that night. It was as though he didn't exist, and then suddenly, he was everywhere.

I'd just bailed on the Halloween party still in full swing behind me. Weaving between the cars crammed into the parking lot behind my ex's frat house, I tapped out a text to my roommate. The night was beautiful and warm—a typical Southern-style Indian summer. From the wide-open windows of the house, music blared across the pavement, punctuated with occasional bursts of laughter, drunken challenges, and calls for more shots.

As tonight's designated driver, it was my responsibility to get Erin back to our dorm across campus in one unmangled piece, whether or not I could stand another minute of the party. My message told her to call or text when she was ready to go. The way she and her boyfriend, Chaz, had been tequila-soaked dirty dancing before they linked hands and tripped up the stairs to his room, she might not be calling me until tomorrow. I chuckled over the thought of the short walk of shame she'd endure from the front porch to my truck, if so.

I hit Send as I dug in my bag for my keys. The moon was too cloud-obscured and the fully lit windows of the house were too far away to provide any light at the far end of the lot. I had to go by feel. Swearing when a mechanical pencil jabbed a fingertip, I stomped one stiletto-clad foot, almost certain I'd drawn blood. Once the keys were in my hand I sucked on the finger; the slight metallic taste told me I'd punctured the skin.

"Figures," I muttered, unlocking the truck door.

In the initial seconds that followed, I was too disoriented to comprehend what was happening. One moment I was pulling the truck door open, and the next I was lying flat on my face across the seat, breathless and immobile. I struggled to rise but couldn't, because the weight on top of me was too heavy.

"The little devil costume suits you, Jackie." The voice was slurred but familiar.

My first thought was *Don't call me that*, but that objection was quickly dismissed in favor of terror as I felt a hand pushing my already short skirt higher. My right arm was useless, trapped between my body and the seat. I clawed my left hand into the seat next to my face, trying again to push myself upright, and the hand on the bare skin of my thigh whipped up and grabbed my wrist. I cried out when he wrenched my arm behind my back, clamping it firmly in his other hand. His forearm pressed into my upper back. I couldn't move.

"Buck, get off me. Let go." My voice quavered, but I tried to deliver the command with as much authority as possible. I could smell the beer on his breath and something stronger in his sweat, and a wave of nausea rose and fell in my stomach.

His free hand was back on my left thigh, his weight settled onto my right side, covering me. My feet dangled outside the truck, the door still open. I tried to pull my knee up to get it under me, and he laughed at my pathetic efforts. When he shoved his hand between my open legs, I cried out, snapping my leg back down too late. I heaved and squirmed, first thinking to dislodge him and then, realizing I was no match for his size, I started to beg.

"Buck, *stop*. Please—you're just drunk and you'll regret this tomorrow. Oh my God—"

He wedged his knee between my legs and air hit my bare hip. I heard the unmistakable sound of a zipper and he laughed in my ear when I went from rationally imploring to crying. "No-no-no-no . . ." Under his weight, I couldn't get enough breath together to scream, and my mouth was mashed against the seat, muffling any protest I made. Struggling uselessly, I couldn't believe that this guy I'd known for over a year, who'd not once treated me with disrespect the entire time I'd dated Kennedy, was attacking me in my own truck at the back of the frat house parking lot.

He ripped my panties down to my knees, and between his efforts to push them down and my renewed effort to escape, I heard the fragile fabric tear. "Jesus, Jackie, I always knew you had a great ass, but *Christ*, girl." His hand thrust between my legs again and the weight lifted for a split second—just long enough for me to suck in a lungful of air and scream. Releasing my wrist, he slapped his hand over the back of my head and turned my face into the leather seat until I was silent, almost unable to breathe.

Even freed, my left arm was useless. I leveraged my hand against the floor of the cab and pushed, but my wrenched and aching muscles wouldn't obey. I sobbed into the cushion, tears and saliva mixing under my cheek. "Please don't, please don't, oh

God stop-stop-stop . . ." I hated the weedy sound of my powerless voice.

His weight lifted from me for a split second—he'd changed his mind or he was repositioning, I didn't wait to find out which. Twisting and pulling my legs up, I felt the spiky heels of my shoes tear into the pliant leather as I propelled myself to the far side of the bench seat and scrambled for the handle. Blood rushed in my ears as my body rallied for all-out fight or flight. And then I stopped, because Buck was no longer in the truck at all.

At first, I couldn't figure out why he was standing there, just past the door, facing away from me. And then his head snapped back. Twice. He swung wildly at something but his fists hit nothing. Not until he stumbled back against my truck did I see what—or who—he was fighting.

The guy never took his eyes off Buck as he delivered two more sharp jabs to his face, bobbing to the side as they circled and Buck threw futile punches of his own, blood streaming from his nose. Finally, Buck ducked his head and rushed forward with bull-like intent, but that effort was his undoing as the stranger swung an easy uppercut to his jaw. When Buck's head snapped up, an elbow cracked into his temple with a sickening thud. He collided with the side of the truck again, pushing off and rushing the stranger a second time. As though the entire fight was choreographed, he grabbed Buck's shoulders and pulled him forward, hard, kneeing him under the chin. Buck crumpled to the ground, moaning and cringing.

The stranger stared down, fists balled, elbows slightly bent, poised to deliver another blow if necessary. There was no need. Buck was nearly unconscious. I cowered against the far door, panting and curling into a ball as shock replaced the panic. I must have whimpered, because his eyes snapped up to mine. He rolled Buck aside with one booted foot and stepped up to the door, peering in.

"You okay?" His tone was low, careful. I wanted to say yes. I wanted to nod. But I couldn't. I was so not okay. "I'm gonna call 911. Do you need medical assistance, or just the police?"

I envisioned the campus police arriving at the scene, the partygoers who would spill from the house when the sirens came. Erin and Chaz were only two of the many friends I had in there, more than half of them underage and drinking. It would be my fault if the party became the focus of the police. I would be a pariah.

I shook my head. "Don't call." My voice was gravelly.

"Don't call an ambulance?"

I cleared my throat and shook my head. "Don't call anyone. Don't call the police."

His jaw hung ajar and he stared across the expanse of seat. "Am I wrong, or did this guy just try to *rape* you"—I flinched at the ugly word—"and you're telling me not to call the police?" He snapped his mouth closed, shook his head once, and peered at me again. "Or did I interrupt something I shouldn't have?"

I gasped, my eyes welling up. "N-no. But I just want to go home."

Buck groaned and rolled onto his back. "Fuuuuuck," he said,

not opening his eyes, one of which was probably swollen shut anyway.

My savior stared down at him, his jaw working. He rocked his neck to one side and then back, rolled his shoulders. "Fine. I'll drive you."

I shook my head. I wasn't about to escape one attack just to do something as stupid as get into a stranger's car. "I can drive myself," I rasped. My eyes flicked to my bag, wedged against the console, its contents spilled across the floor of the driver's side. He glanced down, leaned to pick out my keys from the bits and pieces of my personal effects.

"I believe you were looking for these, before." He dangled them from his fingers as I realized that I still hadn't moved any closer to him.

I licked my lip and tasted blood for the second time that night. Scooting forward into the faint illumination shed by the tiny overhead light, I was careful to keep my skirt pulled down. A wave of dizziness crashed over me as I became fully conscious of what had almost happened, and my hand trembled when I reached out for my keys.

Frowning, he clamped his fist around them and dropped his arm back to his side. "I can't let you drive." Judging by his expression, my face was a disaster.

I blinked, my hand still extended for the keys he'd just confiscated. "What? Why?"

He ticked three reasons off on his fingers. "You're shaking, probably an aftereffect of the assault. I have no idea if you're actually uninjured. And you've probably been drinking."

"I have not," I snapped. "I'm the designated driver."

He raised one brow and glanced around. "Who exactly are you designated for? If anyone had been with you, by the way, you might have been safe tonight. Instead, you walked out into a dark parking lot *alone*, paying absolutely no attention to your surroundings. Real responsible."

Suddenly I was beyond angry. Angry at Kennedy for breaking my heart two weeks ago and not being with me tonight, seeing me to the safety of my truck. Angry at Erin for talking me into coming to this stupid party, and even angrier with myself for agreeing. Furious at the barely conscious asswipe drooling and bleeding on the concrete a few feet away. And seething at the stranger who was holding my keys hostage while accusing me of being brainless and careless.

"So it's my fault he attacked me?" My throat was raw, but I pushed past the pain. "It's my fault I can't walk from a house to my truck without one of you trying to *rape* me?" I threw the word back at him to let him see I could bear it.

"'*One of you*'? You're gonna lump me in with that piece of shit?" He pointed at Buck, but his eyes never left mine. "I am *nothing* like him." That was when I noticed the thin silver ring through the left side of his lower lip.

Great. I was in a parking lot, alone, with an insulted, facially pierced stranger who still had my keys. I couldn't take any more of this night. A sob came from my throat as I tried to remain composed. "May I have my keys, please?" I held my hand out, willing the tremors to subside.

He swallowed, looking at me, and I stared back into his clear eyes. I couldn't tell their color in the dim light, but they contrasted compellingly with his dark hair. His voice was softer, less hostile. "Do you live on campus? Let me drive you. I can walk back over here and get my ride after."

No more fight in me, I nodded, reaching over to get my bag out of his way. He helped gather the lip gloss, wallet, tampons, hair ties, pens, and pencils strewn across the floor and return them to my bag. The last item he picked up was a condom packet. He cleared his throat and held it out to me. "That's not mine," I said, recoiling.

He frowned. "You sure?"

I clamped my jaw, trying not to be furious all over again. "Positive."

He glanced back at Buck. "Bastard. He was probably gonna . . ." He glanced into my eyes and back at Buck, scowling. "Uh . . . conceal the evidence."

I couldn't even contemplate that. He shoved the square package into his front jeans pocket. "I'll throw it away—he's sure as hell not getting it back." Brow still furrowed, he swung his gaze to me again as he climbed in and started the truck. "Are you sure you don't want me to call the police?"

Laughter sounded from the back door of the house and I nodded. Framed exactly within the center window, Kennedy danced with his arms around a girl dressed in a gauzy, low-cut white outfit, wings, and a halo. Perfect. Just perfect.

At some point during my battle with Buck, I'd lost the devil-horned headband Erin had stuffed onto my head while I sat on the bed whining that I didn't want to go to a stupid costume party.

Without the accessory, I was just a girl in a skimpy red-sequined dress that I'd refuse to be caught dead wearing otherwise.

"I'm sure."

The headlights illuminated Buck as we backed out of the parking spot. Throwing a hand in front of his eyes, he attempted to roll to a sitting position. I could see his split lip, misshapen nose, and swollen eye even from that distance.

It was just as well I wasn't the one behind the wheel. I probably would have run him over.

I gave the name of my dorm when asked, and stared out the passenger window, unable to speak another word as we meandered across campus. With a straightjacket hug, I gripped myself, trying to conceal the shudders wracking through me every five seconds. I didn't want him to see, but I couldn't make them stop.

The dorm lot was nearly full; spots near the door were all taken. He angled the truck into a back space and hopped out, coming around to meet me as I slid from the passenger side of my own truck. Teetering on the edge of breaking down and losing it, I took the keys after he activated the door locks and followed him to the building.

"Your ID?" he asked when we reached the door.

My hands shook as I unsnapped the front flap on my bag and withdrew the card. When he took it from my fingers, I noted the blood on his knuckles and gasped. "Oh my God. You're bleeding."

He glanced at his hand and shook his head, once. "Nah. Mostly his blood." His lips pressed flat and he turned away to swipe the card through the door access reader, and I wondered if he meant to follow me inside. I didn't think I could hold myself together for much longer.

After opening the door, he handed me the card. In the light from the entry vestibule, I could see his eyes more clearly—they were a clear gray blue under his lowered brows. "You sure you're okay?" he asked for the second time, and I felt my face crumple.

Chin down, I shoved the card into my bag and nodded uselessly. "Yes. Fine," I lied.

He huffed a disbelieving sigh, running a hand through his hair. "Can I call someone for you?"

I shook my head. I had to get to my room so I could fall apart. "Thank you, but no." I slipped past him, careful not to brush against any part of him, and headed for the stairs.

"Jackie?" he called softly, unmoving from the doorway. I looked back, gripping the handrail, and our eyes met. "It wasn't your fault."

I bit my lip, hard, nodding once before I turned and ran up the stairs, my shoes rapping against the concrete steps. At the second floor landing, I stopped abruptly and turned to look back at the door. He was gone.

I didn't know his name, and couldn't remember ever seeing him before, let alone meeting him. I'd have remembered those unusually clear eyes. I had no idea who he was . . . and he'd just called me by name. Not the name on my ID—Jacqueline—but Jackie, the nickname I'd gone by ever since Kennedy renamed me, our junior year of high school.

• • • • • • • • • •

Two weeks ago

"Wanna come up? Or stay over? Erin is staying at Chaz's this weekend . . ." My voice was playful, singsongy. "His roommate's out of town. Which means I'll be all alone . . ."

Kennedy and I were a month from our three-year anniversary. There was no need to be coy. Erin had taken to calling us an old married couple lately. To which I'd reply, "*Jealous*." And then she'd flip me off.

"Um, yeah. I'll come up for a little while." He kneaded the back of his neck as he pulled into the dorm parking lot and searched for a parking space, his expression inscrutable.

Prickles of apprehension arose in my chest, and I swallowed uneasily. "Are you all right?" The neck rubbing was a known stress signal.

He flicked a glance in my direction. "Yeah. Sure." He pulled into the first open spot, wedging his BMW between two pickups. He never, *ever* wedged his prized import into constricted spots. Door dings drove him insane. Something was up. I knew he was worried over upcoming midterms, especially precalc. His fraternity was hosting a mixer the next night, too, which was plain stupid the weekend before midterms.

I swiped us into the building and we entered the back stairwell that always creeped me out when I was alone. With Kennedy behind me, all I noticed was dingy, gum-adorned walls and the stale, almost sour smell. I jogged up the last flight and we emerged into the hallway.

Glancing back at him while unlocking my door, I shook my head over the charming portrayal of a penis someone had doodled onto the whiteboard Erin and I used for notes to each other and from our suitemates. Coed dorms were less mature than depicted on college websites. Sometimes it was like living with a bunch of twelve year olds.

"You could call in sick tomorrow night, you know." I laid a palm on his arm. "Stay here with me—we'll hide out and spend the weekend studying and ordering takeout . . . and other stress-reducing activities . . ." I grinned naughtily. He stared at his shoes.

My heart sped up and I suddenly felt warm all over. Something was definitely wrong. I wanted him to spit it out, whatever it was, because my mind was conjuring nothing but alarming possibilities. It had been so long since we'd had a problem or a real conflict that I felt blindsided.

He moved into my room and sat on my desk chair, not my bed. I walked up to him, our knees bumping, wanting him to tell me he was just in a bad mood, or worried about his upcoming exams. My heart thudding heavily, I put a hand on his shoulder. "Kennedy?"

"Jackie, we need to talk."

The drumming pulse in my ears grew louder, and my hand dropped from his shoulder. I grabbed it up in my other hand and sat on the bed, three feet from him. My mouth was so dry I couldn't swallow, let alone speak.

He was silent, avoiding my eyes for a couple of minutes that felt like forever. Finally, he lifted his gaze to me. He looked sad. Oh, God. Ohgodohgodohgod.

"I've been having some . . . trouble . . . lately. With other girls."

I blinked, glad I was sitting down. My legs would have buckled and sent me to the floor if I'd have been standing. "What do you mean?" I croaked out. "What do you mean, 'trouble' and 'other girls'?"

He sighed heavily. "Not like *that*, not really. I mean, I haven't *done* anything." He looked away and sighed again. "But I think I want to."

The *hell*?

"I don't understand." My mind worked frantically to make the best possible situation out of this, but every single remotely possible alternative sucked.

He got up and paced the room twice before planting himself on the edge of the chair, leaning forward, elbows on his knees and hands clasped. "You know how important it is to me to pursue a career in law and politics."

I nodded, still stunned to silence and pedaling hard to keep up.

"You know our sister sorority?"

I nodded again, acknowledging the very thing I'd worried about when he moved into the frat house. Apparently, I hadn't worried enough.

"There's a girl—a couple of girls, actually, that . . . well."

I tried to keep my voice rational and level. "Kennedy, this doesn't make sense. You aren't saying you've acted on this, or that you want to—"

He stared into my eyes, so there'd be no mistake. "I want to."

Really, he could have just punched me in the stomach, because my brain refused to comprehend the words he was saying. A physical assault, it might have understood. "You *want* to? What the hell do you mean, you *want* to?"

He bolted out of the chair, walked to the door and back—a distance of a dozen feet. "What do you *think* I mean? Jesus. Don't make me *say* it."

I gaped. "Why not? Why not say it—if you can imagine *doing* it—then why the *fuck* not say it? And what does this have to do with your career plans—"

"I was getting to that. Look, everyone knows that one of the worst things a political candidate or elected representative can do is to become embroiled in some sexual scandal." His eyes locked on mine in what I recognized as his debate face. "I'm only human, Jackie, and if I have these desires to sow my wild oats or whatever and I repress it, I'll probably have the same desire later, even worse. But acting on it *then* would be a career killer." He spread his hands helplessly. "I have no choice but to get it out of my system while I can do it without annihilating my future professional standing."

I told myself, *This isn't happening*. My boyfriend of three years was not breaking up with me so he could bang coeds with shameless abandon. I blinked hard and tried to take a deep breath, but I couldn't. There was no oxygen in the room. I glared at him, silent.

His jaw clenched. "Okay, so I guess trying to let you down easy was a bad idea—"

"This is your idea of letting me down *easy*? Breaking up with me so you can screw other girls? Without feeling guilty? Are you *serious*?"

"As a heart attack."

The last thing I thought before I picked up my econ textbook and hurled it at him: *How can he use such a piece-of-shit cliché in a moment like this*?

chapter Two

Erin's voice woke me. "Jacqueline Wallace, get your ass out of that bed and go save your GPA. For chrissake, if I'd let a guy throw off my academic mojo like this, I'd never hear the end of it."

I made a dismissive sound from under the comforter before peeking out at her. "What academic mojo?"

Her hands on her hips, she was wrapped in a towel, fresh from a shower. "Ha. Ha. Very funny. *Get up*."

I sniffed, but didn't budge. "I'm doing fine in all of my other classes. Can't I just fail this one?"

Her mouth dropped open. "Are you even listening to yourself?"

I *was* listening to myself. And I was every bit as disgusted with my cowardly sentiments as Erin—if not more so. But the thought of sitting next to Kennedy for an hour-long class three days a week was unbearable. I couldn't be sure what his newfound single status would mean in terms of open flirtations or hookups, but whatever it meant, I didn't want to stare it in the face. Imagining the details was bad enough.

If only I hadn't pressed him to take a class with me this semester. When we registered for fall classes, he questioned why I wanted to take economics—not a required course for my music education degree. I wondered if he had sensed, even then, that this was where we'd end up. Or if he'd known.

"I can't."

"You *can* and you *will*." She ripped the comforter off. "Now get up and get in that shower. I have to get to French on time or Monsieur Bidot will question me mercilessly *en passé composé*. I can barely do past tense in English. God knows I can't do it *en français* at ass o'clock in the morning."

I dragged myself out of bed and arrived outside the classroom at straight-up nine o'clock, knowing that Kennedy, habitually punctual, would already be there. The classroom was large and sloped. Slipping through the back door, I spotted him, sixth row center. The seat to his right was empty—my seat. Dr. Heller had passed around a seating chart the second week of class, and he used it to take attendance and give credit for class participation. I would have to talk with him after class, because there was no way I was sitting there again.

My eyes scanned the back rows. There were two empty seats. One was three rows down between a guy leaning on his hand, mostly asleep, and a girl drinking a Venti something and chattering nonstop to her neighbor. The other open seat was on the back row, next to a guy who appeared to be doodling something into the margin of his textbook. I turned in that direction at the same time the professor entered a side door below, and the artist raised his head to scan the front of the classroom. I froze, recognizing my savior from two nights ago. If I could've moved, I would have turned and fled the classroom.

The attack came flooding back. The helplessness. The terror.

The humiliation. I'd curled into a ball on my bed and cried all night, thankful for Erin's text that she was staying with Chaz. I hadn't told her what Buck had done—partly because I knew she'd feel responsible for making me go to the party and for letting me leave alone. Partly because I wanted to forget it had happened at all.

"If everyone will be seated, we'll begin." The professor's statement shook me from my stupor—I was the only student standing. I bolted to the empty chair between the chatty girl and the sleepy guy.

She glanced at me, never pausing in her weekend confession of how trashed she'd been and where and with whom. The guy unsquinted his eyes just enough to notice when I slid into the bolted-down chair between them, but he didn't otherwise move.

"Is this seat taken?" I whispered to him.

He shook his head and mumbled, "It was. But she dropped. Or stopped coming. Whatever."

I pulled a spiral from my bag, relieved. I tried not to look at Kennedy, but the angled seating made that effort challenging. His perfectly styled dirty blond hair and the familiar uncreased button-down shirt drew my eyes every time he moved. I knew the effect of that green plaid next to his striking green eyes. I'd known him since ninth grade. I'd watched him alter his style from a boy who wore mesh shorts and sneakers every day to the guy who sent his fitted shirts out to be pressed, kept his shoes scuff-free, and always looked as though he'd just stepped from the cover of a magazine. I'd seen more than one teacher turn her head as he passed before snapping her gaze away from his perfect, off-limits body.

Junior year, we had pre-AP English together. He focused on me from the first day of class, flashing his dimpled smile in my direction before taking his seat, inviting me to join his study group, inquiring about my weekend plans—and finally making himself a part of them. I'd never been so confidently pursued. As our class president, he was familiar to everyone, and he made a concerted effort to become familiar *with* everyone. As an athlete, he was a credit to the baseball team. As a student, his academic standing was in the top 10 percent. As a member of the debate team, he was known for conclusive arguments and an unbeaten record.

As a boyfriend, he was patient and attentive, never pushing me too far or too fast. Never forgetting a birthday or an anniversary. Never making me doubt his intentions for us. Once we were official, he changed my name—and everyone followed suit, including me. "You're my Jackie," he told me, referencing the wife of John F. Kennedy, his namesake and personal idol.

He wasn't related. His parents were just weirdly political—and also at odds with each other. He had a sister named Reagan and a brother named Carter.

Three years had passed since I'd gone by Jacqueline, and I fought daily to regain that one original part of myself that I'd put aside for him. It wasn't the only thing I'd given up, or the most important. It was just the only one I could get back.

• • • • • • • • • • •

Between trying to avoid staring at Kennedy for fifty minutes straight and having skipped the class for two weeks, my brain was sluggish and uncooperative. When class ended, I realized I'd absorbed little of the lecture.

I followed Dr. Heller to his office, running through various appeals in my head to induce him to give me a chance to catch up. Until that moment, I hadn't cared that I was failing. Now that the possibility had become a probability, I was terrified. I had never failed a class. What would I tell my parents and my advisor? This F would be on my transcript for the *rest of my life*.

"All right, Ms. Wallace." Dr. Heller removed a textbook and a stack of disorderly notes from his battered attaché and moved around his office as though I wasn't standing there. "State your case."

I cleared my throat. "My case?"

Tiredly, he peered at me over his glasses. "You missed two straight weeks of class—including the midterm—and you missed today. I assume you're standing here in my office in order to make some sort of case for why you should not fail macroeconomics. I'm waiting with bated breath for that explanation." He sighed, shelving the textbook. "I always think I've heard them all, but I've been known to be surprised. So go ahead. I don't have all day, and I presume you don't either."

I swallowed. "I was in class today. I just sat in a different seat."

He nodded. "I'll take your word for that, since you approached me at the end of the lecture. That's one day of participation back in your favor—amounting to about a quarter of a grade point. You still have six missed class days and a zero on a major exam."

Oh, God. As if a plug had been pulled, the jumbled excuses

and realizations came pouring out. "My boyfriend broke up with me, and he's in the class, and I can't stand to see him, let alone sit next to him . . . Oh my God, *I missed the midterm*. I'm going to fail. I've never failed a class in my life." As if that speech wasn't mortifying enough, my eyes watered and spilled over. I bit my lip to keep from sobbing outright, staring at his desk, unable to meet the repulsed expression I imagined him wearing.

I heard his sigh in the same moment a tissue appeared in my line of vision. "It's your lucky day, Ms. Wallace."

I took the tissue and pressed it to my wet cheeks, eyeing him cautiously.

"As it happens, I have a daughter just a bit younger than you. She recently endured a nasty little breakup. My whip-smart, straight-A student turned into an emotional wreck who did nothing but cry, sleep, and cry some more—for about two weeks. And then she came to her senses and decided that no boy was going to ruin her scholastic record. For the sake of my daughter, I'll give you one chance. *One*. If you blow it, you will receive the grade you've earned at the end of the semester. Do we understand each other?"

I nodded, more tears spilling.

"Good." My professor shifted uncomfortably and handed me another tissue. "Oh, for Pete's sake—as I told my daughter, there's not a boy on the planet worth this amount of angst. I know; I used to be one." He scribbled on a slip of paper and handed it to me. "Here's the email address of my class tutor, Landon Maxfield. If you aren't familiar with his supplemental instruction sessions, I suggest you *get* familiar with them. You'll no doubt need some one-on-one tutoring as well. He was an excellent student in my class two years ago, and he's been tutoring for me since then. I'll give him the details of the project I expect you to do to replace the midterm grade."

Another sob escaped me when I thanked him, and I thought he might explode from discomfort. "Well, well, yes, of course, you're welcome." He pulled out the seating chart. "Show me where you'll be sitting from now on, so you can earn those quarter points for attendance." I pointed to my new seat, and he wrote my name in the square.

I had my shot. All I had to do was get in touch with this Landon person and turn in a project. How hard could it be?

• • • • • • • • • • •

The Starbucks line in the student union was ridiculously long, but it was raining and I wasn't in the mood to get soaked crossing the street to the indie coffee shop just off campus to get my fix before my afternoon class. In unrelated reasoning, that was also where Kennedy was most likely to be—we went there almost daily after lunch. On principle, he tended to shun "corporate monstrosities" like Starbucks, even if the coffee was better.

"There's no way I'm making it across campus on time if I wait in this line." Erin growled her annoyance, leaning to check out how many people were ahead of us. "Nine people. Nine! And five waiting for drinks! Who the hell are all of these people?" The guy in front of us glanced over his shoulder with a scowl. She scowled back at him and I pressed my lips together to keep from laughing.

"Caffeine addicts like us?" I suggested.

"Ugh," she huffed and then grabbed my arm. "I almost forgot—did you hear what happened to Buck Saturday night?"

My stomach dropped. The night I just wanted to forget wouldn't leave me alone. I shook my head.

"He got jumped in the parking lot behind the house. A couple of guys wanted his wallet. Probably homeless people, he said—that's what we get with a campus right in the middle of a big city. They didn't get anything, the bastards, but damn, Buck's face is busted up." She leaned closer. "He actually looks a little hotter like that. *Rowr*, if you know what I mean."

I felt ill, standing there mute and feigning interest instead of refuting Buck's explanation of the events leading to his pummeled face.

"Well, crap. I'm gonna have to chug a Rockstar to keep from zoning out during poli-sci. I can't be late—we've got a quiz. I'll see you after work." She gave me a quick hug and scurried off.

I scooted forward with the line, my mind going over Saturday night for the thousandth time. I couldn't shake how vulnerable I felt still. I'd never been blind to the fact that guys are stronger. Kennedy had scooped me into his arms more times than I could count, one time tossing me over his shoulder and running up a flight of stairs as I clung to his back, upside down and laughing. He'd easily opened jars I couldn't open, moved furniture I could hardly budge. His superior strength had been evident when he'd braced himself above me, biceps hard under my hands.

Two weeks ago, he'd torn out my heart, and I'd never felt so hurt, so empty.

But he'd never used his physical strength against me.

No, that was all Buck. Buck, a campus hottie who didn't have a problem getting girls. A guy who'd never given any indication that he could or would hurt me, or that he was aware of me at all, except as Kennedy's girlfriend. I could blame the alcohol . . . but no. Alcohol removes inhibitions. It doesn't trigger criminal violence where there was none before.

"Next."

I shook off my reverie and looked across the counter, prepared to give my usual order, and there stood the guy from Saturday night. The guy I'd avoided sitting next to this morning in econ. My mouth hung open but nothing came out. And once again, Saturday night came flooding back. My face heated, remembering the position I'd been in, what he must have witnessed before he'd intervened, how foolish he must consider me.

But then, he'd said it wasn't my fault.

And he'd called me by my name. The name I no longer used, as of sixteen days ago.

My split-second wish that he wouldn't recall who I was went ungranted. I returned his penetrating gaze and could see he remembered all of it, clearly. Every mortifying bit. My face burned.

"Are you ready to order?" His question pulled me from my disorientation. His voice was calm, but I felt the exasperation of the restless customers behind me.

"Grande caffè americano. Please." My words were so mumbled that I half expected him to ask me to repeat myself.

But he marked the cup, which was when I noted the two or

three layers of thin white gauze wrapped around his knuckles. He passed the cup to the barista and rang up the drink as I handed over my card.

"Doing okay today?" he asked, his words so seemingly casual, yet so full of meaning between us. He swiped my card and handed it back with the receipt.

"I'm fine." The knuckles of his left hand were scuffed but not severely abraded. As I took the card and receipt, his fingers grazed over mine. I snatched my hand away. "Thanks."

His eyes widened, but he said nothing else.

"I'll have a Venti caramel macchiato—skinny, no whip." The impatient girl behind me gave her order over my shoulder, not touching me, but pressing too far into my personal space for comfort.

His jaw tensed almost imperceptibly when he shifted his gaze to her. Marking the cup, he gave her the total in clipped tones, his eyes flicking to me once more as I stepped away. I don't know if he looked at me after that. I waited for my coffee at the other end of the bar, then hurried away without adding my usual dribble of milk and three packets of sugar.

Macroeconomics was a survey course, and as such the roster was huge—probably two hundred students. I could avoid eye contact with two boys in the midst of that many people for the remaining six weeks of fall semester, couldn't I?

chapter *Three*

I dutifully emailed the econ tutor when I got back to the dorm after class, and started on my art history homework. While tapping out a response essay on a neoclassical sculptor and his influence on the style, I mumbled a thank-you to my inner neurotic that I'd at least kept up in my non-econ classes.

With Erin at work, I could buckle down to an evening of quiet studying. Here in our microscopic room, she couldn't help being a near constant distraction. While I attempted to cram for an algebra test last week, the following conversation took place: "I *had* to have those pumps for my job, Daddy!" she argued into her cell. "You said you wanted me to learn the value of work while I'm in school, and you always say a person should dress for success, so I'm only trying to follow your words of wisdom."

When she glanced at me, I rolled my eyes. My roommate was a hostess at a swanky restaurant downtown, a position she frequently used as an excuse for overspending her clothing budget. Three hundred dollar shoes, essential for a job that paid nine bucks an hour? I stifled my laugh when she winked back at me. Her father always caved, especially when she employed the D-word—*Daddy*.

I wasn't expecting a quick reply from Landon Maxfield. As an upperclassman and a tutor for a huge class like Dr. Heller's, he had to be busy. I was also certain he'd be none too thrilled to assist a failing sophomore who'd skipped the midterm and two weeks of class, and who had never attended one of his tutoring sessions. I was prepared to show him I would work hard to catch up and get out of his hair as quickly as possible.

Fifteen minutes after I emailed him, my inbox dinged. He'd replied, in the same formal tone I'd chosen after switching back and forth between using his first or last name in the address, finally deciding on *Mr. Maxfield*.

Ms. Wallace,

Dr. Heller has informed me of your need to catch up in macro and the project you'll need to complete in order to replace the midterm grade. Since he's approved you to do this work, there's no need to share the reason why you've fallen so far behind with me. I'm employed as a tutor, so this falls under my job description.

We can meet on campus, preferably in the library, to discuss the project. It's detailed and will require a great deal of outside research on your part. I've been instructed by Dr. Heller as to the level of assistance I should provide. Basically, he wants to see what you can do, alone. I'll be available for general questions, of course.

My group tutoring sessions are MWTh 1-2:00, but those cover current material. I assume you'll need more assistance comprehending the material you missed. Let me know the times you're available to meet for individual tutoring sessions and we'll coordinate from there.

LM

My jaw tensed. Though perfectly polite, the tone of his email reeked of condescension . . . until his signature at the very end: *LM*. Was he being friendly, or casual, or ridiculing my attempt to sound like a serious, mature student? I'd alluded to the breakup in my email, hoping he wouldn't want or ask for details. Now I felt as though he'd not only scoffed at learning the particulars, but also he thought less of me for letting a relationship crisis affect my academic life.

I read his email again and got even madder. So he thought I was too dumb to comprehend the course material on my own?

Mr. Maxfield,

I can't attend your sessions because I have art history MW 1-2:30, and I tutor at the middle school on Thursday afternoons. I live on campus and am available to meet late afternoons Monday/Wednesday, and most evenings. I'm also free on weekends when I'm not tutoring.

I've begun reading the course material on GDP, CPI, and inflation, and I'm working on the review questions at the end of chapter 9. If you want to meet to pass on the project requirements, I'm sure I can catch up on the regular coursework on my own.

Jacqueline

I pressed Send and felt superior for all of about twenty seconds. In actuality, I'd barely glanced at chapter 9. So far, it looked less like comprehensible supply and demand charts, and more like gibberish with dollar signs and confusing shifts tossed in for fun. As for GDP and CPI, I knew what those acronyms signified . . . sort of.

Oh, God. I'd just haughtily dismissed the tutor provided by my professor—the professor who wasn't obligated to give me a second chance, but had.

When my email dinged again, I swallowed before clicking over to it. A new message from Landon Maxfield was at the top of my inbox.

Jacqueline,

If you prefer to catch up on your own, that's your prerogative, of course. I'll gather the information on the project and we can meet, say, Wednesday just after 2:00?

LM

PS—What do you tutor?

His reply didn't seem angry. He was civil. Nice, even. I was so emotional lately that I couldn't judge anything clearly.

Landon,

I teach private lessons to orchestra students—middle and high school—on the upright bass. I just remembered I agreed to assist in transporting two of my students' instruments to regionals this Wednesday afternoon. (I drive a truck, to accommodate transport of my own instrument, and now I'm constantly inundated with requests to move large musical instruments, sofas, mattresses . . .)

Are you free any evening? Or Saturday?

JW

I'd been playing the upright bass since I was ten. In fourth grade, one of the orchestra's two bass players had a peewee football collision the second weekend of school, resulting in a snapped collarbone. Our orchestra teacher, Mrs. Peabody, had looked out over the vast sea of violin players and pleaded for someone to switch. "Anyone?" she'd squeaked. When no one else volunteered, I raised my hand.

Even the half-sized instrument dwarfed me back then; I'd needed a step stool to play it, a fact that had provided my orchestra classmates with endless amusement. The ridicule didn't stop at school.

"Honey, isn't that an *odd* choice of instrument for a girl to play?" my mother asked. Still petulant over my rejection of learning piano—her instrument of choice—in favor of the violin, she was immediately unsupportive of my new preference.

"Yes." I glared at my mother and she rolled her eyes. She'd never lost her disdain of the instrument I came to love to play for the way it grounded and directed the rest of the orchestra. I also loved the disbelief on the faces of fellow contestants at regional competitions, their surety that I wasn't as good as they were because of my gender—and the way I proved that I was *better*.

By the time I was fifteen, I'd reached my full five-and-a-half-foot stature and could perform with a three-quarter-sized instrument, no height adjustment needed, though it was a close thing.

For the past year, I'd been giving lessons to local students, all of them boys—each of them some version of smug and impertinent until they heard me play.

Jacqueline,

Upright bass? Interesting.

I'm busy in the evenings this week, and most weekends as well. I don't want you to lose time on this, so I'll send you the project information later tonight, and we can discuss it over email until we can sync our schedules. Will that work for you?

LM

PS—I'll keep you in mind if I buy a large appliance or need to move.

Landon,

Thank you, yes—that would be great. (Re: sending the project information, I mean, not your brazen resolution to use me for my truck's hauling capacity. You're no better than my friends! They dodge U-Haul rentals and delivery fees, and I get paid in beer.)

JW

Jacqueline,

I'll send the project specifics when I get home, and we can discuss.

The barter system is just primitive economics at work, you know. (And are you old enough for beer?)

LM

Landon,

Far be it from me to knock an effective use of prehistoric economics. And I suppose friends who pay in beer are better than friends who don't pay at all. (Re: my age—I don't believe the job description of Economics Tutor makes you privy to that sort of personal information.)

JW

Jacqueline,

Touché. I'll just have to trust you not to get me arrested for supplying alcohol to minors.

You're right—impoverished, auto-lacking college students like myself should respect tried-and-true methods of transport negotiations.

LM

I smiled at his candid admission of being carless, my face falling when I contrasted it with the sense of self-importance Kennedy got from his car. Right before we graduated, his parents gave his two-year-old Mustang to his sixteen-year-old brother, who'd wrecked his Jeep the weekend before. As an early graduation gift, they replaced Kennedy's Mustang with the brand new BMW—sleek and black, with every available upgrade, including plush leather seats and a stereo system I could hear from a block away.

Dammit. I had to stop linking every single thing that happened to me with Kennedy. Realization dawned then, that he was still my default. Over the past three years, we'd become each other's habit. And though he'd broken his habit of me when he walked away, I'd not broken my habit of him. I was still tethering him to my present, to my future. The truth was, he now belonged to my past only, and it was time I began to accept it, as much as it hurt to do so.

• • • • • • • • • • •

As soon as we hit campus freshman year, Kennedy had pledged his father's fraternity. Despite my boyfriend's need for cliquish affiliation, I'd never shared that aspiration. He didn't seem to mind when I said I preferred not to rush any sororities, as long as I supported his future-politician need for brotherhood. He told me once he sort of liked that I was a GDI girlfriend.

"A GDI? What's that?"

He'd laughed and said, "It means you're goddamned independent."

When he walked out of my room almost three weeks ago, it hadn't occurred to me that he was taking my carefully cultivated social circle with him. Minus my relationship with Kennedy, I had no automatic invitation to Greek parties or events, though Chaz and Erin could invite me to some stuff since I fell under the heading of acceptable things to bring to any party: alcohol and girls.

Awesome. I'd gone from an independent girlfriend to party paraphernalia.

Running into clusters of my former friends was uncomfortable at best. Just outside the main library, tables of frat boys sold coffee, juice, and pastries every morning for a week to raise money for leadership training. Across campus, armed with portable grills, Tri Delts camped out in tents on their lawn to showcase the plight of the homeless. (I suggested to Erin that most homeless people are unlikely to own portable Coleman grills and REI camping gear, and she snorted and said, "Yeah, I pointed that out. My warning fell on deaf ears.")

I couldn't leave my dorm and walk in any direction without passing people with whom I'd had uncomplicated relationships just days before. Now their eyes shifted away when I walked by, though some still smiled or waved before pretending to be deep in conversation with someone else. Even fewer called out, "Hi, Jackie." I didn't tell them I was no longer using that name.

At first, Erin insisted that the snubs were in my head, but after two weeks, she reluctantly concurred. "People feel the need to choose sides when a relationship splits—it's human nature," she said, her second-year psych classes kicking in. "Still. *Cowards*." I appreciated that she was willing to ignore her detached analysis in support of me.

It didn't surprise me that practically everyone chose Kennedy. He was one of them, after all. He was the outgoing, charming future world leader. I was the quiet, cute but somewhat odd girlfriend. . . . After the breakup, I became just a non-Greek undergrad—to everyone but Erin.

Tuesday, we passed the reigning campus power couple—Katie was president of Erin's sorority and D.J. was vice president of Kennedy's fraternity. "Hi, Erin! *Great* outfit," Katie said, as though I wasn't there. D.J. tipped his chin and smiled at Erin, his eyes flicking over me, but he didn't acknowledge my existence any more than his girlfriend had.

"Thanks!" Erin responded. "Fuckheads," she muttered right after, linking her arm through mine.

When I'd moved into my dorm room over a year ago, I'd been horrified to find myself with a roommate who embodied the sorority-girl stereotype. Erin had already claimed the bed nearest the window. Above her headboard, she'd fastened shiny blue-and-gold high school pom-poms to a huge cutout spelling ERIN, which was coated in gold glitter. Surrounding the giant gilded letters were posters covered in photos of cheerleader events and homecomings with hulking football players.

As I stood gaping at her light-reflective side of our tiny room, she'd bounced through the door. "Oh, hi! You must be Jacqueline! I'm Erin!"

Diplomatically, I hadn't voiced the *no shit* comment that popped into my head.

"Since you weren't here, I chose a bed—I hope you don't mind! I'm almost done unpacking, so I can help you." Wearing a university T-shirt that almost exactly matched her upswept coppery hair, she picked up my heaviest bag and swung it onto the bed. "I attached a whiteboard to the door so we can leave messages to each other—my mom's idea, actually, but it sounded like a usable suggestion, don't you think?"

I blinked at her, mumbling, "Uh-huh," as she unzipped my bag and started removing the belongings I'd brought from home. There had to be some mistake. I'd filled out a lengthy roommate attribute preference sheet, and this girl appeared to have *not one* of those desired qualities. I'd basically described myself: a quiet, studious bookworm who would go to bed at a decent hour. A non-partier who wouldn't bring a parade of boys through our room, or make it the floor headquarters for beer pong.

"It's Jackie, actually," I'd said to her.

"Jackie—so cute! I do like Jacqueline, though, I have to admit. So classy. You're lucky, you can choose! I'm sort of stuck with Erin. Good thing I like it, huh? Okay, Jackie, where should we hang this poster of—who is this?"

I'd glanced at the poster in her hands—the likeness of one of my favorite singers, who also played the upright bass. "Esperanza Spalding."

"Never heard of her. But she's cute!" She'd grabbed a handful of tacks and hopped up on my bed to press the poster against the wall. "How 'bout here?"

Erin and I had come a long way in fifteen months.

chapter *Four*

Arriving a minute before econ began Wednesday morning, the last thing I expected to see was Kennedy, leaning on the wall outside the classroom, exchanging phone numbers with a Zeta pledge. Giggling after snapping a picture of herself, she handed his phone back. He did the same, grinning down at her.

He would never smile at me like that again.

I didn't realize I was frozen in place until a classmate shouldered into me, knocking my heavy backpack from my shoulder. "'Scuse me," he grumbled, his tone more *Get out of the way* than *Sorry I ran into you*.

As I bent to retrieve my backpack, praying Kennedy and his fangirl hadn't seen me, a hand grasped the strap and swung the pack up from the floor. I straightened and looked into clear gray-blue eyes. "Chivalry isn't really dead, you know." His deep, calm voice was just as I remembered from Saturday night, and from Monday afternoon, across the Starbucks counter.

"Oh?"

He slipped the strap back onto my shoulder. "Nah. That guy's just an asshole." He gestured toward the guy who'd bumped me, but I could have sworn his eyes raked over my ex, too, who was crossing to the door, laughing with the girl. Her bright orange sweatpants said ZETA across the rear. "You okay?" For the third time, this question, from him, held deeper significance than the usual, everyday implication.

"Yes, fine." What could I do but lie? "Thank you." I turned and entered the room, took my new seat, and spent the first forty-five minutes of class fixing my attention on Dr. Heller, the whiteboard he filled, and the notes I took. Dutifully copying charts of short-run equilibrium and aggregate demand, all of it seeming like so much nonsense, I realized I would have to beg Landon Maxfield for help after all. My pride would only cause me to slide further behind.

Minutes before the end of class, I turned and reached into my backpack as an excuse to sneak a look at the guy on the back row. He was staring at me, a black pencil loose between his fingers, tapping the notebook in front of him. He slouched into his seat, one elbow over the back of it, one booted foot casually propped on the support under his desk. As our eyes held, his expression changed subtly from unreadable to the barest of smiles, though guarded. He didn't look away, even when I glanced into my bag and then back at him.

I snapped forward, my face warming.

Guys had shown interest in me over the past three years, but other than a couple of short-lived, certainly never revealed or acted-upon crushes—one on my own college-aged bass tutor, another on my chemistry lab partner—I hadn't been attracted to anyone but Kennedy. The economics lecture reduced to background babble, I couldn't decide if my response to this stranger was lingering embarrassment, gratitude that he'd saved me from Buck, or a simple crush. Perhaps all three.

When class ended, I packed my textbook into my backpack and resisted the urge to look in his direction again. I fiddled long enough for Kennedy and his fangirl to leave. As I stood to go, the persistently sleepy guy who sat next to me spoke.

"Hey, which questions did he say to do for the extra credit? I must have knocked off for a few seconds right around when he discussed those—my notes are indecipherable." I glanced at the spot he indicated in his notes, and sure enough, the scribbles became less and less readable. "I'm Benji, by the way."

"Oh, um, let's see . . ." I flipped through my spiral and pointed to the assignment details printed across the top of the page. "Here it is." As he copied it, I added, "I'm Jacqueline."

Benji was one of those guys to whom adolescence hadn't been kind. A scattering of acne dotted his forehead. His hair was overgrown and curly—a skilled stylist could tame it, but he was probably a fan of the eight-dollar place featuring flat screens of nonstop ESPN. Given his doughy midsection, I doubted he spent much time in the university's state-of-the-art gym. The T-shirt stretched across his belly gave some sort of "bro" instruction best left unread. Expressive hazel eyes and an engaging smile that crinkled them adorably were his saving grace in the looks department.

"Thanks, Jacqueline. This saves my ass—I *need* those extra credit points. See you Friday." He snapped his notebook closed. "Unless I accidentally sleep in," he added, giving me a genuine smile.

I returned the smile as I moved into the aisle. "No problem."

Maybe I was capable of making friends outside of my Kennedy circle. This interaction, along with the defection of most of *our* friends to Kennedy after the breakup, made me realize how dependent on him I'd become. I was a little shocked. Why had this never occurred to me before? Because I'd never thought Kennedy and I could end?

Foolish, naive assumption. Obviously.

The room had almost cleared, the guy from the back row included. I felt a stab of irrational disappointment. So he'd stared at me in class—big deal. Maybe he was just bored. Or easily distracted.

But as I exited the room, I spotted him across the crowded hallway, talking with a girl from class. His demeanor was relaxed, from the navy shirt, open over a plain gray T-shirt, to the hand tucked into the front pocket of his jeans. Muscle didn't show under the unbuttoned long-sleeved shirt, but his abdomen looked flat, and on Saturday night he'd put Buck on the ground and bloodied easily enough. His black pencil sat atop one ear, only the pink eraser at the tip showing, the rest disappearing into his dark, messy hair.

"So it's a group tutoring thing?" the girl asked, twirling a long loop of blonde hair around and around her finger. "And it lasts an hour?"

He hitched his backpack, twitching wayward bangs out of his eyes. "Yeah. From one to two."

As he gazed down at her, she tilted her head and rocked her weight slightly from side-to-side, as though she was about to dance with him. Or *for* him. "Maybe I'll check it out. What are you doing after?"

"Work."

She huffed an annoyed breath. "You're always working, Lucas." Her pouty tone hit my ears like nails on a chalkboard, as it always has when used by any girl above age six. But bonus—I'd just learned his name.

He glanced up then, as though he sensed me standing there, eavesdropping, and I pivoted in the opposite direction and started walking swiftly, too late to pretend I hadn't been purposely listening to their conversation. I wove through the rush of people in the packed hallway, ducking out the side exit.

No way was I going to those tutoring sessions if *Lucas* attended them. I wasn't sure what he meant—if he meant anything at all—staring at me like that during class, but the overt intensity of his gaze made me uneasy. Besides, I was still in a mourning period over my recently shattered relationship. I wasn't ready to start anything new. Not that he was interested in me that way. I all but rolled my eyes at my own thought processes. I'd gone from a marginal amount of interest to a possible relationship in one jump.

From a purely observational perspective, he was probably used to girls like the blonde in the hallway throwing themselves at his feet. Just like my ex. Kennedy's titles of class and then student body president equated to small-time celebrity status, and he'd relished it. I'd spent the last two years of high school ignoring the envious girls who dogged our relationship, just waiting for him to be finished with me. By the time we'd left town for college, I was so sure of him.

I wondered when I would stop feeling like such a clueless twit for that misplaced trust.

• • • • • • • • • • •

Landon,

I'm having more trouble with the current material than I let on, but I'm not sure if I'll ever be able to make it to one of your tutoring sessions. Too bad for both of us that my ex didn't dump me early enough in the semester to drop this class! (No offense. You're probably an econ major and like this stuff.)

I've started researching online journals for the project. Thanks for decoding Dr. Heller's notes before sending them to me. If you'd have forwarded them without a translation, I'd be searching for a tall building, an overpass, or a water tower from which to yell "good-bye cruel world."

JW

Jacqueline,

Please, no leaping from towering structures. Do you have any idea how much damage that would do to my tutoring reputation?? If nothing else, think of the effect on me. ;)

I create worksheets for the tutoring sessions. I've attached the past three weeks' worth. Use them as study guides, or fill them in and send them back to me, and we'll see where you're getting confused.

Actually, I'm an engineering major, but we have to take econ. I think everyone should, though—it's a good starting point for explaining how money, politics, and commerce work together to create the total chaos that is our economic system.

LM

PS—How did the regional competitions go? And btw, your ex is obviously a moron.

I downloaded the worksheets, turning over his last statement in my mind. Whether Landon knew Kennedy or not—unlikely, given the size of the university and their differing majors—he'd taken my side. Me, a girl so absurdly unhinged by a breakup that she'd skipped class for two weeks.

He was smart and funny, and after only three days, I already looked forward to his name in my inbox, our back-and-forth banter. All of a sudden, I wondered what he looked like. *God*. Just yesterday, I'd left class telling myself to ignore the brooding stares of a guy in class because I needed time to get over Kennedy's desertion, and here I was daydreaming over a tutor who could look like Chace Crawford. Or . . . Benji.

It didn't matter. I needed time to recover, even if Landon was right. Even if Kennedy was a moron.

I clicked on the first worksheet and opened my econ text, and breathed a sigh of relief.

Landon,

The worksheets are definitely going to help. I already feel less scared of failing this class. I did the first two—when you have time, could you look them over? Thank you again for wasting your time on me. I'll try to get caught up quickly. I'm not used to being the student who's a pain in the butt.

I had two freshmen from rival schools in competition with each other at regionals. Both asked me, separately thank God, who was my favorite. (I told each of them, "You are, of course." Was that wrong??) They were very smug with each other when they came to get their basses from my truck, and I prayed that neither would mention the favorite status in front of the other. BOYS.

Engineering? Wow. No wonder you seem so brainy.

JW

Jacqueline,

The worksheets look great. I marked a couple of minor mistakes that could trip you up on an exam, so check those.

Ah, sounds like your freshmen have crushes on you? Not surprised. A bass-playing college girl would have rendered me speechless at 14.

Of course I'm brainy! I'm the all-knowing tutor. And in case you're wondering—yes, you're my favorite. ;)

LM

• • • • • • • • • • •

Saturday night, Erin was once again threatening to drag me out of our room, ignoring my protests and reluctance. This time, three of us were heading to the strip to hit some clubs with our fake IDs.

"Don't you remember how the party last weekend went for me?" I asked when she shoved a clingy black dress into my outspread arms. Of course she didn't remember; I hadn't told her. All she knew was that I'd bailed early.

"Jacqueline, babe, I know this is hard. But you can't let Kennedy win! You can't let him make you a hermit, or keep you scared of falling for someone new. God, I *love* this part of it—the hunt for a new guy, everything unknown, untried—the mass of hot prospects in front of you, waiting to be discovered. If I didn't lust after Chaz so hard, I'd be jealous of you."

The way she described it, the process sounded like an expedition to an exotic continent. I didn't share her feelings, not in the least. The idea of finding a new guy sounded exhausting and depressing. "Erin, I don't think I'm ready—"

"That's what you said last weekend, and you did fine!" She frowned, thinking, and for the hundredth time, I almost told her about Buck. "Even if you did leave early." She rehung the black dress I didn't intend to wear, and I held my tongue, losing my chance again. I wasn't sure why I couldn't tell her. I was mostly afraid she'd be infuriated. More unreasonably, I was afraid she'd be disbelieving. Neither response was something I wanted to contend with; I just wanted to forget.

I thought of Lucas, annoyed that his presence in econ was making that process impossible, because he was irrevocably connected to the horror of that night. He'd not looked at me at all Friday—as far as I knew. Every time I snuck a look back at him, he appeared to be sketching rather than taking notes, his black pencil held low between his fingers, a concentrated expression on his face. When class ended, he stuck the pencil behind his ear, turned and walked from the classroom without a backward glance, first one out the door.

"Now *this* will show off the goods," Erin said, breaking into my reverie. Next up was a stretchy, low-cut purple top. Yanking it from the hanger, she tossed it to me. "Put on your skinny jeans and those badass boots that make you look like a gangbanger's girlfriend. This fits your tough, I'm-a-challenge mood better anyway. You have to dress to attract the right guys, and if I make you too cute, you'll flick them all away with glares and irritated rolls of your big blue eyes."

I sighed and she laughed, pulling the black dress over her own head. Erin knew me far too well.

• • • • • • • • • •

I'd lost count of the number of drinks Erin had pressed into my hand, telling me that since she was the designated driver, I was required to drink for two. "I can't touch any of these hotties, either—so I have to live vicariously. Now finish that margarita, stop scowling, and stare at one of these guys until he knows he won't lose a limb if he asks you to dance."

"I'm not scowling!" I scowled, obeying and tossing the drink back. I grimaced. Cheap tequila refused to be concealed by an abundance of even cheaper margarita mix, but that's what you get for no cover charge and five dollar drinks.

Still relatively early, the small club we decided to occupy for the night wasn't yet overcrowded with the hundreds of college students and townies it would hold soon. Erin, Maggie, and I claimed a corner of the near-vacant floor. Having downed the drinks and dressed the part, I moved to the music, gradually loosening up while laughing at Erin's cheer poses and Maggie's ballet movements. The first guy to interrupt us approached Erin, but she shook her head as her lips mouthed the word *boyfriend.* She turned him toward me and I thought: That's me—boyfriend-less. No more relationship. No more Kennedy. No more *You're my Jackie*.

"Wanna dance?" the guy yelled over the music, fidgeting as though he was ready to bolt if I turned him down. I nodded, choking back the pointless, almost physical pain. I was no one's girlfriend, for the first time in three years.

We moved to an open space a few feet from Erin and Maggie—who also had a boyfriend. It didn't take long to figure out that the two of them planned to point every guy who asked one of them to dance at *me*. I was their pet project for the night.

Two hours later, I'd danced with too many guys to remember, dodging wandering hands and turning down any drinks not handed to me by Erin. Crowded around a tall table near the floor, we leaned hips on the barstools surrounding it, watching the surrounding hookup activity. As Maggie returned from bopping and pirouetting her way to the bathroom and back, I asked if we could go yet, and Erin fixed me with a look she usually reserved for ill-mannered steakhouse patrons. I smirked at her and sipped my drink.

I knew when the next guy walked up behind me, and that Erin and Maggie approved, because their eyes widened simultaneously, focusing over my shoulder. Fingers grazed the back of my arm, and I took a deep breath and exhaled it slowly before turning around. Good thing, too—because it was Lucas who stood there, his eyes dropping to my cleavage for a split second. He crooked an eyebrow and gazed into my eyes with a faint smile, unapologetic for looking. The heels on my boots were killing my feet, but they weren't tall enough to bring me eye-to-eye.

Rather than raising his voice like everyone else, he leaned close to my ear and asked, "Dance with me?" I felt his warm breath and inhaled the scent of his aftershave—something basic and male—before he withdrew, his eyes on mine, waiting for my answer. An enthusiastic nudge between my shoulder blades told me Erin's vote: *Go dance with him*.

I nodded, and he took my hand and made his way to the floor, maneuvering through the crowd, which parted easily for him. Once we reached the worn oak floor, he turned and pulled me close, never letting go of my hand. As we found the rhythm of the slow-paced song, swaying together, he took my other hand in his and moved both hands behind my back, gently holding me captive. My breasts grazed against his chest and I struggled not to gasp at the subtle contact.

I'd barely let anyone else touch me at all tonight, adamantly refusing all slow dances. Dizzy from weak-but-plentiful margaritas, I closed my eyes and let him lead, telling myself that the difference was the alcohol in my blood, nothing more. A minute later, he released my fingers and spread his hands across my lower back, and my hands moved to his biceps. Solid, as I knew they would be. Tracking a path, my palms encountered equally hard shoulders. Finally, I hooked my fingers behind his neck and opened my eyes.

His gaze was penetrating, not wavering for a moment, and my pulse hammered under his silent scrutiny.

Finally, I stretched up toward his ear, and he leaned down to accommodate my question. "S-so what's your major?" I breathed.

From the corner of my eye, I watched his mouth twitch up on one side. "Do you really want to talk about that?" He maintained the closeness, our torsos pressed together chest to thigh, ostensibly waiting for my answer. I couldn't remember the last time I'd been so full of pure, unqualified desire.

I swallowed. "As opposed to talking about what?"

He chuckled, and I felt the vibrations of his chest against mine. "As opposed to *not* talking." His hands at my waist gripped a little tighter, thumbs pressing into my ribcage, fingers at the small of my back.

I blinked, one moment not understanding what his words implied, and the next knowing unreservedly.

"I don't know what you mean," I lied.

He leaned closer still, his smooth cheek whispering against mine as he murmured, "Yes, you do." Struck again by his scent—clean and subtle, unlike the trendy colognes Kennedy favored, which always seemed to overpower any scent I wore—I felt an impulse to bring my fingertips to his face and trail them over his freshly shaven jaw, the sexy scruff from yesterday gone. His skin wouldn't redden mine now if he kissed me, hard. I would feel nothing but his mouth on mine—and maybe that slim ring at the edge of his lip . . .

The errant thought made my breath catch.

When his lips touched just south of my earlobe, I thought I might pass out. "Let's just dance," he said. Pulling back just far enough to stare into my eyes, he drew my body against his, and my legs obeyed where his said to go.

chapter Five

"Holy *fuckburgers*. Who *was* that *hot guy*?" Erin carefully maneuvered her daddy-furnished Volvo sedan around the people weaving drunkenly through the parking lot. "If I wasn't stone cold sober, I'd think he was a figment of my sex-starved imagination."

"Psshh," I mumbled, eyes closed, my spinning head lolling back against the headrest. "Don't even talk to me about *sex-starved*."

Erin grabbed my hand and squeezed. "Aw, shit. I'm sorry, J. I forgot."

It had been three weeks since my breakup, but I wasn't about to disclose the fact that it had been more like four weeks . . . maybe five, since the last time we'd been at all intimate. I should have seen Kennedy's lack of interest for the sign it was, rather than giving him justifications in my head—he was busy with frat obligations, while I fit in at least two hours of practice a day, more when I had ensemble rehearsal. He had his straight-A grade point average to maintain, and I had music lessons to give.

A minute later, Maggie piped up from the back seat. "You haven't answered the question, *Jacqueline*!" Her speech was almost as slurred as mine, my name pronounced in three distinct syllables, like three separate words. "Who was that beautiful guy, and more importantly, why didn't you solve your sex-starvedness with him? Holy hell, I think I'd be willing to boot Will outta bed for a night with him!"

"Slut," Erin said, rolling her eyes into her rearview mirror.

Maggie laughed. "In this case . . . Hell. Yeah."

They both grew quiet, staring at me, waiting for me to reveal who he was. I mentally sorted through everything I knew about him. He'd saved me from Buck's attack, which I hadn't told anyone about. He'd beaten the crap out of Buck, which I likewise hadn't told anyone. He'd stared at me all through economics on Wednesday, and then ignored me completely on Friday, which I hadn't told anyone. He worked at the Starbucks. And he kept asking me if I was okay . . . but he hadn't asked me that tonight.

Tonight had been something else altogether. By unspoken agreement, we'd danced several dances without stopping—slow, fast, and everything in between. His hands never left my body, triggering an upsurge of longing I'd not felt in a very long time—longer than four or five weeks ago. His hands hadn't wandered inappropriately, his fingers not even teasing beneath the fabric of my top at the waist, but they'd seared the skin beneath regardless.

And then he disappeared. Bending, his lips next to my ear, he thanked me for the dances, led me back to my table, and vanished into the throng of people. I hadn't seen him again, and could only assume he'd left the club.

"His name is Lucas. He's in my economics class. And he draws stuff."

Maggie began giggling and slapped the leather seat. "He draws stuff? What kind of stuff? Naked girls? That's pretty much the extent of most guys' artistic endeavors. Usually not even whole girls. Just *boobs*."

Erin and I laughed along with her. "I don't know what he draws. He was just . . . sketching something in class Friday. I don't think he listened to the lecture at all."

"Oh no, Erin!" Maggie leaned as far up as her seatbelt would allow. "Sounds like that god of a man is a *bad student*. We know what that means for Jacqueline."

I frowned. "What does it mean?"

Erin shook her head, smiling. "Come on, J—have you ever in your life been attracted to a bad boy? Or a boy who's, um, academically challenged? In other words, a boy who isn't—gasp!—a *brainiac*?"

My mouth fell open. "Shut up! Are you saying I'm an intellectual snob?"

"No! We didn't say you were—we don't mean that. We just mean . . . you sure didn't look indifferent to this Lucas guy tonight, while you two danced together for like *ever*, and it sounds like he's maybe not your usual type—"

"My only 'type' has been Kennedy for the past three years! Who knows what my type is?"

"Don't get huffy. You know what I mean—you don't even *crush* on dumb guys."

"Well, who does?" I rebelled against the idea that Lucas was dumb. Maybe he was unmotivated in economics, but nothing about him seemed unintelligent.

"Hello!?" Maggie called. "Do you even *know* Will?" We all dissolved into fits of giggles. Maggie's boyfriend was a sweet guy, and he could probably bench press a small Honda, but he wouldn't be winning any acclaim for his GPA.

"Chaz is brainier than me—but that's not saying much," Erin said.

I've tried repeatedly to get her to quit knocking her B-average intellect, but at some point in her life, she became convinced that she's not smart. I poked her in the arm, as I had every time she's spouted that self-deprecating nonsense.

"Ow! I'm just being honest!"

"No, you're not."

"*Anyway*," Erin continued, "I've been known to slum it and shop in the gag-him-and-bag-him aisles, believe it or not." Maggie hooted a laugh behind us as Erin continued. "Have y'all seen the guy who took me to senior prom?" We'd all seen her photos of that guy—the Adonis in a tux, his arm around her silk-clad waist. "What a body—holy cow, I just wanted to lick his abs. He was in remedial classes, but let me tell you, he was *gifted and talented* at plenty of nonacademic occupations."

I was pretty sure my face was on fire—as it was whenever my roommate elaborated so explicitly—and Maggie was laughing so hard she was having trouble breathing. They'd both come to college single and sexually experienced. Kennedy and I had been sleeping together since winter break of senior year, but I'd never been with anyone else. I'd had no complaints about our sex life, though the occasional magazine article or something Erin said made me wonder if there was more to it than I knew.

"And all of this proves . . . ?"

Erin grinned at me. "It proves you're ready for a long-overdue Bad Boy Phase."

"Ooohhh," Maggie sighed.

"Um. I don't think—"

"*Exactly*. Don't think. You're gonna seduce this Lucas guy and rebound the hell out of him. That's the thing about bad boys—they don't have any qualms about being the rebound guy because they don't hang around for long anyway. He probably *lives* for being the rebound guy—especially in a situation like this, where he'll get to teach you all sorts of naughty stuff."

Maggie endorsed Erin's crazy idea with one heavily sighed word. "*Lucky*."

I thought of Lucas's hands at my waist, his mouth grazing my ear, and I shivered. I recalled his penetrating gaze Wednesday during class, and the breath in my lungs went shallow. Maybe I was experiencing alcohol perspective, and everything would look different tomorrow—but at the moment, Erin's crazy idea was starting to sound almost *not* crazy.

Oh, hell.

• • • • • • • • • • •

I was a ball of nerves as I approached the classroom Monday morning, unsure if I should initiate the man-snaring strategy I'd agreed to test on my unsuspecting classmate, or abandon it fully while I still could. He walked into the room ahead of me, and I watched his eyes flick over my recently assigned seat, and the vacant one next to Kennedy, who was already seated, thank God. I had about thirty seconds to reconsider the whole thing.

Erin and Maggie hadn't let up on the thankfully short drive back to the dorm, feeding each other's enthusiasm and swearing envy over what I was about to do. Or *who* I was about to do. Since Erin had nothing to drink on Saturday but Diet Dr. Pepper, she'd sprung out of bed Sunday morning unhungover and chock-full of plans for Operation Bad Boy Phase.

I pretended more of a hangover than I had, just to put her off, but Erin with an idea was not readily put off. Determined to impart her how-to-seduce-a-guy knowledge whether I wanted it or not, she'd shoved a bottle of orange juice into my hands as I grumbled and pulled myself to a sitting position. I wanted to tug the covers over my head and plug my ears, but it was far too late for that.

She plopped next to me. "First, you have to approach this with *no fear*. Seriously, they can smell fear. It totally puts them off the scent."

I frowned. "Off the scent? That's so . . ." I tried to think of a more suitable word than *aaauugh*, but my brain hadn't booted up yet.

"That's so *true*, you mean? Look—guys are dogs. Women have known this since the beginning of time. Guys don't want to be chased; they chase. So if you're going to catch one, you have to know how to make *him* chase *you*."

I squinted at her. *Archaic, sexist, demeaning* my brain declared, filling in for *aaauugh*, too late. This viewpoint shouldn't have surprised me—I'd heard her say these sorts of things before. I just never considered those off-the-cuff remarks to be part of a creed.

I chugged half of the OJ before commenting. "You're serious about this."

She cocked an eyebrow. "This is where I *don't* say 'as a heart attack,' right?"

• • • • • • • • • • •

Go time.

I took a deep breath. I had three minutes until class started. Erin said I needed one minute, no more than two. "But two is pushing it," she insisted, "because then you look *too* interested. One is better."

I slid into the seat next to him, but perched on the edge, making it obvious that I had no intention of remaining. His eyes snapped to mine immediately, dark brows disappearing into that messy hair falling over his forehead. His eyes were almost colorless. I'd never seen anyone with eyes so light.

He was definitely startled by my appearance next to him. Good, according to Erin and Maggie.

"Hey," I said, a subtle smile on my lips, hoping I appeared somewhere between interested and indifferent. According to Erin and Maggie, that impression was a vital part of the strategy.

"Hey." He opened his econ text, concealing the open sketchbook in front of him. Before he obscured it, I caught a detailed illustration of the venerated old oak tree in the center of campus and the ornamental wrought iron fence surrounding it.

I swallowed. *Interested and indifferent*. "So, it just occurred to me that I don't remember your name from the other night. Too many margaritas, I guess."

He wet his lips and stared at me a moment before answering, and I blinked, wondering if he was purposefully making my loosely sustained *indifference* more challenging to maintain. "It's Lucas. And I don't think I gave it."

In the next moment, Dr. Heller entered noisily near the podium, catching his handled case in the door. An audible "Dammit" echoed through the lecture hall, thanks to the planned acoustics of the room. Lucas and I smiled at each other as our fellow classmates tittered.

"So . . . you, um, called me Jackie, before?" I said, and his head tilted slightly. "I actually go by Jacqueline. Now."

His brows drew down slightly. "Okay."

I cleared my throat and stood—surprising him again, judging by his expression. "Nice to meet you, Lucas." I smiled again before turning away and darting to my assigned seat.

Keeping my attention on the lecture and defying the compulsion to peek over my shoulder was excruciating. I was sure I felt Lucas's eyes boring into the back of my head. Like an out-of-reach itch, the sensation nettled me for fifty minutes straight, and it took herculean effort to refrain from turning around. Unknowingly, Benji helped by making distracting observations on Dr. Heller, like tallying the number of times he said "Uuummm" during the lecture with marks at the top of his notebook, and pointing out the fact that our professor was sporting one navy and one brown sock.

Instead of lingering at the end of class to see what Lucas would do (speak to me or ignore me?), instead of waiting for Kennedy to leave (funny, I'd paid scant attention to him for the past hour—that was a first), I swung my backpack onto my shoulder and practically sprinted from the room without looking at either of them. Emerging from the side door into the crisp fall air, I sucked in a deep breath. Agenda: Spanish class, lunch, Starbucks.

Erin: How'd OBBP go?
Me: Got him to tell me his name. Went back to my seat. Didn't look at him again.
Erin: Perfect. Meet you after next class for more strategizing before coffee. ;)

• • • • • • • • • • •

When Erin and I joined the line at the Starbucks, I didn't see Lucas.

"Rats." She craned her neck, making sure he wasn't one of the people behind the counter. "He was here last Monday, right?"

I shrugged. "Yeah, but his work schedule is probably unpredictable."

She elbowed me lightly. "Not so much. That's him there, right?"

He came through a door to the back with an industrial-sized bag of coffee. My physical reaction to him was unnerving. It was as though my insides all twisted up tight at the sight of him, and when they unwound, everything restarted at once—my heart rate accelerating, lungs pumping air, brain waves running amok.

"Ooh, J, he's got *ink*, too," Erin murmured appreciatively. "Just when I didn't think he could get any hotter . . ."

My eyes fell to his forearms, flexing as he sliced the bag open. Tattooed designs wrapped around his wrists, contiguous symbols and script running up both arms and disappearing into the sleeves of the gray knit shirt, which were shoved above his elbows. I'd never seen him without his sleeves pulled to the wrists. Even Saturday night, he'd worn long sleeves—a faded black button-down, open over a white T-shirt.

I'd never been attracted to guys with tattoos. The notion of needles injecting ink under the skin and the confidence to make permanent imprints of words and symbols was foreign to me. Now, I wondered how far the tattoos spread—just the sleeves of his arms? His back? His chest?

Erin tugged my arm as the line moved forward. "You're botching our carefully crafted *indifferent* act, by the way. Not that I can blame you." She sighed. "Maybe we should bail now before he—"

I glanced at her when she fell silent, watching a devious smile cross her face as she turned to me.

"Keep looking at me," she said, laughing as though we were having an amusing conversation. "He's staring at you. And I mean *staring*. That boy is undressing you with his eyes. Can you feel it?" Her expression was triumphant.

Could I feel his stare? *I can now, thanks,* I thought. My face heated.

"Oh my God, you're blushing," she whispered, her dark eyes widening.

"No shit." My teeth gritted, voice tight. "Stop telling me he's—he's—"

"Undressing you with his eyes?" She laughed again and I'd never wanted to kick her more. "Okay, okay—but J, do *not* worry. You've got this. I don't know what you've done to him, but he's ready to sit up and beg. Trust me." She glanced in his direction. "Okay, he's starting a new batch of coffee now. You can do your own staring."

We stepped closer; there were only two people in front of us. I watched Lucas replace the filter, measure out the coffee, and set the controls. His green apron was haphazardly secured in the back—more of a knot than a bow. The ties drew my eyes to his hips in his worn, low-slung jeans, one pocket holding a wallet to which a loose chain was attached. It disappeared under the apron, linking to a front belt loop, no doubt.

He turned then, eyes on the second register as he punched buttons and brought it to life. I wondered if he planned to ignore me as I had him during class. It would serve me right, playing this game. Just as the guy in front of me began his detailed drink order to the girl at the first register, Lucas's gaze swung up to meet mine. "Next?" The steel gray of his shirt set off the gray in his eyes, the blue disappearing. "Jacqueline." He greeted me with a smirk, and I worried that he could read my mind, and the devious plans Erin had implanted in it. "Americano today, or something else?"

He remembered my drink order from a week ago.

I nodded, and he flashed a barely there grin at my bemusement, ringing up the order and printing the cup with a Sharpie. Instead of passing it on, though, he made the drink himself while Erin gave her order to his coworker.

He added a protective sleeve and a lid and handed me the cup.

I couldn't read his trace of a smile. "Have a nice day." Looking over my shoulder, he said, "Next?"

I joined Erin at the pick-up counter, confused and sulking.

"He made the drink for you?" She retrieved her drink and followed me to the condiment counter.

"Yeah." I removed the lid and added sugar and milk while she shook cinnamon over her latte. "But he just handed it over like I was any other customer and took the next guy's order." We watched him interact with customers. He didn't once glance my way.

"I could have sworn he was so into you he couldn't see straight," she mused as we left, rounding a corner to join the mass of people flowing through the student center.

"Hey, baby!" Chaz's voice pulled both of us from our thoughts. He snatched Erin out of the flow of people and I followed, laughing at her delighted squeal until I noticed the guy standing next to him.

My face went hot, blood pounding in my ears. As our friends kissed hello and began talking about what time they each got off work tonight, Buck stared down at me, his mouth turning up on one side. My breath came in pants and I fought to keep the rising panic and nausea under control. I wanted to turn and run, but I was immobilized.

He couldn't touch me here. He couldn't hurt me here.

"Hey, Jackie." His piercing gaze roamed over me and my skin crawled. "Lookin' good, as always." His words gushed flirtation, but all I felt was the threat underneath, intended or not.

The bruises had faded from his face, but weren't entirely gone.

One yellowish streak ringed his left eye, and another brushed along the right side of his nose like a pale smear. Lucas had given him those, and only the three of us knew it. I stared back, mute, the coffee clutched in my hand. I'd once thought this boy handsome and charming—the all-American veneer he wore fooling me as thoroughly as it fooled everyone else.

I raised my chin, ignoring my physical reaction to him, and the fear causing it. "It's Jacqueline."

He cocked one eyebrow, confused. "Huh?"

Erin grabbed my elbow. "Come on, hot stuff. Don't you have art history in like five minutes?"

I stumbled slightly as I turned and followed her, and he issued a soft, taunting laugh as I passed him. "See you around, *Jacqueline*," he teased.

My name in his mouth sent a tremor through me, and I trailed behind Erin into the sea of students. Once I could move, I couldn't get away from him fast enough.

chapter *Six*

Erin: Do you still have your coffee cup?
Me: Yes?
Erin: Take the sleeve off
Me: OMG
Erin: His phone number?
Me: How did you know???
Erin: I'm Erin. I know all. ;)
Actually, I just wondered why he wrote on your cup if he was going to make your drink.

If Erin hadn't texted me during class, that cup, and his number, would have been pitched into the hallway wastebasket.

So . . . Lucas wasn't writing an unnecessary drink order onto my cup, he was giving me his phone number. I entered it into my phone, wondering what I was meant to do with it. Call him? Text him?

I thought about what I knew of him: He'd come out of nowhere the night of the party. After putting a stop to the attack, some further protective trait had obliged him to see me safely back to the dorm. He'd somehow known my name that night—my nickname—but I'd never noticed him before.

He sat in the back row in econ, sketching or staring at me instead of paying attention to the lecture. Saturday night, the firm touch of his hands as we danced made my head swim, before he disappeared without explanation. He'd undressed me with his eyes, Erin said, in the middle of Starbucks—where he worked. He was cocky and self-assured. Tattooed and too hot for words. He looked and acted like the Bad Boy Erin and Maggie believed him to be.

And now, his number was programmed into my phone. It was as though he knew all about Operation Bad Boy Phase, and he was as willing and eager to fill that role as my friends believed he'd be.

But I didn't know him. I didn't know what he thought of me. If he thought of me. The girl talking to him after class last week wanted him. In the club, girls had openly stared as he passed, some of them turning around in his wake to assess him further. He could have danced with any of them, probably gone home with most of them. Why me?

• • • • • • • • • •

Landon,

I've attached an outline of my research paper. If you have a chance, could you make sure it's not too broad, or too focused? I'm not sure how many economies outside the US to include. Also, the J-curve is a little confusing. I get that we can see it after the fact, but isn't economics based on prediction, like the weather? I mean, who cares if we can only see what happened after the fact—if the weather guy can't predict what's going to happen tomorrow, he's probably going to get fired, right?

I did the worksheets, too. Sorry I'm sending you so much at once, and on a Monday. I should have sent it earlier, but I went out with some friends Saturday and didn't get it done.

JW

Jacqueline,

No problem. I'm either working, studying, or in class practically every waking hour. I hardly notice what day it is. I hope you enjoyed your night out.

I know I initially said I didn't need details of your breakup (if that was rude, I didn't mean it that way); it must have been bad to make you ditch class for two weeks. I can tell skipping is atypical for you.

I've attached a WSJ article that explains the J-curve better than the text. You're exactly right, without the ability to predict, economics isn't economics, it's history. And while history has its place in the predictable probabilities of both economics and meteorology (clever analogy, btw), it's hardly useful if you need to know whether or not to invest in foreign currency or bring your umbrella to school.

LM

I stared at the email, trying and failing to compare Landon to Lucas. They seemed as opposite as night and day, but I only knew half of each of them. I didn't know much about Lucas beyond his striking looks and his ability to beat the shit out of someone. During art history, I'd found myself wondering what would have happened in that interaction with Buck if Lucas had been with me. I wondered if Buck would have dared to look at me like that. To say what he'd said: *Lookin' good*. The thought of Buck's cold eyes examining me made my stomach turn.

Feeling shallow for caring, I speculated again what Landon might look like, and how much impact that might have on what I thought of him. His compliments made me stare at my laptop and smile. He'd said my ex was a moron, and now he seemed to be interested in our breakup. In me. That, or I was reading too much into it.

Landon,

We were together almost three years. I never saw it coming. I followed him here to school, instead of trying for a performing arts school. My orchestra teacher nearly had a stroke when I told him. He pleaded with me to audition at Oberlin or Julliard, but I didn't. I can't blame anyone but myself. I trusted my future to my HS boyfriend, like an idiot. Now I'm stuck somewhere I'm not supposed to be. I don't know if I just believed that much in him or that little in myself. Either way, pretty freaking stupid, huh? So there's my weepy little story.

Thank you for the article.

JW

Jacqueline,

Not stupid. Overly trusting, maybe, but that reflects on his lack of trustworthiness, not on your intelligence. As for being somewhere you're not supposed to be—maybe you're here for a reason, or there is no reason. As a scientist, I lean toward the latter. Either way, you're off the hook. You made a decision; now you make the best of it. That's all you can do, right? On that note, I'm off to study for a statistical mechanics quiz. Who knows, maybe I'll be able to prove scientifically that your ex isn't worthy of you, and you're exactly where you should be.

LM

• • • • • • • • • • •

When Erin came through the door, I was half-asleep and surrounded by conjugated Spanish verbs printed on colored index cards. I scooped most of them up just before she bounced onto the edge of my bed.

"So? Did you call him or text him? Did you use the stuff we went over? What did he say?"

I sighed. "Neither."

She lay back on the bed, flinging her arms wide dramatically as I snatched up cards before she creased them. "You chickened out."

I stared at the cards in my hand. *Yo habré, tú habrás, él habrá, nosotros habremos* . . . "Yeah, maybe."

"Hmm. You know, this is better. Don't call. Make him chase you." She laughed at my creased brow. "Guys like Chaz are so much easier. Hell, I could *tell* him to chase me and he would."

We laughed at the visual that produced, because it was probably true. I thought about Kennedy. About what kind of guy he was. He'd chased me in the beginning, but he didn't have to try very hard to catch me. I was swept off my feet by him, swept along in his dreams and plans, because he'd made me part of them. Until a few weeks ago.

"Aw, shit, J. I know what you're doing. Don't think about him. I'm gonna make some cocoa. Get back to"—she sat up, picking up a card I hadn't grabbed hastily enough—"*ugh*, Spanish verbs."

Erin filled mugs with tap water in the bathroom and stuck them in the microwave to heat. I stared at the blurry cards in my hand. Damn Kennedy. Damn him, damn him. It would serve him right to see me with someone like Lucas. Someone so different, but equally hot. More so, if I started calculating details.

Operation Bad Boy Phase was *on*. But I wasn't calling Lucas, or texting him. If Erin was right—if he was a chaser—he hadn't done enough chasing yet.

When she handed me the mug, I took a deep breath and smiled. She'd piled mine with marshmallows from the little stash of them we both occasionally dug into without bothering to make cocoa. "So if I don't text him, what's next?"

She smiled and squeaked a triumphant little squeal. "He must be digging the good girl thing you've got going on . . ." Her eyes widened. "Jacqueline—maybe he'd noticed you in class before the breakup. You changed seats, right? Making it obvious you two broke up. This is *perfect*." I was back to confused and she was laughing. "He's *already* chasing you. Now all you have to do is keep running. Just not too fast."

I licked chocolate from my upper lip. "Erin, you're dangerous."

She smiled wickedly. "I *know*."

• • • • • • • • • • •

Wednesday, I got to the classroom before the eight o'clock class let out. As soon as most of the students had filed out the door, I slipped in and took my seat, determined not to pay attention to Lucas when he came in. To that end, I flipped through my index cards, though I was more than ready to ace the quiz in Spanish.

When Benji slid into his seat on my left, I didn't pause in my review. I refused to be distracted from *not* paying attention to Lucas's seat and whether he was in it or not.

"Hey, Jacqueline." That wasn't Benji's voice.

The seats were bolted to the floor, with right-handed desktops. Lucas leaned slightly over the side of Benji's, pushing into the very margin of my space. My breath caught, and I focused on letting it out, appearing unaffected. "Oh, hi."

He bit his lower lip once, briefly. "I guess you didn't notice the phone number on your coffee cup."

I glanced at my phone, sitting on the edge of my textbook. "I noticed." I watched his reaction, knowing I was practically *telling* him to chase me.

He smiled, his light eyes crinkling slightly at the corners, and I tried not to swoon visibly. "I see. Turnabout is fair play. How 'bout you give me yours?"

I arched a brow at him. "Why? Do you need help in economics?"

He bit his lip in earnest that time, stifling a laugh. "Hardly. What makes you think that?"

I frowned. Could I be attracted to a guy who cared so little about doing well in class? "I guess it's not my business."

He leaned his chin into the palm of his hand. The tips of his fingers were tinged with gray, probably from drawing with that pencil sitting over his ear. "I appreciate your concern, but I want your number for reasons completely unrelated to economics."

I picked up my phone and found his number, and sent him a text that said: Hi.

"Dude, you're in my seat." Benji's tone was matter-of-fact but unperturbed.

Lucas's phone vibrated in his hand, and he smiled as my text popped up, giving him my number. "Thanks." He unfolded himself from the chair and addressed Benji. "Sorry, man."

"No prob." Benji was one of the most easygoing people I'd ever met. His attitude said *slacker*, but I'd gotten a look at the midterm crammed into his notebook—he'd made a high B, and for all his talk about skipping class and sleeping in, he'd yet to miss one. After Lucas sauntered back to his seat, Benji leaned over the edge of his desktop, closer than Lucas had. "So what was *that* about?" His eyebrows rocked up and down and I tried not to grin.

"I'm sure I don't know what you mean," I replied, fluttering my lashes in my best Southern belle impersonation.

"Careful, little lady," he drawled. "That fella seems a bit dangerous." He shook a too-long curl out of his eyes, smiling. "Not that there's anything wrong with a bit of danger."

My lips pinched into half a smile. "True."

I congratulated myself for taking a singular peek over my shoulder, halfway through the fifty-minute class. Lucas wasn't looking at me, so I couldn't help staring. Pencil in hand, he was sketching intently, first shading and then carefully smearing with his thumb. His dark hair fell around his face as he concentrated on his work, the lecture and the classroom disregarded as though he was alone in his room. I imagined him sitting on his bed, knees up, pad balanced on his thighs. I wondered what he was sketching. Or who.

He glanced up and caught my gaze. Held it.

His mouth pulled into that ghost of a smile and he stretched his neck and rolled his shoulders, returning my stare. Glancing at the pad, he tapped the end of his pencil against it and sprawled back in his seat, lashes fanning down as he examined his work.

Dr. Heller finished the chart he was free-handing onto the whiteboard, and the lecture resumed. Lucas tucked the pencil over his ear and picked up a pen. Before shifting his attention to our professor, he smiled at me again, and a jolt of excitement shot through me.

At the end of class, a different girl than last week intercepted him on his way out the door, and I bolted without a backward look. My adrenaline kicked in, my body sensing my need to escape and giving wings to it. Glancing over my shoulder, I ducked through the side exit and slowed down, feeling silly. Erin and Maggie insisted that I should elude his grasp for a few days more, make him pursue me—but he wasn't going to *literally* give chase.

I texted Erin that I'd be getting crap coffee in the cafeteria before my afternoon class instead of going by the Starbucks. She texted back:

GENIUS. I'll meet you there. Sisters in solidarity and all that shit.

• • • • • • • • • • •

By the end of art history, I was beginning to doubt Erin's notion that Lucas wanted to play this game. Maybe he wasn't a dog. Or I wasn't a cat. Or I was just really bad at this. I sighed, stuffing my phone into my bag. I'd clicked it to check for a message at least thirty times during class.

I'd always disparaged the games people played in pursuit of love—or the next hookup. The whole thing was a competition to see who could get how far, and I could never figure out if there was more luck or skill involved, or some unknowable combination of the two. People rarely said what they thought or revealed how they felt. No one was honest.

Easy for me to say, from my high horse of the perfect relationship with Kennedy. Erin had called me on that months ago, when I told her she was being ridiculous over a guy—plotting to decipher what he wanted from a girl before systematically breaking down his defenses. I had to admit she was right. I had no idea what it was like to be a young, single adult, so I wasn't entitled to judge.

Until now.

This angst was absurd, but I couldn't shake it. He'd stared at me in class. I felt confident when I left economics, and miserable now. Why? Because he hadn't shoved the redhead out of his way at the end of econ to come after me? Because he hadn't texted me at some point during the barely three and a half hours since I'd seen him? That didn't even make sense.

By the time I was heating soup in the microwave for dinner, I'd resigned myself to having failed at keeping Lucas's interest. I pushed the pretty girl who'd rushed up to him at the end of the class from my mind, once I started imagining him leaving the class holding her hand, or more. "Dumbass," I muttered at myself.

From the end of my bed, my laptop dinged an email alert, and an answering flutter came from my stomach. It was probably nothing—a notice about flu shots from the health center, or another note from one of my old high school friends, who were all "so devastated" that Kennedy and I were over (which they all figured out when he changed his Facebook relationship status—*twenty minutes* after he'd broken up with me).

I'd disabled my account immediately, and I had yet to reinstate it. The thought of seeing his glib status updates and having photos of him pop up in my feed was demoralizing. Even if I hid him, we knew too many of the same people. There'd be no hiding his activities completely. I began getting sympathetic and condescending emails and texts the next day, so I was justifiably apprehensive whenever I checked my inbox.

Cringing, I pulled it up . . . and smiled.

Jacqueline,

Are you going to make it to the session tomorrow (Thursday)? In case you won't, I've attached the worksheet I'm planning to go over. It's new, separate stuff, and you needn't be completely caught up to get it. (Speaking of, you should be all caught up within a week or so.)

LM

PS—I've been thinking about that proof I spoke of last time—that you're where you're supposed to be. And it occurred to me, can you prove you'd be better off somewhere else? If you'd have left the state, your relationship would have ended still. Maybe you'd have even blamed yourself, not knowing that it was doomed because of him, either way. Instead, you're here. You got dumped, skipped class, and met the best econ tutor at the university! Who knows, maybe I'll make you fall in love with economics. (What's your major, btw?)

Landon,

I'm a music education major. I hate that saying: "Those who can, *do*, those who can't, *teach*." As a tutor, I know that's BS. Still. I wanted to *do*. I imagined joining a symphony orchestra, or a progressive jazz band . . . And instead, I'm going to teach.

I won't be at your session—I have lessons with my middle school boys tomorrow. (I think I'd be more impressive to them if I could fart the scales instead of plucking them on the bass.)

Sorry to inform you, but I plan to make it through this class and be done with econ. No reflection on your genius tutoring skills, I swear. Thank you for the worksheet. You're too kind.

JW

Jacqueline,

If you want to do, then do. What's stopping you?

So I'm kind, huh? Never heard that before. People usually think I'm a pretentious a-hole. I must admit, I tend to encourage that estimation. So please promise to keep your opinion to yourself. Reputations can be ruined so easily, you know. ;)

LM

PS—Do the worksheet. Before Friday. I'm giving you a very serious look through this screen. DO THE WORKSHEET. If you have problems with any of the material, let me know.

Landon,

What's stopping me? Well, I've blown the chance to go to a serious music school. And I'm stuck in a state that doesn't always foster the arts (something I'll probably spend my entire teaching career fighting). It seems impossible to go out now and "do." I guess I should rethink that.

Your secret geniality is safe. My lips are sealed.

JW

PS—I'm DOING the worksheet, but I'm giving you a very petulant look through my screen. Slave driver. Sheesh.

I was grinning when I clicked Send. Maybe I was playing an entirely different game of chase, and Lucas and his infuriatingly enigmatic smile could take a flying leap. Erin and Maggie could keep their make-him-chase-you advice and use it themselves, because I, apparently, sucked at it in real life. Through email, though . . . My happy expression slid away as I realized the stark truth—I was flirting with someone online. I had no idea what he looked like, or what type of person he was.

That wasn't exactly true. I knew exactly what type of person he was, even though I'd never laid eyes on him. He was kind. And intelligent. And straightforward.

Of course, he hadn't beaten a would-be rapist to a bloody pulp for me. Or made my insides melt when he put his hands on my waist. He probably didn't have tattoos on his arms or glacier-gray-blue eyes and a liquefying stare.

At ten p.m., my phone trilled a text alert.

Lucas: Hi :)

Me: Hi :)

Lucas: What's up?

Me: Nothing. Homework.

Lucas: I wanted to talk to you after class, but you disappeared.

Me: I have another class right after. One of those profs who stops talking, stares at you and waits until you get to your seat if you're late.

Lucas: I would probably just walk to my seat even slower. ;) You should come by the SB Friday. It's usually dead. Americano, on the house?

Me: Free coffee? I can't pass that up. I'll try to stop by. When do you work?

Lucas: All afternoon. Til 5.

Me: K

Lucas: See you Friday, Jacqueline

chapter *Seven*

Lucas was fifteen minutes late to class on Friday, and we had a pop quiz first thing—which he missed. My first thought was how irresponsible it was to miss a quiz . . . and then I remembered that I missed the *midterm*. I couldn't exactly point any fingers.

He slipped through the back door as Dr. Heller walked up the center aisle, collecting quizzes. He took the stacks from the left row and then turned to the right, where Lucas sat. "I need to see you after class," he said, his voice low.

Inclining his head once, Lucas pulled his text from his backpack and replied in the same subdued tone. "Yes, sir."

I didn't look back at him during the remainder of class, and when it was over, he packed up his backpack and walked down the outside aisle to the front. While waiting for Dr. Heller to finish his conversation with another student, Lucas's eyes lifted and found me. His smile was as unreadable as always, scarcely there at all. But his gaze was focused, pegging me like a dart to a board.

Turning his attention to our professor, he broke the stare. I released the breath I hadn't realized I was holding and escaped the classroom, undecided on whether to follow through with stopping by Starbucks that afternoon.

I considered the quiz I'd just aced, thanks to Landon's insistence that I complete the worksheet he sent two nights ago. Doing that worksheet had been all sorts of help—on a quiz he must have known about. I didn't think he'd crossed a line and told me something he shouldn't have, but his toe was definitely on the line. For me. Swept along and invisible among thousands of other students on this enormous campus, I was struck by the fact that for some reason, he'd gone out of his way to help me. For some reason, I mattered to him.

• • • • • • • • • • •

Erin: Chaz and I are leaving soon. You gonna be ok this weekend? You're going to SB this afternoon, RIGHT? If he asks you out, GO FOR IT. Clear the palate! Don't forget you'll have the room to yourself all weekend. WINK WINK.

Me: You kids have fun. I'll be fine! I'll keep you posted.

Erin: You'd better! I'll be back Sunday afternoon. Or evening, depending on the level of hangover Sunday morning. Heh heh. TEXT ME LATER.

I'd forgotten Erin's road trip with Chaz was this weekend. His brother was in a band, and they were playing at a festival tomorrow near Shreveport, so they had reservations at a bed-and-breakfast for the weekend. Erin had told Maggie and me about it last month while we waited to look at Mercury and Venus through a telescope during an evening astronomy lab.

"A *bed-and-breakfast?*" Maggie arched a brow. "What's next, monogrammed towels?"

Erin scowled. "It's romantic!"

"Exactly." Maggie laughed. "And you're going with *Chaz*. How'd you even talk Mr. Sports Stats into that, anyway?"

Erin's full lips made a prim little bow and she combed a hand through hair so red I could tell its color even while standing in this dark field on the outskirts of town. "I told him that bed-and-breakfasts have ginormous whirlpool tubs, and that I'd be willing to do unspeakably sinful things to him in it."

A strangled sound came from one of the two nerdy guys behind us in line, both wearing tortured expressions and staring at Erin. We stifled laughs.

Maggie sighed. "Poor Chaz. He never had a chance . . . he's gonna be standing in front of a bunch of people saying 'I do' someday without knowing how it happened."

"Ugh! I don't think so. When it's time to settle down, I'm getting somebody like . . ." Erin looked over her shoulder at the eavesdroppers behind us. "Like one of them."

The boys looked at each other and stood up a little straighter. With a smirk in Erin's direction, one of them fist-bumped the other.

• • • • • • • • • •

I doubted Erin would give me a second thought during her romantic weekend. I was on my own. I deliberated, finally turning toward the student union while pulling my jacket tighter against the sudden November chill. Frat parties held this weekend wouldn't be open-window, not that I'd know firsthand. There was no way in hell I was going anywhere Kennedy might be. Or Buck.

The coffee smell invaded my senses before the Starbucks came into view. Rounding the corner, my eyes went to the counter, where two employees stood talking. When I didn't see Lucas, I wondered if he'd switched shifts and forgot to text me.

There was only a handful of customers—one of whom was Dr. Heller, reading the paper in the corner. I had nothing against my professor, but I didn't exactly want him witnessing my attempts to flirt with the guy who skipped the quiz and got called out for it just this morning. I stood just behind a display of coffee mugs and travel cups.

Just as he had Monday, Lucas pushed through the door to the back as my eyes brushed over it. My fingers and toes tingled at the sight of him. Underneath the green apron, he wore a close-fitting light-blue T-shirt, long-sleeved, not the university-branded sweatshirt he'd worn this morning in class. His shirtsleeves were pushed past his elbows again, leaving the tattoos visible. I moved to the counter, my eyes skimming from his forearms to his face. He hadn't seen me yet.

One of the girls at the register straightened. "Can I help you?" Her voice held a bite of annoyance, as though she was snapping her fingers to get my attention.

"I've got it, Eve," Lucas said, and she shrugged and returned to her conversation with her coworker, but they both eyed me with even more hostility than a moment before. "Hey, Jacqueline."

"Hi."

He glanced toward the corner where Dr. Heller sat. "What can I get for you?"

His tone wasn't the tone of a guy who'd specifically asked me to come by. Maybe he was behaving circumspectly for his coworkers' benefit.

"Um, a grande americano, I guess."

He grabbed the cup from the stack and made the drink. I tried to hand him my card, but he shook his head once. "That's okay. I've got it."

His coworkers exchanged a look I pretended not to see.

I thanked him and retreated to the opposite side of the shop from Dr. Heller, setting up my laptop to work on my econ project. I had to glean information from multiple sources to defend the position my research paper was taking. It was due before Thanksgiving break, less than two weeks away.

If I never had to make up another midterm, it would be too soon.

After an hour, I'd bookmarked a dozen sources on current international economic happenings, my coffee was gone, and Lucas hadn't come over once. I was expected at the high school for my weekly Friday afternoon bass lessons in half an hour. Shutting down my laptop, I turned to unplug the power cord from the wall.

"Ms. Wallace." At Dr. Heller's unexpected greeting, I jumped, knocking over my empty cup. "Oh! So sorry to have startled you!"

"Oh, that's okay. I'm a little jumpy—from, uh, the coffee." *And from thinking for one split second that you were Lucas.*

"I just wanted to let you know that Mr. Maxfield tells me you're almost caught up, and making headway on the project. I'm glad to hear it." He lowered his voice and glanced around conspiratorially. "My colleagues and I don't actually *want* to fail anyone, you know. Our goal is to frighten—I mean *encourage*—the less, er, serious students to produce. Not that I believe you're one of those."

I returned his smile. "I understand."

He straightened and cleared his throat. "Good, good. Well, on that note—have a *productive* weekend." He chuckled at his joke and I managed to avoid rolling my eyes.

"Thank you, Dr. Heller."

He walked to the counter and spoke to Lucas as I wound the power cord and stowed the laptop in my backpack. The conversation between them was earnest, and I was concerned when Dr. Heller seemed to gesture toward me at least once. I wondered if our professor believed that Lucas was one of those less serious students he could intimidate into becoming more dedicated. If so, I didn't want to be used as some sort of example.

As I walked out, I looked over my shoulder, but Lucas didn't shift his gaze my way at all, and his expression was tense. His coworker, wiping down a counter a few feet away, smirked at me.

When I left the high school two hours later, I switched on my phone, endeavoring to look forward to a weekend alone while it powered up. Clearly, the trip to Starbucks was a bust. Lucas had been, if possible, even more puzzling and cagey than he was before.

While working on the project, I'd emailed Landon to thank him for sending the worksheet Wednesday, and for insisting that I do it. Not wanting to trigger a possible guilt complex, I didn't directly refer to the tip-off he'd knowingly given me, in case he was the rigorously honest type of guy he seemed to be. I hadn't heard from him since Wednesday, but maybe he would email this afternoon or tonight. Maybe he'd be free this weekend, and we could finally meet.

I had one text from Erin that she and Chaz had arrived in Shreveport—along with lots of insinuation about what I could do with a room to myself—and Mom had texted to ask about my Thanksgiving plans. Kennedy and I had alternated spending the day at his house or mine the past three years. Somehow, this translated into confusion about whether I was coming home this year. When I texted her back that yes, breaking up with a guy generally means no more shared holidays, I expected an apology to follow. I should have known better.

Mom: Don't be snippy. Your dad and I planned and paid for a trip to Breckenridge that weekend, because we thought you could stay at the Moores'. I guess we'll have to cancel.

Me: Go ahead and go. I'll go home with Erin or something.

Mom: Ok. If you're sure.

Me: I'm sure.

Wow. My boyfriend dumps me, and the first chance Mom has to be tangibly supportive, she and Dad are taking off alone to go skiing. Way to make me feel wanted and included, Mom. As if Kennedy's rejection wasn't enough to deal with. Jesus.

I tossed my phone in an empty cup holder and drove back to campus, prepared to watch reality TV and work on economics all weekend.

When I got to my room, I saw that Lucas had texted while I was driving back.

Lucas: Sorry I didn't say goodbye
Me: It was awkward with Dr. Heller there I guess.
Lucas: Yeah. So, I'd like to sketch you.
Me: Oh?
Lucas: Yeah
Me: Okay. Not, like, sans clothes or anything right?
Lucas: Haha no. Unless you're up for that. J/k. Is tonight ok? Or tomorrow night?
Me: Tonight is good.
Lucas: Cool. I can be there in a couple of hours.
Me: Ok.
Lucas: What's your room number?
Me: 362. I'll need to let you into the building.
Lucas: I can probably get in. I'll text you if I can't.

chapter Eight

Lucas's knock was light. I was so nervous that I was trembling when I got up to answer the door.

He'd said he wanted to sketch me, but I wasn't sure if that's all he wanted to do, or if it was code for more. Erin would never let me hear the end of it if I had him in our room and didn't at least kiss him, though Lucas didn't strike me as the sort of guy who usually had to stop at kissing. Plenty of girls saw college as some sort of exploratory period, and many would be more than happy to explore Lucas. But it had taken me over a year to work up to sex with Kennedy, and he was the only guy I'd ever slept with. I wasn't ready to go there with Lucas, not yet anyway—rebound or not.

I took a breath.

He knocked again, a little harder, and I stopped thinking and opened the door.

Fringes of dark hair stuck out from his dark gray beanie. In the diffuse hallway lighting, his eyes took on the nearly colorless quality they'd had that first night, when he peered into my truck after he'd fought with Buck. He hunched his shoulders, hands in his front pockets, sketchpad under one arm. "Hey," he said.

I stepped back into the room, holding the door wide.

Olivia and Rona lounged in their own doorway across the hall, eyeballing Lucas, gaping at me, watching him enter my room while Erin was gone. Olivia arched a brow and glanced at her roommate.

The whole floor would know I had a hot guy in my room within five minutes.

I let the door swing shut as Lucas tossed his sketchpad on my bed and stood in the center of the room, which seemed to shrink with him in it. Without moving, he examined Erin's side of the room, the walls above her bed covered in photos, the Greek letters of her sorority above the glittery letters of her name. Taking advantage of his distraction, I studied him: cowboy boots, scuffed to hell; worn jeans; heather-gray hoodie. He turned his head to scan my side of the room, and I stared at his profile—recently shaved jaw, parted lips, dark eyelashes.

Facing me, his eyes flicked over me and then to the laptop on my desk, which I'd hooked to a small set of speakers. I'd set up a playlist of tracks from my collection and set it to play quietly. Another of Erin's suggestions. She'd titled the playlist OBBP, and I belatedly hoped he didn't inspect the list and ask what that meant. I wouldn't tell him, of course, but my blush-prone parts would probably incinerate.

"I like this band. Did you see them last month?" he asked.

Kennedy and I had seen them, in fact—the night before we broke up. They were one of our favorite local groups. He'd been weird that night. Distant. At concerts, he'd usually tuck my back to his chest, legs spread just enough to accommodate my feet between his, his arms locked around my middle. Instead, he'd stood next to me, like we were friends. After we broke up, I realized that he'd made up his mind before that night—that his reserve was evidence of the wall between us; I just hadn't seen it yet.

I nodded, vanquishing Kennedy from my thoughts. "Did you?"

"Yeah. I don't remember seeing you there—but it was dark, and I maybe had a beer or two." He smiled—white teeth, just imperfect enough to indicate that he hadn't suffered through the orthodontics I had. Pulling off the cap and dropping it on my bed, he placed the pencil on his sketchbook and slid both hands through his flattened hair, and then shook it out, resulting in a bed-head look. *Good God.* When he drew the hoodie over his head, his white T-shirt pulled up a bit with it, and I got my answer on how far the tattoos extended. Four lines of script, too small to read, snaked around his left side. Some sort of Celtic-looking design balanced it on the right. Bonus: I now knew what Erin meant by *lickable* abs.

The hoodie joined the cap, and his T-shirt fell back into place. Picking up the sketchbook and pencil, he turned to me, and I noted that the ink on his forearms continued over his biceps and under the short sleeves of his shirt.

"Where do you want me?" More breathless than I'd intended, my question seemed a brazen proposition. Wow. Could I be any more obvious? Maybe I should just come out and ask him if he wanted to be my Kennedy rebound, no strings attached.

My insides went liquid from his ghost of a smile—the one that was becoming more and more familiar. "On the bed?" he said, his voice gruff.

Oh, God. "Okay." I moved to perch on the edge of the mattress as he swept the hoodie and the cap to the floor. My heart was pounding, waiting.

He peered at me, head angling to the side. "Um. You look really uneasy. We don't have to do this if you don't want to."

We don't have to do what? I thought, wishing I could ask him if using me as a model was a pretense, and telling him that if so, it was a pretense he didn't need to maintain. I looked him in the eye. "I want to."

He stuck the pencil over his ear, looking unconvinced. "Mmm. What position would be the most comfortable for you?"

I couldn't say aloud the answers that popped into my head at that question, but the flush that spread across my face like wildfire gave me away. He caught his lower lip in his teeth, and I was sure it was to contain a laugh. Most comfortable position? What about with my head stuck under a pillow?

He glanced around my room and went to sit on the floor, against the wall, facing the foot of my bed. Knees up, pad on his thighs, he was just as I imagined him in class the other day. Except he was in my room, not his own.

"Lie down on your stomach and rest your head on your arms, facing me."

I did as he told me. "Like this?"

He nodded, eyeing me as if absorbing details or searching for flaws. Coming onto his knees, he moved close enough to fan his fingers through my hair and let it fall over my shoulder. "Perfect," he murmured, scooting back to his position against the wall, a few feet away.

I stared at him as he sketched, his eyes moving back and forth from my face to the pad. At some point, his gaze began to move over the rest of me. As if his fingertips skimmed over my shoulders and down my back, my breath caught in my throat and I shut my eyes.

"Falling asleep?" His voice was soft. Near.

I opened my eyes to find him on his knees next to me, sitting back on his heels. My heart picked up the pace again at his nearness. "No." He'd left the pad and pencil on the floor behind him. "Are you . . . done?"

He shook his head slightly. "No. I'd like to do another, if you don't mind." At my nod, he said, "Turn onto your back."

I rolled over slowly, afraid he'd be able to see my heart hammering through my thin sweater. He grabbed the pad and pencil from the floor and stood. Staring down, he let his eyes roam over me, and I felt vulnerable, but not in danger. I knew so little about him, but there was one thing I felt unequivocally: safe.

"I'm going to arrange you, if that's okay?"

I swallowed. "Uh . . . sure." My hands seemed affixed to my ribcage, my shoulders hunched almost to my ears. *What, this isn't how you want me positioned?* I barely contained the nervous twitter that bubbled up at the thought.

His fingers encircled the wrist nearest him, and he brought my arm over my head, bent it as though it had been thrown back. Taking the opposite hand, he splayed my fingers over my abdomen, sat back, stared at me a moment, and then moved it, too, over my head, crossing my wrists, as though I was bound. I struggled to breathe normally. *Impossible*. "I'm going to move your leg," he said, his eyes on mine, waiting for my nod. His hands on my knee, he angled it out, leaving it flush against the mattress.

He picked up the pad and turned the page. "Now tilt your face toward me a bit—chin down—that's good. And shut your eyes." I fought to remain relaxed, knowing that as long as I heard the scratch of his pencil across the page, he wasn't going to touch me. I lay unmoving, eyes closed, listening to the rasp of lead on paper, broken by the soft brush of his finger, smearing a line or a shadow.

From the laptop on my desk, my inbox dinged, and my eyes flashed open. Without thinking, I rose to my elbows. *Landon?* But there was no way I could check.

Lucas was watching me closely. "Do you need to check that?"

Landon had ignored my email all afternoon, when in the past he'd answered so promptly that I was probably spoiled. But Lucas was sitting in my room. On my bed. I lay back, returned my arms to their prior position, and I shook my head. I didn't close my eyes this time, and he didn't ask me to.

He returned to sketching, concentrating on my hands a long while, and then my face. He stared into my eyes, back and forth between that intense examination and his drawing. When he stared at my mouth for long moments—drawing, staring, drawing, staring—I wanted to reach up, grab his T-shirt, and pull him down to me. My hands clenched involuntarily and his gaze flicked there and back.

Eyes blazing, he looked down at me. "Jacqueline?"

I blinked. "Yes?"

"The night we met—I'm not like that guy." His jaw was rigid.

"I know tha—" He placed a finger over my lips, his expression softening.

"So I don't want you to feel pressured. Or overpowered. But I do, absolutely, want to kiss you right now. Badly." He trailed his finger over my jaw and down my throat, and then into his lap.

I stared at him. Finally comprehending that he was waiting for a response, I said, "Okay."

He dropped the pad onto the floor and the pencil followed, his stare never unlocking from mine. As he leaned over me, I felt a heightened awareness of every part of my body that touched a part of his—the edge of his hip pressed to mine, his chest sliding against mine, his fingers tracing from wrists to forearms and then framing my face. He held me in place, lips near my ear. When he kissed the sensitive spot, my breath shuddered. "You're so beautiful," he whispered, moving his mouth to mine.

His lips were warm and firm, pressing against mine, and when his tongue began a gentle onslaught against the line of my lips, I opened them. Tongue delving into my mouth, his hands traveled in opposite directions—one to my still-crossed wrists, pressing them into the mattress above my head, one skimming down my side, digging into my waist. He kissed me harder, claiming the responses he coaxed from me. My head swam, and I was drawing in short bursts of air as if I was surfacing every few seconds before diving deeper. Just when I thought I couldn't take the intensity, he lessened the pressure and sucked my lower lip softly, brushed his tongue over it, and then he repeated the movement. I fidgeted beneath him and his tongue slipped between my lips again and repeated its closer examination—caressing my tongue, my teeth, the roof of my mouth.

If someone had asked, *How does this compare to kissing Kennedy?* I would have answered, "Who?"

Lucas's hands each grasped a wrist and pulled my arms around his neck. Responding by doing something I'd dreamed of doing more than once, I pushed my hands into his hair, mussing it further. He drew me up, scooping me onto his lap as he scooted his back against my pile of pillows at the head of the narrow bed, one booted foot still on the floor, the other drawn up under me. Leaning me back, his hand cradling my head, he kissed a path down my neck and into the V of my sweater. My head fell back as I panted and tried to form a rational thought.

His hand drifted under the soft knit to slide along my ribs, roaming over the satin cups of my bra, his fingertips skimming the skin above, the curves of flesh, the cleavage augmented by my folded-up position. Pushing the hem above my breasts, he moved his lips to the places his fingers had been and ran his tongue along the line of skin just above the edge of my bra.

My hands tightened in his hair as his fingers skimmed the front clasp. Hadn't I worn this easy-access bra for this very reason? My body wanted him, but my mind protested—a first kiss, to feeling me up, to . . . what?

Erin's voice in my head said, *Rebound the hell out of him!* and I choked an untimely laugh.

Lucas raised his head and cocked an eyebrow at me. "Ticklish?" he asked, incredulous.

I was entirely horrified, and couldn't imagine a bigger tragedy in that moment than having ticklish breasts—unless it was having the stupidest sense of humor on the planet. I bit my lip, trying not to laugh again, thinking, *Oh my God*. I shook my head.

His gaze flicked to my teeth, clamped on my bottom lip. "You sure? Because it's either that . . . or you find my seduction techniques . . . humorous."

I barked another laugh, unable to contain it, and he shook his head as I sat on his lap, my chest half-bare, mortified. I jerked my hand from his hair and slammed it over my imprudent mouth.

Then, he smiled. Behind my palm, I smiled back, begging him silently not to make me laugh again—because just under the surface, the repressed hysterics were preparing to mutiny.

"Maybe I should just tickle you and get it over with." He appeared to mull over the idea.

"Please don't," I said, alarmed. Like most people, I wasn't an attractive sight when tickled. I knew this, because my aunt had filmed my jackass older cousin tickling me into a writhing, pleading mess on my eleventh birthday. My face had turned a blotchy scarlet, spit trailing from the corner of my mouth, the sounds of protestation I uttered almost inhuman.

"No?"

"No. Please, no."

Sighing, he took my hand from in front of my face and pressed it to his chest, leaning forward swiftly and kissing me. I noticed he'd carefully pulled my sweater back down, though that didn't stop him from stroking his fingertips across my abdomen beneath it, or palming my breasts through the bra, his thumb stroking over a nipple while his mouth moved with mine, leaving me lightheaded. Against my hand, his heart thumped in time with mine.

I forgot all about laughing.

• • • • • • • • • • •

My lips were sensitive and tingly. Touching them brought rushes of gooey memories—his hands, and what they'd done in concert with his mouth—the crazy-making kisses, and the few words he'd spoken. *You're so beautiful*.

I wanted to see the sketches, so he showed them to me. They were good. Amazingly good. I told him so and earned his barely there smile.

"What will you do with them?" I asked, more than a little belatedly.

"Redo them in charcoal, probably."

I waited for more. "And then?"

He shrugged into his hoodie and stared down at me. "Tack them to my bedroom wall?"

My lips parted, but I had no idea what to say. *Bedroom wall?*

His eyes returned to the pad, turned to the second drawing. "Who wouldn't want to wake up to this?"

That statement had a 99 percent chance of meaning what it seemed to suggest, but I wasn't sure enough to reply in kind, so I said nothing. He closed the sketchpad and laid it on the bookcase near the door. Taking my chin in his hand, he rubbed his thumb across my lower lip gently.

"Ah, crap." He pulled his hand away and looked at his fingers.

"I forgot what my hands look like after drawing." He looked at my shirt. "You may have little gray marks . . . everywhere."

Assuming I now had a gray lip and possibly faint streaks of gray across my abdomen and the upper curves of my breasts, I couldn't think what to say beyond, "Oh."

He balled his hands into fists, set one under my chin to raise it again and used the other to tug me closer. "Don't worry, no fingers." Dragging my body against his, he kissed me, his back against the door to my room. In this position, there was no hiding what his body wanted from me. I pressed against him and he groaned into my mouth and wrenched his mouth from mine, breathing raggedly. "I have to go now, or I'm not going."

This was the moment for me to say *Stay*, but I couldn't. Kennedy flashed through my mind, saying something oh-so-similar not that long ago. Even more insane was the thought of Landon, and a possible email waiting for me. Neither of those things should matter. Not in this moment.

Lucas straightened and cleared his throat. Kissing my forehead and the tip of my nose, he opened the door. "Later," he said, and was gone.

I gripped the doorframe and watched him walk away, pulling the beanie over his tousled hair. Every girl he passed glanced up. Some turned and watched until he reached the stairwell door, before whipping their heads around to see where he'd come from. I retreated into my room and left them to their speculation.

The interrupting email wasn't from Landon, it was from Mom—and contained my parents' itinerary for their ski trip to

Colorado. A ski trip that I hadn't been invited to join. A ski trip scheduled for the only mid-semester weekend I'd planned to spend at home—a holiday weekend, no less.

Still, I had a difficult time stirring up any real anger when I opened her email, for two reasons. One, I was oddly disappointed that it wasn't Landon's name in my inbox, and two, I was so high from being thoroughly kissed by Lucas that I didn't care about a holiday eleven days in the future, or how I'd be spending it.

• • • • • • • • • • •

By Sunday evening, I was eating spoonfuls of peanut butter for dinner, watching *He's Just Not That Into You*, and telling myself I was clearly no exception to *anyone's* rule. Landon still hadn't emailed, and I hadn't heard from Lucas, either.

Erin was due back any moment, and I was eager for her boisterous, colorful presence in our room. Too much quiet left me depressed and consuming condiments for meals.

My inbox dinged and I debated whether to pause the movie to check it. I wasn't in the mood for another of my mother's efforts to shed her remorse about deserting me on a major holiday. So far, she'd tried logic ("It was your year to go to Kennedy's"), emotional blackmail ("Your father and I haven't had a trip alone in twenty years"), and one grudging invitation to join them ("I suppose we could get you a ticket. But you'd have to sleep on the sofa or a cot, because the rooms are undoubtedly booked"). I ignored the first two and said *No, thanks* to the third.

What next—an attempt to buy me off? A proposed shopping trip wouldn't be out of the question—she'd used that before. Last week, I'd bookmarked a pair of boots online that my private lesson pay and my allowance wouldn't quite cover. I paused the movie and clicked my inbox.

Jackpot. But not Mom. Landon.

Jacqueline,

I'm glad you felt confident about the quiz. Whenever you get a draft of your paper together, I'd be happy to look it over before you turn it in. I've attached the worksheet for tomorrow's session, which I just finished making. If you have any questions, let me know.

LM

I reread the email, pouting. There was nothing remotely flirtatious in it. It could have come from a professor. He didn't account for why it had taken him all weekend to answer me when he usually answered within a couple of hours, if not sooner. He didn't tease me about anything, or ask any non–econ related questions. I felt as though I'd imagined every shred of familiarity we'd developed over the past couple of weeks.

Landon,

Thank you. I'll send the draft by Saturday morning. I hope you had an enjoyable weekend.

JW

E A S Y

Jacqueline,

Getting it to me by Saturday is fine. I'll try to get it back to you quickly so you can get it in to Dr. H before the break. My weekend was good. Especially Friday. How was yours?

LM

Landon,

Good. A bit lonely (my roommate was out of town all weekend, and she just got home and is bursting to tell me all about it), but productive. Thanks again for all your help.

JW

chapter *Nine*

Once again, Lucas was approached by a girl at the end of class. What the hell? Did every girl in our class feel a need to converse with him? But then a guy walked up next to her, his arm wrapping around her shoulder. Alarmed, I realized what my visceral reaction implied: jealousy. Over a guy I barely knew, with whom I'd exchanged more saliva than sentences.

As I passed the last aisle, Lucas gave me a tight smile with a slight lift of his chin and shifted his attention back to the couple in front of him. Conflicted, I was equal parts relieved and disappointed.

I asked Erin's advice over lunch.

"He's holding his cards damned close." Sipping her typical Jamba Juice lunch, she mulled over possible causes for his reserve. "It's almost like . . . he's resisting being attracted to you. Don't get me wrong, lots of guys get standoffish—but usually not until they've closed the deal." She gave me a close look. "Are you *sure* nothing more happened Friday night?"

I heaved a sigh and clunked my forehead with the heel of my hand. "Oh *yeah*, I totally forgot that part where we had wild sex all night Friday."

She rolled her eyes, and then her brows rose. "Hey. What if he has a girlfriend?"

I frowned. I hadn't considered that. "I guess that's possible."

My mind went to one thing I couldn't say: What if what happened the night we met made me appear as pathetic and foolish as I felt, and he couldn't get past it? Those terrifying minutes haunted me still, and running into Buck a few days ago only amplified the threat. It wouldn't be the last time I'd see him. He was in the same frat as Kennedy. He was friends with Chaz and Erin, and my entire former circle of friends. He was almost unavoidable.

"A girlfriend would definitely put a kink in our plans," Erin mused.

Out of the blue, I wondered if Landon Maxfield had a girlfriend. He hadn't mentioned one, but why would he? There was no reason for him to insert *Hey, btw, I have a girlfriend* into one of our email exchanges. I could find some way to ask. He seemed so candid that I was sure he'd answer.

"J?" Erin's voice broke into my thoughts.

"Huh? Sorry."

She arched a brow, slurping up the last of her smoothie. "What are you thinking about? I know that calculating look, and as your official wingwoman, I need in on whatever you're plotting."

I picked at the sandwich in my hand, pulling the tomatoes out and stacking them in the corner of my tray. I couldn't tell her about Buck. But I could confess my building interest in Landon. "You know my econ tutor?"

She nodded, confused, and suddenly, forming an online-only attraction while attending a university where there were thousands of single guys seemed like the most ridiculous thing ever in the history of ridiculous things.

"Well, sometimes it seems like we're flirting. And once, he said Kennedy was a moron."

She arched one brow. "He knows Kennedy?"

"No—I mean he said, 'Your ex is a moron.' I don't think he actually knows *him*. It was more of a . . . complimentary statement about me." I took a bite of my turkey bacon guacamole sandwich.

"Hmm." Erin leaned both elbows onto the table between us. "Well, it's a given that he can't be as hot as Lucas. But he's a tutor, so he must be smart—God knows *that's* right up your alley. Is he cute at all?"

"Er," I said, still chewing.

She narrowed her eyes. "Oh my God. You've never *met* him, have you?"

I closed my eyes and sighed. "Not exactly."

"Not exactly?"

"Okay, not at all. I have no idea what he looks like, all right? But he's intelligent and funny. And he's been really nice, and helped me so much—I'm almost caught up in class, except for that project—"

"Jacqueline, you can't fall for a guy without ever seeing him! What if his looks are a dealbreaker? He could look like"—she scanned the food court and zeroed in on a creepy-looking guy in a ratty T-shirt and sweats loping past our table—"*that* guy."

I crossed my arms, offended on Landon's behalf. "*That* guy looks like a social outcast. Landon is too smart to look like that."

She covered her eyes and shook her head. "Okay. We'll make *Landon* Plan B." She eyed me, wearing her conspiracy-theory expression—eyes narrowed, lips puckered. "What do you really know about this Landon guy?"

I laughed. "A lot more than I know about that Lucas guy."

"Except what he looks and tastes like." She waggled her brows.

"Ugh! Erin. You have a one-track mind."

She smiled deviously. "I prefer to think of it as target-driven."

We skipped the Starbucks—part of Erin's plan, though she lamented the sacrifices she was making on my behalf as we choked down cups of cafeteria coffee. Leaving me with strict instructions not to text or email either of them, she gave me one swift hug before being swallowed by a group of her sorority sisters—all of whom acted as though we were distant acquaintances at best—as they set up an afternoon bake sale.

A month ago, I'd been sanctioned as Kennedy's GDI girlfriend; now I was only poor Erin's non-Greek roommate.

• • • • • • • • • •

Laundry rooms were located on each floor of the dorm, but since everyone on my floor decided to run loads at the same time, the washers were all full. Heaving the overflowing mesh bag into the stairwell, I hopped it down the concrete steps one at a time, hoping the residents a floor down were less moved to cleanliness, at least tonight.

Ten minutes later, I headed back upstairs with my empty bag. Stopping just inside the stairwell when my phone buzzed, I answered a message from Maggie reminding me to email a link she needed for a Spanish assignment we were doing together. Itching to text Lucas or email Landon, I shoved my phone down into my front pocket. I'd promised Erin I'd do neither. She knew how boys' minds worked, while my years with Kennedy left me woefully unprepared for these sorts of complex maneuvers. Frankly, the rules for hooking up didn't seem that much less tricky to me than the rules for finding a committed relationship, but what did I know.

The door beneath me opened and shut as I rounded the corner, and ascending footsteps sounded behind me. There were hundreds of residents in my building, and though we all used the elevator or the main stairs for coming and going from the building, most of us employed the persistently dank stairwell when moving between floors. The creeped-out, claustrophobic sensation was something I felt every time, and I forced myself not to sprint for the door at the top.

I jerked to a stop, realizing that I was moving forward, but my laundry bag wasn't. Assuming it was hooked on the handrail, I turned to liberate it and was almost eye to eye with Buck. The end of the bag was caught in his fist.

I gasped and my heart stopped, as though the moment was suspended in slow motion, and then it began pounding like heavy machinery in my chest. He stepped up to the stair just beneath me—and sneered down at me. "Hey Jackie." Bile rose in my throat at the sound of his voice, and I swallowed. "Or no. I guess it's Jacqueline now, right? Isn't that what you said? A rose by any other name would smell as sweet . . ." When he leaned closer, I tried to back up the stairs and tripped, sprawling. I used the opportunity to scramble backward and up toward the door, but he reached down and pulled me up easily, both hands gripping my shoulders.

"Don't touch me," I choked.

He smiled as though he was hypnotizing small, trapped prey. Toying with me. "C'mon, *Jacqueline*, don't be like that. You've always been real nice to me. I just want you to be a little bit nicer, that's all."

His words weren't slurred this time. He was sober and resolute, and the malevolence in his eyes told me that I would pay for my escape the night of the party. I would pay for what Lucas had done.

I shook my head. "No. I'm saying *no*, Buck. Just like last time."

His eyes narrowed, and I could barely hear the curse he hissed from the blood pulsing through my ears. *Run. Run. Run*, it seemed to say, and I wished I could obey. I let go of the bag, and it fell at our feet.

"I know what happened that night wasn't your fault." He shrugged. "You're a pretty girl, and obviously that guy had the same idea I did. He just got the jump on me 'cause I'd been drinking." His breath fell over my face, hot, feral. He wouldn't trip if I twisted from his grip and ran. "So did he fuck you in your truck, or did you let him take you back to your room? I know Erin was with Chaz that night. Just like she'll be tonight."

I flinched from his vulgar words. I hadn't gotten a text from Erin yet, but it wasn't impossible that she was staying with Chaz tonight, or that Buck would know before I would.

One arm snaked around and grasped my hip, squeezing it

painfully. The pain was nothing compared to the degradation of being pawed against my will.

"The stairwell is rank and uncomfortable, but doable. Why don't we go to your room, instead? I'll make it good for you, baby."

His threat was obvious. If I said no, he would rape me right here. "S-someone could come into the stairwell any moment."

He laughed. "True. Too bad you aren't wearing that little skirt you had on the other night. I could put you against this wall and do you in two minutes without taking a thing off of you."

My head spun. I strained against him, trying to move, even just a little, but couldn't.

"Wouldn't be the first time I've been caught with some hot little freak in an off-the-wall position. And hey—bonus—if you want to get Kennedy back for dumping you, then turning into the girl who'll do anything, anywhere, with anyone, would make him crazy." He shrugged. "You already started with that piece of shit—and who knows who else? So we can do it here, if that's what you want."

"No," I said, and his eyes flared. "My room." My breath panted out, shaky and hopefully mistaken for horniness in his pea-brained assessment. He smiled, and I almost threw up. I've never *wanted* to vomit more, but my body fought it down instinctively.

Arm around my waist, he turned me toward the door at the top, grabbing the laundry bag from the floor. I asked myself if I was willing to do what I was about to do. If I was prepared to scream, fight, and claw him in the hallway, humiliate myself in front of everyone, in hopes that he wouldn't succeed in getting me into my room. If he did that, I was done for. The walls weren't soundproof, but everyone was used to hearing all sorts of noises emanating from neighboring rooms. If anyone even heard anything over their music, televisions, and video games, they'd likely think nothing of it.

We emerged into the hallway, and I evaluated the people I was about to depend on. My room was six doors from the stairwell. Two guys at the opposite end of the hall were practicing kickflips on a skateboard. Olivia stood in the middle of the hall, talking to Joe, a guy from the fourth floor. When she spotted us, her mouth dropped open before she snapped it closed, and Joe looked over his shoulder, lifted his chin at Buck, and turned back to her with a low chuckle. This was bad.

Kimber, who roomed two doors down, came into the hallway with her laundry. I stopped. It was now or never. Buck took a step forward before realizing I was holding my ground. He turned back toward me. "C'mon, J," he coaxed.

"No. You aren't going into my room, Buck. I want you to leave now."

The shock registered on his face. Kimber, Olivia, and Joe froze, waiting to witness firsthand whatever was about to go down.

Buck's hand was at my elbow. "That's not what you said a few minutes ago, babe. Let's have this talk in private." He tried to pull me forward, but I wrenched my arm from his meaty hand.

"I want you to leave. Now." I glared, my chest heaving.

Indecision played across his features. Five people were watching. He put both hands up, palms out. "Don't be mad, okay? I tried to tell you that brick would be cold and rough. It's not *my* fault you couldn't wait five minutes." Tossing the bag over my shoulder, he said, "Call me later when you cool down, pretty girl." He bumped fists with Joe and sauntered to the stairwell, and I waited until he disappeared through the door to move.

My face burning, I unlocked my door while Olivia whispered not-so-discreetly behind me. "Ohmygod, they just *did it* in the stairwell? She had some other guy in her room like, Friday night! I wonder if she was screwing around on Kennedy and that's why he—"

I shut my door, leaned against it, and slid to the floor, quaking. Tears skated in tracks down my face and my breath shuddered out, leaving my chest aching. I wanted to run away. To go home. To be ignorant of getting dumped, of having my dreams dashed, of constantly feeling too inexperienced and stupid to deal with my own life.

I'd outwitted Buck this time, making it twice that he hadn't gotten what he wanted, and he was pissed. Popular and good-looking, he could almost take his pick of girls, and from what I'd heard and witnessed, he used that advantage to the fullest. I was no prettier than girls like Olivia, who constantly threw themselves in his path. There was no reason for him to fixate on me.

There had been some early rivalry between Buck and Kennedy, but I couldn't remember what it was. Something that happened when they were pledges. Would he harass me like this because of some grudge against my ex?

He might, if he thought he could get under Kennedy's skin by doing it.

I was going to have to tell Erin. She would be furious with me for keeping this to myself, and I dreaded her reaction, but I had no choice. Not anymore.

• • • • • • • • • • •

"Jacqueline, are you hooking up with *Buck*?" Erin hissed as the door to our room shut behind her.

I imagined I could feel the blood draining from my face. "Where did you hear that?"

She made a noise—*pshh*. "Where did I *not* hear it? Why didn't you tell me this morning during astronomy? And why *Buck* of all people? I mean he's hot and all—"

"I didn't." I swallowed with difficulty, and my eyes were filling. "I didn't, Erin."

She blinked at my expression and crossed the room in three strides, grabbing my arms. "J, what's the matter? What happened?"

I sank onto my bed and she sat with me, her eyes wide.

"I . . . have to tell you something."

"Okay . . . I'm listening . . ."

Where to start? Last night? Two weeks ago?

"When I left the Halloween party early—a couple of weeks ago? Buck followed me." I chewed a loose piece of skin on my lip and knew it was bleeding. The taste of blood brought that night back more vividly and my face flushed hot. "He was drunk. He pushed me into my truck." I held myself rigidly, forcing the words out as her mouth fell open.

"He *what?*" Her grip on my arm tightened.

"He was going to r-rape me—"

"Going to?"

I shut my eyes. Licked the blood from my lip. "Lucas showed up out of nowhere. He stopped him."

"Oh my fucking God."

In the silence that followed, I finally opened my eyes. Erin still gripped one of my arms as she stared at the worn carpet beneath our feet.

"Do you believe me?" The tears wouldn't stay dammed, though I felt sure I would run dry soon. The last time I cried—before Kennedy broke up with me, before the past month—had been over a year ago, when I fractured my femur snowboarding. Before that, when our old dog, Cissie, died.

"Jacqueline, how can you . . . of course I believe you! What kind of question is that?" She glared at me, insulted. "And by the way, why the *hell* didn't you tell me this before now? Because you didn't think I'd believe you?" Her lip quivered, transforming her expression from offended to injured.

"Chaz and Buck are best friends, and I thought I could just . . . avoid him . . ."

"Jacqueline, this is exactly the sort of stuff women need to share with each other! I don't give a shit if he *was* drunk—"

"There's more."

She sat, staring and silent.

"Last night, he caught me in the stairwell." Erin's eyes grew round and I shook my head. "Nothing happened. I tricked him into coming upstairs by saying we could go into the room. When we got into the hallway, with other people around, I told him to leave." I covered my face with my hands and choked out the rest. "He made it sound like we'd done it in the stairwell. Olivia heard him . . ."

"I get the picture," Erin said, grabbing my hands. "That gossipy whore has no right to spread rumors about anyone. I don't care about her. But be honest with me, J. Did he hurt you? Did he?" Her eyes flashed.

I shook my head. "He just scared me."

She sighed, her forehead creased in thought, and then she straightened. "Wait. So that lying bastard ran into Lucas's *fists* multiple times, not a couple of homeless thugs?"

"Yeah."

The hurt crept across her face—I could see it in her eyes. "Why didn't you tell me?"

My shoulders slid up and down, almost imperceptibly. "I don't know. I'm sorry."

Her answer was to put her arms around me. "And Lucas? You knew him before all of this?"

I leaned against her, tucked my head under her chin. "No. I'd never seen him before that night. Our econ class is huge, and it's not like I was looking around at other guys. I had Kennedy." My hands flipped palm up on my lap. "Or, I thought I did."

Erin's arms tightened. "Of course you did."

chapter *Ten*

"Do you go to the tutoring sessions? I've only been a couple of times, but I don't remember seeing you there." Benji's voice snapped my attention from Lucas.

"Huh?"

He chuckled as I shoved my econ text into the backpack at my feet, embarrassed at having been caught sneaking a glance at Lucas. Again.

"Tutoring sessions? I wish I could, but I have another class at the same time. We've emailed, though—I needed help catching up, after my two-week hiatus from sanity."

Suddenly I realized—if Benji had attended the tutoring sessions, that meant *he had seen Landon*. I'd also deduced, from a few deliberately transparent comments, that Benji was gay. So he might not be opposed to answering questions such as *Exactly how hot is the econ tutor?*

"So you've been to a couple of sessions, huh?"

He nodded, and I decided to start with something way more fundamental.

"Is there any chance the tutor is, you know, gay?" I held my breath, waiting for his answer.

"What, like I hand out a survey?" He laughed when I blinked, worried I'd just offended him. "I'm just messing with ya. I'm pretty sure he doesn't play for my team. Though if he did, he'd be a little out of my league." He sucked in and patted his stomach, which was made somewhat flat by his efforts. "Nothing a couple of weeks at the gym and giving up bread for the weekend wouldn't take care of."

I rolled my eyes. "Shut up."

He sighed. "I love being a guy. Need to lose five pounds? Go without ketchup for a couple of weeks. Problem. Solved."

We shouldered our backpacks and trudged up the stairs. "I really hate you right now."

He laughed, more so when my eyes scanned the space between Lucas's seat and the door. He was gone. "So, you're trading emails *and* intense do-me stares in class. I'm guessing you aren't the only girl—or guy—in Heller's class who thinks the tutor's hot like a spicy tamale, but you may be the only one where the feeling is mutual."

I heard his teasing words, but nothing registered after I made the connection that had been right in front of me. "Lucas . . . is the tutor?"

Benji halted with me, both of us buffeted by people parting around us. "Holy *shit.*" He dragged me from the heavy flow of foot traffic. "You didn't know he was the tutor?" He smiled. "I guess you'll be going to the sessions now, huh? I mean, technically, you're off-limits, but you aren't the only one in that staring game or I wouldn't tease you." He leaned his face down and looked into my eyes. "Jacqueline? What the hell?"

I considered the emails he wrote to me as Landon, and Lucas's stares, his texts . . . and most notably, the sketching and *makeout* session five days ago. After which he hadn't texted. Or emailed. Or told me he was *Landon*!

"I didn't know." Like I needed one more damned thing to make me feel like an utter idiot.

"Hello, Ms. Obvious, I sorta deduced that from your dazed and confused expression. Maybe he thought you knew?"

I shook my head. "He *knew* I didn't know." I frowned. "And what do you mean, that I'm off-limits?"

He lifted one shoulder. "My roommate tutored freshman chemistry. Tutors have to attend the class they're doing sessions for, but they aren't allowed to, you know, *fraternize* with those students. Conflict of interest. Not as big of a deal as TAs or professors—who are advised against hooking up with any student at all. Still, it's not like it doesn't happen. We're all human."

I stared at the floor. "Am I just completely freaking *clueless*? How did I not know?"

Benji tucked a finger under my chin. "Um. I'm getting the distinct feeling there's been some *fraternizing* going on." He sighed at the look on my face. "Look, if you never attended a tutoring session, and neither of his alter egos *told* you he was the same guy, how were you supposed to know, exactly?"

The tension in my shoulders deflated. "I guess you're right."

"Of course I'm right. Now what?"

My jaw locked. "No idea. But one thing's for sure—I'm not telling him I know."

Benji shook his head, one arm around my shoulders as we merged back into the stream of students. "When I registered for econ, I had no idea that I'd be in for this level of reality-show drama. It's like a big fat *bonus*."

• • • • • • • • • •

Erin: I signed us up for a self-defense class

Me: What??

Erin: Put on by the campus po-po. Saturdays 9-noon, starts this week, skips the weekend after Thanksgiving, then 2 more.

Me: Okay.

Erin: We get to beat the shit outta guys in those big puffy suits!!! I've always wanted to really kick the crap outta some guy's nuts. Now I can do it guilt-free!

Me: You're a sick girl.

Erin: Guilty as charged. :)

• • • • • • • • • •

On Friday, I didn't look in Landon/Lucas's direction once. Not one single time. It had been a week since our university-prohibited makeout. Was that the pull for him? That I was forbidden fruit? I'd show him forbidden.

When we were packing up, Benji looked over my shoulder, his eyebrows rising into the dark curls falling over his forehead.

"Hey, Jackie."

Kennedy hadn't spoken to me in over a month, the last words between us involving a trite cliché and the very textbook I was currently holding. I pulled a steadying breath through my nose and turned. "Kennedy." I waited, sure he had some reason to approach me, though I had no idea what it was.

"Are you heading home for Thanksgiving? If so, we should carpool. You know, make that four-hour drive a little less monotonous."

"You want us to drive home . . . *together*?"

He shrugged and flicked his head to the side with a faintly dimpled smile. Kennedy tossing his hair out of his eyes was an arresting sight, and he damn well knew it. At the moment, though, it kind of pissed me off.

Benji cleared his throat and touched my elbow. "See ya Monday, *Jacqueline*."

I smiled at him. "Have a good weekend, *Benjamin*."

He winked at me and bumped by Kennedy without apology.

"What's his deal?" my ex scowled.

"What do you really want, Kennedy?" I shifted my backpack and stared up at him, conflicted by my contradictory desires in that moment. I wanted to punch him in the face. I wanted to fall into his arms and wake up from the nightmare of him casting me aside.

"I'd like for us to be friends at the end of this. You mean a lot to me." The gentleness in his eyes was almost a physical caress. I'd known him so well, and for so long.

This speech was unanticipated—too much, too soon. My eyes teared up. "I don't know if I can ever do that, Kennedy. And I don't want to drive home with you next week. Excuse me." I edged around him and started up the aisle to the door.

"Jackie—"

"It's *Jacqueline*," I said without turning, leaving him behind.

• • • • • • • • • • •

Landon,

I'm sending this a little early, though of course I don't imagine you're sitting around on a Friday night waiting for economics projects to pour in. But I'm going to be busy tomorrow morning, so I thought I'd go ahead and send it.

Thank you again for looking it over before I turn it in.

JW

Jacqueline,

As a matter of fact, you've distracted/saved me (temporarily, at least) from an infuriating search for a bug somewhere within hundreds of lines of code that doesn't quite work. I'd *much* rather look over your econ project. I'll have it back to you by Sunday evening, if not sooner.

LM

I stared at the L of his signature, picturing him as the guy I knew he was—Lucas. As Landon, his flirting had been subtle; as Lucas, it was overt. What game was he playing? I had no way of knowing if this situation was a first for him, or if he frequently stepped outside of those tutor-student boundaries. The night we met, that horrible night, he'd known who I was. He'd called me Jackie, the name he must have heard Kennedy call me. When I first emailed him for economics help, he must have known, too, but he'd given me no hint.

According to the university's website, restrictions on socializing were to protect—or prevent—students from trading sexual favors for grades, or the appearance of such a thing. But Landon was helping me learn the material, and I was doing the work. When it came to my grade in Dr. Heller's class, there was nothing improper going on. He knew it. I knew it.

But even consensual fraternization, as Benji called it, was theoretically against the rules.

I could get Landon Maxfield in serious trouble. When he came to my room, I thought he was just another student in the class, and he'd continued that deception.

He'd kissed me, touched me, and I'd let him. I'd wanted him to.

I shut my laptop and stared at my phone. We'd made out a week ago. Here, in my room. And hadn't texted me once since then. I wanted to know why.

Me: Did I do something wrong?

I waited several minutes, looking at photos on my phone—many of which included Kennedy. I wondered if it was weakness that made it tough to delete them, or if I just wanted to keep the evidence that we'd seemed in love—that we'd looked in love, even while it was all ending.

Lucas: No. Been busy. What's up?
Me: I guess you haven't had time to redo the sketches.
Lucas: Actually, I did one of them. I'd like you to see it.

Me: I'd like to see it. Is it tacked to your wall?
Lucas: Yes. Listen, I'm out right now, ttyl?
Me: Sure

According to his email, he was working on what sounded like a huge CSE project, and according to his text, he was out partying. I had no idea which was true. I'd believe he was blowing me off . . . except for this: *I'd like you to see it*. I reread the text, opened my laptop, and reread his email, but felt no closer to figuring him out.

• • • • • • • • • • •

Erin came storming into our room at one a.m., on her cell. "You know what? I think you don't respect my opinion about a *lot* of things."

Luckily, I was awake, watching online video clips of self-defense classes. Despite Erin's eagerness for nut-kicking and my own need to learn this stuff, the last thing I wanted to do in the morning was get up and go punch and kick some guy in a puffy suit. I couldn't see how that would correlate into getting away from someone like Buck. If I'd have been able to break his grip on me either night, let alone kick him, I would have.

The door shut behind my clearly furious roommate as she flung her bag onto her bed, kicking off her heeled pumps. "Well, *I* can't be with someone who's decided to stand behind a fucking *rapist*."

Oh, God. I closed out of YouTube and pushed my laptop off my lap.

"Yes, Chaz, that's what I really think." She unbuttoned her white blouse so forcefully, I was sure she would rip off a button or two. "*Fine*. Think whatever you want. I'm done." Punching her phone, she growled at it and tossed it on her bed before turning to me, yanking her shirt off. "Well. I guess *that's* over."

My mouth agape, I sat, speechless, while she shoved her black skirt down over her hips and kicked it in the general direction of the laundry hamper. She slipped bracelets from her arms and removed her earrings, dropping them on a desk littered with jewelry, tarot cards, gum packets, and paperback novels.

"Erin, did you just—break up with Chaz? Over *me*?"

She pulled on a T-shirt that fell to mid-thigh and clearly belonged to Chaz. Scowling, she ripped it back over her head, wadded it up, and hurled it. "No. I broke up with Chaz because he's a fucking twat-headed jackass."

"But—"

"Jacqueline." She held up one palm like a traffic cop signaling *stop*. "Don't say it. I broke up with Chaz because he proved what's important to him. 'Bros before hos.' Well fuck that. I won't come second to a bunch of his dumbass friends, and I certainly won't come second to some dickhead who's a walking affront to all women. Besides . . . it was never gonna be a permanent thing, right? Who does that in college anyway?"

She spun around and rummaged through the top drawer of our tiny built-in wardrobe, ostensibly searching for a non-previously-Chaz-owned T-shirt. I heard one muffled sniff and knew she was crying. Damn Chaz. Damn Buck. Damn Lucas/Landon/whoever the hell he was.

• • • • • • • • • • •

The campus Self-Defense for Women classes were held in one of the classrooms on the first floor of the activities building. We found the room and I tossed my coffee cup in the hallway trash can, Erin yawning after a sleepless night—which I knew because her restless fidgeting and sniffling had kept me awake. Around four a.m., she'd crawled into bed with me, curling into spoon position against me as I swept the hair back from her face. Mercifully, she'd fallen asleep almost immediately, and I'd followed suit.

"Hey. Isn't that . . . ?" Erin spoke without moving her lips, like a ventriloquist. Clad in black sweatpants and a black T-shirt, Lucas stood at the front of the room with two older men.

"*Yes*," I hissed as we took our seats and I stared down at the packet of course material, the cover of which depicted a man attacking a woman who was poised to defend herself. "Erin, I don't think I can do this."

"Yes, you *can*," she countered, so quickly that she must have been anticipating my response.

"Good morning, ladies." The smaller, older guy began, silencing any further protest from me. "I'm Ralph Watts, the Assistant Chief of Police on campus. This feeble-looking guy to my left is Sergeant Don, and the ugly one is Lucas, one of our parking enforcement officers." Everyone chuckled, as Don and Lucas were far from feeble or ugly. "We're pleased that you've given up a Saturday mornings to increase your knowledge of personal safety."

I snuck a look at Erin when she nudged me with her knee.

"Parking enforcement officer? Jesus, how many jobs does he *have*?" she mumbled from the side of her mouth.

"No shit," I mumbled back. She didn't even know about the tutoring job.

"Could be hot . . ." she whispered. "Especially if there's a uniform. Or handcuffs."

I sighed.

Glancing around the semicircle of folding chairs, I noted that there were only about a dozen of us—a mix of students, professors, and administrative staff. The oldest was a white-headed black woman who had to be the age of my grandmother. I told myself that if she could come in here to learn how to kick potential rapist ass, so could I.

Even if Lucas was standing across the room, alternately staring at me—according to Erin—or avoiding my eyes completely.

The first hour and a half, basic self-defense principles were discussed. Ralph told us that 90 percent of self-defense involves reducing the risk of attack in the first place. "In an ideal world, we could all go about our business without fear of being assaulted. Unfortunately, that ideal is not representative of reality."

My face heating, I recalled Lucas admonishing me for walking across the dark parking lot behind the frat house texting, instead of paying attention to my surroundings. I circled "90%" in blue ink until I'd obscured the words on either side. But then I remembered the last thing he'd said that night: *It wasn't your fault*.

We were encouraged to propose safety guidelines and write them all down—locking doors, walking or exercising with a friend, wearing shoes that don't hinder running. Erin's suggestion of "Avoid assholes" was popular.

"Three things are necessary for an assault: an assailant, a victim, and opportunity. Remove *opportunity* and you take a huge leap in reducing the likelihood of the assault." Ralph clapped his hands together once. "Alrighty, let's take a short break, and when we come back, it's time to do some of the butt kicking you ladies signed up to inflict on Don and Lucas."

chapter *Eleven*

"Many of you are probably convinced that without a weapon, you have no hope against an aggressive male." Ralph spoke from the opposite side of a set of mats on which Don and Lucas faced each other. The rest of us spread out along the outer edge of the mats, prepared to watch whatever they were about to do. Lucas still hadn't acknowledged my presence.

"The truth is, you have several weapons at your disposal, and we're gonna show you how to utilize them to your best advantage. Big, mean Don here will be the assailant, and Lucas, with all that pretty hair, will be the intended victim."

Giggling erupted from several girls standing near Lucas as he pinned his lips together in good-natured irritation and raked his dark hair back out of his face.

"Your weapons are your hands, feet, knees, and elbows, and your head—and I don't just mean what's inside it, although that comes into play. Your forehead and the back of your head, when they come into contact with susceptible areas on your assailant, can leave him seeing stars." Using Don as an example, he pointed out the obvious vulnerable spots ("*Yes*," Erin hissed when he indicated the groin), and then the less obvious places, like the top of the foot and the forearm.

Ralph called out the moves Lucas employed to defend himself as he and Don acted out half a dozen choreographed attacks, time-lapsed to clearly demonstrate what they were doing. I felt more hopeless, not less, as I watched them. Lucas's muscular body was trained to execute those blocks and hits, to absorb blows from an assailant. I'd watched him beat the crap out of Buck—when I could barely dislodge him long enough to scream, let alone inflict any damage.

"The goal here is not to beat the guy up." Ralph smiled at Erin's disappointed grumble. "Our objective is to give you time to escape. Gettin' the hell outta Dodge is your goal."

We divided into pairs to practice wrist blocks and parries. The three instructors circled the room, assisting and repositioning. I was relieved when Don walked up to watch Erin and me as we took turns trying to slow-motion slap each other. "Keep your eyes on the assailant," he reminded me. He turned to Erin. "Put a little more oomph into that attack. She can block it."

I was shocked to find he was right. Erin almost hit me the second time because I was so surprised I'd completely blocked her first attempt.

Don nodded. "Good job."

We smiled stupidly at each other and switched assailant and victim roles. "So when do we get to the junk-kicking?" Erin asked.

Don shook his head and sighed. "I swear, there's one in every class. Kicks will be next time." He pointed at her. "And I'm makin' sure you're in Lucas's line for that."

She put on her innocent face. "Don't y'all wear those padded Michelin-man suits?"

"Yes . . . but those pads don't block *all* feeling."

"Heh-heh," Erin said, and Don quirked one eyebrow at her.

I looked around the room during this exchange, watching Lucas with a couple of the giggly girls. "Like this?" one of them asked, blinking up at him like she didn't know she'd positioned her hand incorrectly.

"No . . ." He turned her palm around and adjusted her elbow. "Like that." His voice was almost inaudible with all of the slapping, blocking, and laughter scattered through the wide-open room. Even so, I felt his words like a soft stroke down my back. I could hardly connect this guy—his shaggy hair, his tattoos, the pure sexuality in the way he walked and the low thrum of his voice—with Landon, an engineering senior who said (or wrote) that my ex was a moron and teased me about fourteen-year-old orchestra students crushing on me. All while helping me pass a class I'd have failed without him.

I was attracted to the whole of him—each side incongruent with the other. But the whole of him was also a liar. The fact that our professor called him by a different name than the Assistant Chief of Police was perplexing, too. The preface of his official email address was LMaxfield. No help there.

He looked up and caught me staring, and for the first time that morning, neither of us looked away until Erin said, "J, pay attention! Just *try* to slap me." I broke the stare and turned to her. She moved around to face me, her back to Lucas, and rolled her eyes. "Does the concept of playing hard-to-get totally escape you?" she whispered. "Let. Him. Chase."

"I'm not playing that game any longer."

She glanced over her shoulder and back. "Girlfriend, I don't think *he* knows that."

I shrugged.

We practiced defensive stances and simple hand strikes, and though I felt silly at first, Erin and I were soon yelling "NO!" along with our classmates, and shoving the heels of our hands into each other's chins or hammering a fist (very slowly) down onto each other's noses.

"The last thing today will be ground defense. We'll watch Don and Lucas illustrate the first position and defense, and then each pair come grab a mat and we'll circulate while you practice."

Lucas lay face down on the mat and Don knelt over him, holding him down with his weight. My heart rate spiked and my breaths came irregularly, just watching. I didn't want to be in that position again. I couldn't do it in front of a classroom of people. I couldn't do it in front of Lucas.

Erin uncurled my fist with her fingers and took my hand. "J, you've gotta do this one. You be the attacker first. It'll be okay."

I shook my head. "I don't want to. It's too much like—" I swallowed.

"Which is exactly why you've got to do it." Before I said anything else, she squeezed my hand. "Hey, help *me* do it, okay? And then we'll see how you feel."

I nodded. "Okay."

I helped Erin, but I could only stand to play the victim once. I did the moves—and dislodged her fairly easily. As an ex-cheerleader, Erin was strong, but she was no Buck. I had no faith that this move would dislodge someone of his size and strength.

I couldn't look at Lucas—not during this final exercise, and not as we filed out the door.

• • • • • • • • • • •

"You sure you don't wanna go? I could use you to keep me from testing those moves we learned this morning on Chaz, if he has the balls to show up at this party."

I looked up from the novel I was reading, because Landon still hadn't sent my econ project back (funny how I continued to think of him in terms of *Lucas* and *Landon*), and I was weirdly caught up on homework. My roommate had never understood my compulsion to read when I had free time, especially if there were campus social events to attend. "No, Erin, I really don't want to go to a sorority thing, believe it or not. Not to mention the fact that no one would be thrilled to see me there."

Hands on hips, she frowned down at me. "You're probably right. But you're coming with me to the Brotherhood Bash in a couple of weeks, right? Bitches got nothing to say about me bringing you then. Frat rules apply—additional booze and broads welcome."

"Aww, what a sweet and not at all demeaning sentiment."

She laughed while she pulled on platform heels. "I know, right? What a bunch of pricks." Her smile fell. "Seriously, though, I could use a buffer between me and Chaz that night. Not that he'll, you know, bother me. But I know some girls who've just been waiting for me to be out of the way. They'll be on him like ticks on a country dog, and I really don't wanna see it."

I nodded. "I understand—and *eww* on that visual . . . though it's revoltingly appropriate. Can't you just skip the brotherhood thing? You could have the Asian flu. Or malaria. I'll vouch."

Tossing her hair over her shoulder, she grabbed her purse and walked to the door like a runway model—not the slightest wobble. "Nope. It's a huge deal. Besides, I've gotta face it sometime. Plus, I already RSVP'd for us both. And I have a couple of weeks to mentally prepare for it." She yanked the door open. "We're going power shopping after break, though. I'm gonna make that asshole gnaw his own hand off that night, dammit."

As the door shut behind her, my phone trilled a text alert.

Lucas: Do you still want to see the charcoal?
Me: Yes
Lucas: Tonight?
Me: Ok
Lucas: I'll be outside your place in 10? Pull your hair back and wear something warm.
Me: You aren't bringing it over?
Lucas: I was bringing you to it. Unless you don't want to.
Me: I'll come down, but I need 15 minutes.
Lucas: I'll wait. No rush.

I tore around the room like an insane person, stripping off my flannel PJs and snatching a clean bra and panties from the clean-but-not-put-away laundry pile. Warm clothes . . . Sweats? No. Jeans. Black UGGs. The soft sapphire sweater that made Erin say, "That makes your eyes *pop*." After brushing my teeth,

I brushed my hair and secured it at the nape—though I wasn't sure why.

Grabbing my black wool peacoat on the way out the door, I left the building by the main exit. I hadn't been in the stairwell since Buck caught me there, even when it meant extra steps.

Lucas was at the curb, leaning against a motorcycle, arms crossed over his chest. Along with his now-familiar boots and jeans, he wore a dark brown leather jacket that made his hair look black. Watching me with those light eyes, his gaze didn't waver from me, no matter the distracting Saturday night noises of residents coming and going. He didn't hide the unhurried top-to-bottom scan that left parts of me molten and longing for him to touch me like he had in my room.

Swallowing the lump in my throat, I reminded myself of his deception in a failing attempt to douse the desire spreading through me like lava—slow-moving, heavy, and hot. My trepidation about his motorcycle helped cool it to some degree. I'd never been on one before, and couldn't say I'd ever intended to change that fact. When I walked up to him, he held out an extra helmet.

"I guess this is the reason for the hair guidelines," I said, taking the helmet and examining it hesitantly.

"You can take it back down when we get to my place, if you want. I didn't figure you'd want to stuff it under the helmet . . . or leave it loose and let it get all tangled on the ride."

I shook my head, wondering if I needed to undo the straps completely or just loosen them.

"Never been on a bike before?"

From the corner of my eye, I saw Rona and Olivia exit the

building behind a group of boys. Both girls stopped and stared at Lucas, and then me, while I pretended not to notice them. "Um. No . . ."

"Let me help you with that, then."

After I put my bag's strap over my head and settled it crosswise over my chest, he took the helmet and placed it on my head, securing the straps under my chin.

I felt like a bobblehead.

Once we were both helmeted and on the bike, I reached my arms around him and clasped my hands over his abdomen, marveling at how firm it was.

"Hold on," he said, shoving the kickstand back. His suggestion was unnecessary as the engine roared to life—I had a death grip on his torso, my entire front pressed securely against his back, my chin tucked and my eyes squeezed shut. I tried to imagine I was on a roller coaster—perfectly safe and attached to a track instead of hurtling through the streets on a flimsy five hundred pounds or so of metal and rubber, hoping some drunk in an SUV wouldn't run a red light and flatten us.

The ride to his place—an apartment over a detached garage—took less than ten minutes. My hands were numb from the combination of the grasp each had on the other and the chilled November air rushing over them. As I stood rubbing them together, he parked the bike on a paved section between the garage and the open steps before turning and taking my hands in his, one at a time, and massaging warmth into them. "I should have reminded you to wear gloves."

I pulled my hand from his and pointed to the house not more

than fifty feet away. "Do your parents live there?"

"No." He turned to walk up the wooden stairway and I followed. "I rent the apartment."

He unlocked the door to a huge studio with a wall, but no door, defining what I assumed was the bedroom in the far right corner. A small open kitchen was on the left, a bathroom between the two. On the sofa, a huge orange tabby cat regarded me with characteristic feline apathy before hopping down and stalking to the door.

"This is Francis." Lucas opened the door and the tom wandered lazily outside, stopping on the landing to clean a paw.

I laughed, moving to the center of the room. "*Francis?* He looks more like a . . . Max. Or maybe a King."

He shut and locked the door, his ghost smile turning his mouth up on one side. "Trust me, he's superior enough without a macho name to back it up."

He shrugged his jacket off as he crossed the room to me, and I stared up at him, starting to unbutton my coat. "Names are important," I said.

He nodded, dropping his eyes to my fingers. "Yes." I pushed the oversized buttons through the slits slowly, top to bottom, as though there was nothing beneath. Sliding his thumbs inside the lapels, he dragged the coat from my shoulders, his thumbs brushing down the arms of my sweater. "Soft."

"It's cashmere." My voice was nearly breathless, and though I wanted to follow up on my statement about names, wanted to press him to tell me why he was misleading me, I couldn't jar the words from my throat.

The coat fell past my fingertips and he turned aside, tossed it on top of his jacket. "I had an ulterior motive for bringing you here."

I blinked. "You did?"

Grimacing, he took my hands. "I want to show you something, but I don't want to freak you out." He breathed a sigh. "This morning—that last thing—the ground defense . . ." He watched me closely, and I tried to look away, anywhere but his eyes, because my face was burning, humiliated, but I couldn't tear my eyes from his. "I know you don't believe it would work. I want to show you it will."

"What do you mean, show me?"

His hands tightened on mine. "I want to teach you exactly how to execute it. Here. With no one else watching."

It was the replication of the position itself, but also the thought of him watching that had been so unnerving this morning, but he couldn't know that.

"Trust me, Jacqueline. It works. Will you let me show you?"

I nodded.

He led me to the center of the floor space, pulled me down to my knees next to him. "Lie flat. On your stomach." Heart pounding, I obeyed. "The majority of men have no martial arts training whatsoever, so they won't be able to counter the moves correctly. And even those who do won't be expecting what you're going to do. Remember what Ralph said—the key is to get away."

I nodded, my cheek on the carpet, my heart slamming against the floor.

"Do you remember the moves?"

I shook my head, shutting my eyes.

"It's okay. I could tell you were freaking out in class. Your friend did the right thing, not forcing you. I don't want to force you either. I just want to help you feel more in control."

I took a deep breath. "Okay."

"If you find yourself in this position, you want to do these moves automatically, without wasting time or energy trying to buck him off."

I stiffened as his inadvertent use of Buck's name.

"What?"

"That's his name. Buck."

I heard him inhale through his nose, like he was trying to maintain control. "I will remember that." He was silent for a moment. "The first move seems counterproductive because it provides no leverage. But that's the thing—you're taking *his* leverage away. Choose the side you want to roll onto, and put that arm straight up above your head, like you're standing and reaching for the ceiling."

I put my left arm up as he described.

"Good. Now, with your opposite arm, you give *yourself* leverage, and you remove his already precarious balance. Palm flat on the ground, elbow up. Shove down and roll to your side, throwing him off."

I followed his instructions—easy to do, with no weight on top of me.

"Can we try it? I'm going to push your shoulders down and use my weight to hold you there. If you have a problem, just say so and I'm off. Okay?"

I fought my panic. "Okay."

His gentleness as he knelt over me, holding my shoulders to the floor, was so contrary to Buck's violence that I almost cried. He lay over me, his breath in my ear. "Arm straight up." I obeyed. "Palm flat, and push off, hard, and roll onto your side."

I did as he said, and he tumbled off. "Perfect. Let's try it again."

We went through the moves again, and again, and again, and each time he was more forceful and harder to displace, but still, I threw him off, every time. Until I mistakenly pushed up with my hips, trying to rise.

He exhaled harshly. "That won't work, Jacqueline—though it's the natural response to something unwanted on top of you. The only sure way to dislodge a man in this position is rolling to the side. I'm too strong for you to move me by pressing up. You have to fight that inclination."

Finally, we tried it more for real than any other time. He shoved me down, and my arm shot up and out, but I had a difficult time getting my hand free for leverage. Finally, I switched arms and got the opposite palm to the floor, shoved, and rolled, throwing him off and to the side. "Shit!" He laughed, facing me as we lay on the floor. "You swapped sides on me!"

I smiled at his praise, and his gaze flicked to my lips.

"This is the part where you'd get up and run like hell." His voice was gravelly.

"But won't he chase me?" We lay on our sides, two feet of carpet between us, neither making a move to sit up.

He nodded. "He might. But most of these guys don't want challenging prey. Only a handful will go after you if you run away screaming."

"Ah."

He reached out, took my hand. "I was supposed to show you your portrait, I think."

"So it won't seem like you brought me here under completely false pretenses?"

His eyes flared and my breath caught. "I do want you to see the charcoal, but I admit that was secondary to what we just did. Do you feel more confident now that it'll work?"

"Yes."

He leaned up on his elbow, closing the distance between us, pushing his hand into my hair and moving it to cup my face. "I did have one other concealed motive for bringing you here." Leaning down slowly, his lips met mine and the fire that had been embers since he left my room over a week ago flamed. I opened my mouth and his tongue pressed inside, stroked mine and withdrew. Turning his head, he moved his mouth over mine, sucking my lower lip into his mouth, caressing it with his tongue and releasing it to pay attention to the upper. His tongue ran over the sensitive space above my top teeth and I gasped.

And then his hands started moving.

chapter *Twelve*

My head nestled against his shoulder, both hands skimmed down to my hips, urging me closer until there was no space between us. His lips continued to move against mine, unrelenting and sweet, and my head swam as he swept his tongue through my mouth, his hand gripping my thigh, drawing it between his so that our legs were scissored together. I leaned into him and he moaned, one hand kneading my hip and the other stroking up beneath my sweater, warm fingers splayed across my lower back.

One of my arms crushed between us, I lay the other against his chest, fingering the front placket of his flannel shirt, covertly sliding buttons from buttonholes, feeling the variation between the smooth surface of the flannel and the bumpy texture of the thermal knit shirt beneath it. Shirt unbuttoned, I peeled it aside and slid my hand beneath the thermal to his hard stomach. His breath caught and I pulled away to lean on my elbow and look down on him.

"I want to see your tattoos."

"You do, huh?" His eyes burned into mine. When I nodded, he withdrew his hand from beneath my sweater and sat up, crooking an eyebrow at me when he looked down on his unbuttoned shirt.

My face warmed at his smirk and he chuckled, removing the shirt and tossing it aside.

Reaching behind his neck, he removed the white thermal the way boys do—pulled forward over the back of his head—unworried about ruined mascara or blush smeared on the fabric. He dropped this shirt, inside out, on top of the flannel one and lay back on the floor, offering himself up for my inspection.

His skin was smooth and beautiful, his torso segmented with definitions of muscle and ornamented with the two tattoos I'd seen in my dorm room—an intricate octagonal design on his left side, and four scripted lines on his right. There was one other—a rose over his heart, the petals dark red, the dark green stem slightly curved. On his arms were mostly designs and patterns, thin and black like wrought iron.

I ran my fingers over each one, but he didn't turn and I couldn't read the poem-like lines snaking around his left side. It looked like a love poem, and I was jealous of whoever inspired the sort of devotion he must have felt to make those words so permanent. I wondered if the rose represented her as well, but I couldn't ask.

When my fingers trailed down his abdomen to the line of hair below his navel, he sat up. "Your turn, I think."

Confused, I said, "I don't have any tattoos."

"I figured as much." He stood and reached a hand down to me. "Would you like to see the drawing now?"

He was asking me to go to his bedroom. I felt like I should come back with something smart, like *Should I call you Lucas or Landon in bed?* but I couldn't manage it. I reached up and took his hand, and he pulled me up effortlessly. Without releasing my hand, he turned toward the bedroom, and I followed.

Dim light from the outer room illuminated the furniture and the wall adjacent to his bed, where at least twenty or thirty drawings were tacked up. He switched on a lamp and I saw that the entire surface of the wall was covered in cork. I wondered if he'd installed it or if it was already there, and when he went looking for a place to live, he knew immediately that this was meant to be his.

The two uncorked walls were painted an earthy taupe, and his furniture was dark and not at all typical college-boy—from the queen-sized platform bed to the solid desk and hutch.

I moved into the narrow space between his bed and the wall of drawings, searching for myself, but distracted by the others—renditions of familiar scenes like the downtown skyline, unfamiliar faces of children and old men, and a couple of Francis in repose.

"These are amazing."

He came to stand next to me just as my eyes found my own face among the others. He'd chosen to charcoal the one of me on my back, looking up at him. Its placement was low on the right side of the wall. Seemingly, this display spot would indicate lower importance, but I was acutely aware of where it was located in relation to his bed—directly across from his pillow.

Who wouldn't want to wake up to this? he'd said.

I sat on his bed, staring at it, and he sat, too. I was abruptly aware of his bare chest and his statement in the other room: *Your turn, I think*. Turning to him, I saw that he was watching me.

I'd been so sure that this sort of moment would summon

debilitating memories of Kennedy—of his kiss, of our years together. But the truth was, I didn't miss him. I couldn't dredge up a single twinge of sorrow. I wondered if I was either anesthetized to the grief of losing him—which would be worrisome—or if I had cried so much and grieved so deeply in the past several weeks that I was over it. Over him.

Lucas leaned to me and the Kennedy bubble burst entirely. His breath in my ear, he ran his tongue along the curved edge, sucking the fleshy lobe and my small diamond stud into his mouth, and my eyes drifted closed while I babbled a weak sound of longing. Nuzzling my neck, he lapped gentle kisses down the side, his hand coming up to cradle the weight of my head, which had fallen to the side. His weight left the bed as he knelt on the floor and pulled my boots from my feet before resuming his seat and removing his own.

His lips played over mine, and he pulled me to the center of the bed and laid me flat. I opened my eyes when he drew back and stared down at me. "Say stop whenever you want to stop. Understand?"

I nodded.

"Do you want to stop now?"

My head moved back and forth on the pillow.

"Thank God," he said, his mouth returning to mine, his tongue plunging inside as I dug my fingers into his solid arms. I stroked his tongue with mine, sucking it deep into my mouth, and he groaned, wrenching away long enough to lift me slightly and remove my sweater. Teasing one fingertip over the swell of my breast, he followed the arc with his lips.

When I pushed against his shoulder he stopped, his eyes unfocused. I pushed him onto his back and straddled him, feeling him hard and ready through our two pairs of jeans. His hands smoothed up my waist and pulled me down, and we kissed deeply as I rocked against him. Minutes later, he flicked the hooks free at the back of my bra and tugged the straps down my arms. It wasn't off completely before he slid me higher and took a nipple in his mouth.

"Oh," I gasped, going limp in his arms.

We rolled again and I was under him, his hands tracing and circling, followed by his mouth. Then he unbuttoned my jeans and touched the zipper and everything crashed around me.

I tore my mouth from his. "Wait."

"Stop?" he panted, watching me.

I bit my lip and nodded.

"Stop everything, or just go no further?"

"Just . . . just no further," I whispered.

"Done." He gathered me into his arms and kissed me, one hand tangled in my hair and the other caressing down my back, our hearts pulsing out a cadence that the musician in me translated into a concert of lust.

• • • • • • • • • • •

I kept my eyes open on the ride home. Peeking over Lucas's shoulder, I watched the scenery fly by—and it was exhilarating, not frightening. I trusted him. I had since that first night, when I let him drive me home.

Kennedy would have never stopped like that. Not that he had ever forced me or come close to doing so. If I asked him to stop, he'd stop and lay back, a hand over his face, calming himself and saying, "God, Jackie, you're going to kill me." After that, there was no further physical activity—no kissing, no touching. And I always felt guilty.

I thought the guilt would go away once we were actually sleeping together, because it was rare when I'd ask for a reprieve from sex, but if anything, my self-reproach was worse. He'd stop, abruptly, like it pained him. It was all or nothing. He'd take a few deep breaths, click on a game, or channel surf, or we'd go get something to eat. And I would feel like the world's worst girlfriend.

Lucas had continued the makeout session for another hour. Before it was over, he'd slid his hand between my legs, over my jeans. "This okay?" he asked, and at my breathless affirmative answer he stroked his fingers there while kissing me deeply, and somehow made me come through a layer of denim. I was shocked, and a little embarrassed, but one glance at his face told me he savored my body's response, and his ability to trigger it. He would not let me return the favor.

"Leave me something to anticipate," he'd whispered.

Now he was leaving me at the front of my building, wide awake from the cold drive, though he'd placed my hands under his jacket during the ride, so they wouldn't be frozen. He put the helmets and his gloves aside and pulled me closer, his hands under my jacket, over my sweater. "Did you like the charcoal?"

I nodded. "Yes. Thank you for showing me your drawings . . . and the defense move."

Resting his forehead to mine, he closed his eyes. "Mmm-hmm." He kissed the tip of my nose, and then moved his lips to mine.

It almost hurt to kiss him—almost. I sighed into his mouth.

"You'd better get inside before . . ." He kissed me again, more hungrily, and I curled my hands between us against his hard chest.

"Before . . . ?"

He inhaled and exhaled through his nose, his mouth a tight line, his hands gripping my waist. "Just. Before."

I kissed the edge of his jaw and pulled away. "Good night, Lucas."

He remained leaning against the Harley and watched me. "Good night, Jacqueline."

I walked up the steps to my building, and not until I got to the door did I look up and see Kennedy standing there on the top step, his narrowed, curious eyes flicking between Lucas and me.

"Jackie." He stared down at me as I stepped up next to him. "I came by, thought we could talk. But Erin said you were out, and she wasn't sure if you'd be back at all?" I'd left Erin a scribbled note telling her where I was. She must have enjoyed rubbing my night out in Kennedy's face. He looked back toward the curb, but I didn't turn to see if Lucas was there or gone.

"Why didn't you text first? Or call?"

He shrugged, combing his hair back from his forehead with one hand, the other stuffed into the front pocket of his jeans. "I was in the building."

I angled my head. "You were in the building, and thought you'd just stop by and I'd be in my room?" I had planned to be in my room, but that was beside the point.

"No, of course I didn't assume you'd be there," he backpedaled. "I *hoped* you'd be there." He looked toward the curb again. "Is . . . that guy waiting for you, or something?"

I turned then and saw Lucas, arms crossed over his chest, still leaning against his motorcycle. I couldn't make out his facial features from this distance, even with the flood lights surrounding the dorm. But his body language spoke volumes. I lifted a hand and waved, to let him know I wasn't being threatened. "No. He was just dropping me off."

After a smirk of disdain in Lucas's direction, Kennedy turned his sharp green eyes to me. "He doesn't look as though he understands the concept of 'dropping off,' if you ask me."

"Well, I didn't ask you. What do you want, Kennedy?"

Some guy going inside called out, "K-Moore!" and Kennedy acknowledged him with a lifted chin before answering me. "I told you, I want to talk."

I crossed my arms, starting to feel the chill in the air I hadn't felt pressed to Lucas. "About what? Haven't you said everything that needs to be said? Do you want to devalue me some more? Because I have to tell you, I'm not real super amenable to that."

He sighed as though tolerating some sort of distraught outburst, a familiar consequence of me being *inflexible*—his word—that I'd seen many times in the past three years. I'd forgotten about that until seeing it again. "There's no need to be inflexible," he said then, as though reading my mind.

"Really? I think there are plenty of reasons for my inflexibility. Or stubbornness. Or obstinacy. Or pigheadedness—"

"I *get* it, Jackie."

My hands made fists at my hips. "It's. *Jacqueline*."

He stepped closer, his eyes flaring. For a split second, I thought he was angry—but that wasn't anger in his eyes. It was desire. "I get it, Jacqueline. I hurt you. And I deserve everything you're saying, and everything you feel." He raised his hand to my face and I stepped back, out of his reach, my thoughts chaotic. Dropping his hand, he added, "I miss you."

chapter *Thirteen*

Snapping my mouth closed, I spun to swipe my card and enter the dorm, and Kennedy followed me through the door. I turned to tell him I didn't want to talk and saw Lucas grabbing the door just before it snapped shut. Stepping next to me, he glared at my ex and the air was charged between them the moment Kennedy turned and noticed him.

"You okay, Jacqueline?" Lucas asked, his eyes never wavering from my ex.

"Lucas—" I started to reiterate verbally that Kennedy was no physical threat to me when he huffed an arrogant laugh, peering at Lucas.

"Wait—aren't you the maintenance guy? The one who repaired the AC at the house?" He glanced at me, and back to Lucas. "What would administration think about you sniffing around the students?"

The look on Lucas's face was murderous, but he held his ground without reaction, ignoring Kennedy's question as though it hadn't been asked. He turned his eyes to me, waiting for my answer.

"I'm fine. I promise." I held my breath, hoping he'd believe me. People near the door were already nudging each other and whispering.

"Are you hooking up with *this guy*, too?" Kennedy interjected.

"Too?" I asked, but I knew what he meant before he confirmed it.

"In addition to Buck."

The edges of my vision closed in. "What?"

Kennedy took my arm just above the elbow, as though he meant to escort me away, and Lucas's hand shot out, grabbing his wrist and removing his hand from me easily.

"What the fuck?" Kennedy's voice was a low growl as he jerked his arm from Lucas's grip. He put himself slightly in front of me, facing off with Lucas, and everyone within sight of the developing spectacle was stock-still and gawking. The two of them looked evenly matched, but I knew Lucas's proficiency firsthand. Kennedy would lose, and Lucas would be expelled.

I stepped around my ex and laid a hand on his forearm. It was rock-hard beneath my fingers. "Kennedy, *leave*."

"I'm not leaving you with this—"

"Kennedy, *leave*."

"He's a *maintenance* man, Jackie—"

"He's a *student*, Kennedy." I decided not to point out that Lucas was in our econ class, in case he recognized him as the class tutor and reported him for going out with me.

Kennedy inclined his head, his expression transforming into concern—slightly furrowed brow, eyes searching mine. "We'll talk next week. When we're home." His meaning was clear and directed at Lucas. The two of us were about to spend several days in our hometown, where he would have unrestricted access to me, without the nuisance of interference.

I wanted to tell him I had nothing to say to him, not now or then, but my jaw was clenched so tightly that I couldn't speak. Still unsure what I was even doing over Thanksgiving break, I ignored his implication that we would be alone then. Judiciously, he didn't try to touch me again, though his lethal expression matched Lucas's as they faced off. I didn't exhale until he went through the door.

Onlooker disappointment was palpable. A few hung around to see if there would be a bonus row between Lucas and me. The adrenaline was clearly still pumping through him—his body was taut, like the hard wire of my bass strings, and when I reached a hand to his forearm, it was granite under layers of leather and flannel.

"I'm okay, honest." I sighed heavily. "Well, as okay as I can be after that." I squinted up at him. "Exactly how many jobs do you have, anyway? Barista, self-defense guru, fixit guy, parking enforcement officer—and by the way, does that mean *you* gave me the ticket I got last spring for two measly minutes of double parking when I ran into the library to return a book?"

His shoulders relaxed with my teasing tone, and I was rewarded with the ghost smile. "I plead the fifth on that. I write a *lot* of parking tickets. The, um, fixit thing is rare. And I volunteer time for the self-defense gig."

What I'd left off this list, and what he didn't add: *economics tutor*.

"I guess we should add one more, huh?" I said, watching him closely. He had a superb poker face. No reaction at all. "Personal defender of Jacqueline Wallace?"

The faint smile appeared again.

"Another volunteer position, Lucas?" I asked coyly, brows rising. "How will you have time for studying? Or anything fun?"

His hands reached for me, gripping my hipbones and pulling me forward. He stared down at me, his voice low. "There are some things I will make time for, Jacqueline." Leaning, he kissed the spot just in front of my ear, the spot that made my breath go shallow. And then, he turned and jogged out to his motorcycle, leaving me standing in the entryway. Once he was outside the pool of light surrounding the building, I couldn't see him. I turned and walked to my room in a daze.

• • • • • • • • • • •

Jacqueline,

Your paper is good. Solid research. I think Dr. H will be pleased with it. I noted a couple of small inconsistencies, and one place you may have left out a citation. Other than that, I think it's a valid, well-supported argument.

I've attached the worksheet for tomorrow's session. You're caught up now, and you seem to have a good grasp on the new material, but I'll continue to send you the worksheets for the last two weeks of class, if you'd like.

I assume you're going home over the break? I'll be heading home Wednesday morning. No Wi-Fi there, so I'll be out of pocket until Sunday.

LM

Landon,

Looks like I may get this paper turned in early—what a relief. Thank you for your help. Yes, please continue to send the worksheets.

My parents are going skiing over break, but I'd rather go home for a few days and hang out with old friends than stay here on campus. They'll be boarding Coco, Mom's evil-tempered little dog, so it should be peaceful and quiet.

Are you flying home? I remember you saying you were carless.

JW

Jacqueline,

Your parents are going skiing and not taking you? You'll be at home for Thanksgiving alone?

I'm hitching a ride from someone with a car. Home isn't far, though it seems like another world at times.

LM

Landon,

My parents thought I'd be at my ex's. We've traded off the last couple of years rather than trying to join both family meals; this was his year. My BFF's family will be at her grandparents' cabin outside Boulder, and I'm not in the mood to burden anyone else.

I'd rather be alone. That's weird, huh?

JW

Jacqueline,

Not weird to me. But maybe I'm just weird, too, and I wouldn't know.

I'll miss your emails.

LM

Landon,

Ditto. Have a good break.

JW

• • • • • • • • • • •

I couldn't look back at Lucas during class Monday without thinking about Saturday night. His hooded stares made me think he was having the same issue. After I caught him staring holes into the back of Kennedy's head, I didn't turn back around. When class ended, Kennedy turned and smiled at me. I forced my lips into a line and turned my back to him to pack up. This class, this semester could not end soon enough, for too many reasons to count.

"Can I just say—your ex is gorgeous, but he seems like a conceited *asshat*." Benji crammed his spiral into a backpack that looked as though it could erupt with loose papers any moment.

I zipped my backpack. "Yeah, he totally is." We waited for Kennedy to pass before moving into the aisle, and I studiously avoided making eye contact. I was more than a little worried about his assertion that we would talk while we were both home; I couldn't imagine what he could have to say that I'd want to hear.

Following our classmates up the steps, everyone animated with anticipation of the coming long weekend, Benji told me he'd be flying home to Georgia and coming out to his father—the only member of his family he hadn't told. "Mom's known I was gay since I was thirteen."

I was worried on his behalf. "Will your dad be . . . upset?"

He smiled. "I think he knows. He's just not sure if that means I'm going to show up in a dress or something." The thought of Benji in a dress wasn't a pretty picture, and I couldn't hold back my laugh. He laughed too, adding, "I know, right?"

Lucas was gone, or so I thought, until Benji and I emerged into the busy hallway and I spotted him leaning on the far wall, near the side door I usually took to escape the building. He watched us approach, but he seemed acutely aware of everyone else as well. I imagined him watching for Dr. Heller.

"You haven't told him you know yet, have you?" Benji asked, speaking from the side of his mouth.

I shook my head.

"Don't make him suffer too much. He looks sorta vulnerable."

I chuckled. "Right. A tough, muscular guy like that—who's trained to beat people up, and lies about who he is to girls—is so vulnerable."

He squeezed my arm just above the elbow and smiled. "He's either an asshat to rival all asshats before him, or there's a reason for those lies."

I sighed. "I wish I was a mind reader."

"You might not, once you know what's in there."

"If I ever do."

Benji shrugged in agreement and veered off toward the long hallway leading to the south exit, turning to call, "Have a good break, Jacqueline."

"You, too."

I reached Lucas and he turned to follow me, leaning close to push the door open. "Can I see you tonight?" he murmured.

I wondered if I was turning into a booty call. Or if that's all it had ever been to him—if that was his reason for not telling me he was Landon Maxfield. "I have a test tomorrow in astronomy. We have study group in our room tonight."

I glanced up at him, walking beside me with his hands stuffed into the front pockets of his jeans. His gaze continuously scanned over the crowd of people, as though he was on guard.

"Tomorrow night?" He stared down at me as we neared the building, and I noted that he seemed to know exactly where I was going.

"I have an ensemble rehearsal tomorrow. I usually spend Sunday mornings in the music hall, but I missed yesterday." I hadn't told Lucas I played the bass. I'd told Landon.

"You slept in?"

I nodded.

"Me, too."

We reached the entry and stopped to the side of the door. "I have to get my bass packed up, too, since I'm taking it home with me." Waiting to see if he'd react, I watched his eyes, which matched the gray-blue of the overcast sky as his gaze drifted over the faces around us. "I'll have plenty of time to rehearse during break."

"When are you leaving town?" He flicked his hair from his eyes, avoiding the subject of my instrument completely.

"Wednesday morning. You?"

"Same." He shifted, on edge, his lower lip caught between his teeth, and then all of a sudden, he settled and stilled. His eyes met mine, unwavering. "Text me if you're done early. Or your plans change. Otherwise, I'll catch you after break." He hitched the shoulder over which his backpack was slung and added, "Later, Jacqueline," before turning and blending into the flow of students, his dark head rising above most of them.

• • • • • • • • • • •

"Hold up. So tutor-guy *Landon* and hottie OBBP *Lucas* are the *same guy*?" Maggie's eyes were so rounded with shock that I could see white all the way around her light brown irises.

"What I don't understand is why you didn't call him on that shit *immediately*." Erin had her talk-show-participant face on. Any moment, she would call me *girrrrl* and start recounting the ass kicking she'd be doing if she was in my shoes. Ever since she'd broken up with Chaz, she was much less tolerant of guys stepping out of line. Or appearing to.

I huffed a sigh and wished I'd never told them. "What happened to *gag-him-and-bag him* and *rebound* and *Operation Bad Boy Phase*?" The three of us sat on a comforter on the floor of the dorm room, drinking coffee and eating Oreos, astronomy texts and notes spread all around us, untouched for the last half hour as we discussed Landon/Lucas instead of gas giants and celestial navigation.

"He's supposed to be *your* booty call. Not the other way around." Erin's voice resonated with authority.

"Yeah." Maggie chimed in. "Why don't you text him that you want to meet up later?"

I rolled my eyes. "Because I have an exam at nine thirty in the morning—which we're supposed to be studying for right now. And also, I think I need a little distance . . ."

Erin peered at me. "Oh *hell* no—you're getting emotionally involved, aren't you?"

I lay back with my hands covering my face. "Ughhhh!"

"By the way—speaking of booty calls, what's this I hear about you and Buck? He's definitely bad boy material," Maggie mused. "Did you add him to the OBBP stable without telling us?"

I gave Erin a pleading look between my fingers.

"Buck's full of shit. You know that, Maggie," she scoffed.

Maggie nodded. "True . . . Plus, I messed around with him freshman year. He wasn't very good, from what I recall. Too slobbery." She shuddered. "What is it with slobbery kissers? Are they trying to drown us in spit? I mean, Jesus, *swallow* every now and then."

Her hand squeezing my shoulder, Erin laughed, and while I could hear the contrived ring to it, Maggie didn't. I knew where Erin's mind was going. I hadn't given her many details, and she hadn't asked for any. It was difficult enough to speak about that night in generalities. The point was what had happened, and what had almost happened, not the particulars of it.

"So you aren't hooking up with him?" Maggie pressed. She was only curious, but it rankled to have my name joined with Buck's in any way.

"Like Erin said—he's full of shit." I was curious myself. Morbidly so, perhaps. "Why? Is he saying something about me?"

She shrugged. "Trisha said her little sister's boyfriend said Buck was hassling Kennedy about it. Those two are like those big goats that butt heads over the girl goats. I think Buck's still pissed that he was *legacy* and Kennedy still beat him out for pledge class president."

That was the complication I couldn't remember before—the all-important initial conflict between them. The start of their weird brotherly rivalry. I frowned. "But Kennedy was legacy, too."

Maggie licked Oreo crumbs from her fingers. "Yeah, but Buck was legacy *and* his daddy was pledge class prez. He thought he had it wrapped up."

I sat up, becoming furious as Buck's motivations became clearer. His reasons for hurting me were nothing more than goading my ex. "And that translates into the need for Buck to spread lies that I'm *screwing* him?" Not to mention the fact that he'd actually assaulted me.

"I didn't say it made any *sense*."

Erin pulled her notes onto her lap. "Okay ladies, which constellations do we think we'll have to plot on the star chart portion of this test?"

Giving my best friend a grateful look for the change of subject, I shoved thoughts of Buck as far away from my consciousness as I could manage to do.

chapter Fourteen

After three months away, the house smelled funny. Like dog . . . combined with the Chanel cologne Mom always wore, plus some other undefinable scent that my mind classified as *home*. Still, it was foreign. I didn't quite belong here anymore, and my body knew it.

I lugged my bass inside, still nestled safely within its wheeled traveling case. With no parents and no Coco, there was little reason to move it any farther than the living room. I parked it against the wall, where it stood like another piece of furniture. The lights in the house were timer-set, since Mom and Dad were gone. I decided to let them go on and off at will, with the exception of the kitchen lighting and the lamps in my bedroom, which probably wouldn't come on at all otherwise.

There was food in the pantry and freezer, but barely anything in the fridge. My parents had cleared out all of the perishable stuff before their trip, not knowing I was coming home tonight, since I never told them. Mom texted me earlier that they were boarding their plane, adding:

Have fun with Erin. We'll see you next month.

Having never double-checked my plans, she'd somehow come to the conclusion that I was going home with my roommate.

I heated a box of organic vegetarian lasagna for dinner and transferred a ground turkey patty from the freezer to the fridge for my Thanksgiving lunch. There was half a package of tater tots in the freezer, too, and I found an unopened bottle of cranberry juice cocktail in the pantry. I moved it to the fridge. Ta-da! Thanksgiving for one.

After watching a couple of sitcom reruns, I switched the television off, scooted the walnut coffee table from its perfectly centered spot on the hand-knotted Tibetan rug, and unpacked my bass. Improvising with a plant stand when I couldn't find my music stand, I ran through the beginnings of a prelude piece I'd begun composing for my year-end solo.

The last thing I expected to hear while scribbling notes onto staff paper was the doorbell. I'd never been afraid to be at home alone, but then I'd never been so completely alone here before. I debated pretending no one was home, but of course whoever was there had heard me playing and quitting after the doorbell rang. I laid the bass on its side and crept to the solid door, standing on my toes to look through the peephole. Kennedy stood, smiling straight at me, illuminated by the glow of the dual lights of the veranda. He couldn't see me, of course, but he'd answered this door many times and knew the view from the inside almost as well as I did.

I unlocked and opened the door, but didn't move from the doorway. "Kennedy? What are you doing here?"

He glanced behind me and heard the utter quiet of the house. "Are your parents out?"

I sighed. "They aren't here."

He frowned. "Aren't here tonight, or aren't here over break?"

I'd forgotten how readily Kennedy could zero in on what *wasn't* said. That characteristic probably accounted for most of his debate wins. "They aren't here at all—but why are *you* here?"

He leaned a shoulder into the door frame. "I texted first but you didn't answer." I probably hadn't heard the text alert. Little could be heard over the sound of my bass once I began playing. "During dinner, Mom reminded me to make sure I had you over by one tomorrow—and yes, that means I never told them we broke up. I started to tonight, and then I thought this might be a welcome escape from Evelyn and Trent. Where are they, anyway?"

I ignored his question. I couldn't help but notice that he said *we broke up* as though our breakup was a mutual decision. As though I hadn't been the blindsided idiot of the equation.

"You want me to come to Thanksgiving lunch and pretend we're all fine, just so you don't have to tell your parents we broke up?"

He smiled just enough to make the dimple appear. "I'm not *that* big of a coward. I can tell them if you want, and say I've invited you to come as a friend. But we don't have to disclose anything to them if you don't want to. Trust me, they're too oblivious to pick up on anything. My little bro's had a weed habit for over a year—parties so hard he'd put most of the brotherhood to shame—and they have no idea."

"Aren't you worried about him?"

He shrugged. "His grades are still decent. He's just bored. Besides, he's not *my* kid."

"But he's your little brother." I understood sibling relationships only in theory, since I'd never had one, but I assumed logic would dictate some sense of responsibility. Kennedy seemed to feel none.

"He wouldn't listen to anything I have to say."

"How do you know?" I pressed.

He sighed. "I don't know. Maybe because he never has. C'mon. Come tomorrow. I'll pick you up right before one. It'll be better than . . . whatever frozen thing you'd planned to microwave?"

I rolled my eyes and he chuckled.

"I still don't understand why you didn't tell them. It's been over a month."

He shrugged again. "I don't know. Maybe because I know how much my family loves you." *That* was bullshit. I raised an eyebrow and he laughed. "Okay, well they were used to you—used to *us*. I guess you told your parents?"

I curled my toes into the cold marble floor, the chill from outside seeping into the entryway. "I told Mom. I assume she told Dad. They seemed vaguely annoyed, though I don't know if the annoyance was directed at you for dumping me or me for not managing to hold on to you." I wanted to pinch myself for the dejected words that made it sound as though I was pining for him.

In actuality, Mom and I had revisited the quarrel we had when I first told her my college plans. She hadn't approved, claiming that smart girls forge their own educational paths; they don't follow their high school boyfriend to college. "But do what you like. You always have," she'd said, stalking from my room. We hadn't discussed it again until Kennedy broke up with me.

"I guess it doesn't do any good now to point out that I was

right about him." She'd sighed over the phone. "And your ill-advised decision to follow him there."

Whenever I appeared to have won an argument, Mom would say something like, "Even broken clocks are right twice a day." I'd tossed this bit of wisdom back in her face, and just like she had when I announced my college plans, she'd heaved a sigh like I was hopelessly clueless and dropped the subject. Little did she know that in that moment, I agreed with her completely, for once. Following my boyfriend to State was possibly the most dim-witted thing I'd ever done.

Kennedy stood with his thumbs hooked through his belt loops, looking contrite. "I assume you don't have plans to have Thanksgiving supper with Dahlia's family, or Jillian's, or you'd have already said so."

Preferring to wait until the holiday festivities were over, I hadn't yet called my high school friends to let them know I was home. Jillian had flunked out of LSU at the end of freshman year, after which she'd moved home to train for management at Forever 21 and get engaged to some guy who managed a mall jewelry store. Dahlia was in the second year of her nursing program in Oklahoma. We'd all grown apart since graduation. It was odd, how unconnected I felt to each of them now, when we'd been joined at the hip for four years of high school.

Now Dahlia had her nursing undergrad crowd in a neighboring state, and Jillian had a blue stripe in her hair, a full-time job, and a fiancé. Both were shocked when Kennedy and I broke up. They were among the first to text and call, commiserating—or trying to, even though we hadn't been close in over a year. I hoped we could hang out and hopefully *not* discuss Kennedy ad nauseum.

"I don't have plans with anyone. I thought it would be nice to be home *alone*." I emphasized the last word, staring up at him.

"You can't be here all by yourself on Thanksgiving."

I hated the pity underlying his assumption, and I glared up at him. "Yes, I can."

The dark green of his eyes scanned over my face. "Yes, you can," he agreed. "But there's no reason for you to. We can be friends, right? You'll always be important to me. You know that."

I so didn't know that. But if I said no, if I insisted on staying at my parents' house alone and eating a microwaved turkey patty for Thanksgiving, it would look like I couldn't get over him. Like I was so damaged that I couldn't be around him.

"Fine," I said, almost instantly regretting it.

• • • • • • • • • • •

"So, are you and my dickwad brother back together, or what?" Carter asked, under his breath.

If he wasn't so big, Carter would have been a carbon copy of his older brother—same green eyes and mop of dirty blond hair. But where Kennedy was tall and lean, Carter had sprouted to an equal height, but with the girth and muscle of a running back. Having known him since he was a wiry fourteen-year-old—when Kennedy still towered over him—his transformation was mind-boggling. I remembered him as a quiet, scowling boy, eclipsed by his older brother. He was clearly done with that phase.

I glanced behind us as we set the table, relieved that no one else was within earshot. "No."

He followed behind me, placing forks on top of the napkins I'd folded. "Too bad for him."

My eyes widened a bit at this, and when I looked at him, he smirked. "What? Anyone can see you're too good for him. So why are you here?"

"Um, thanks. And my parents went to Breckenridge."

He recoiled, astonished. "Fuck, are you serious? And I thought *my* parents were the biggest assholes in this town."

I couldn't help but grin, though I curbed it as much as possible. Carter had always seemed unmanageable and emotional next to the rest of his logical, coolheaded family. I'd never considered what an outsider he must have felt like with them—the impetuous middle child between Kennedy and his little sister, Reagan, who gave the impression that she'd been born a thirty-year-old accountant.

"Language, Carter," Kennedy said, rounding the corner.

"Fuck off, Kennedy," Carter retorted, not missing a beat.

Fully containing my reaction was impossible. My jaw was like rock in the attempt, but a small snort escaped, which earned a big, full-wattage grin from Carter. He winked at me before scooting off to the kitchen to help his mother. I blinked, imagining that the poor girls at my former high school must collapse against the lockers when he sauntered past.

Kennedy was scowling.

"What happened to 'he's not my kid'?" I asked, placing the last spoon before turning to him. "It's okay to berate him for dropping the F-bomb, but you wash your hands of helping him kick an alleged drug problem?" I was definitely asking for it. Debating with Kennedy was unwinnable.

He inclined his head. "Good point."

I blinked again, thinking that the Moore boys were going to shock me to death by the time I left town.

Grant and Bev Moore were as oblivious as Kennedy had promised. They didn't seem to detect the strained air between their son and me in the four hours I spent with them, or the absence of our usual PDA. He didn't sling an arm across the back of my chair during the meal, and though he pushed my chair in when I sat—as he'd been raised to do—he didn't kiss my cheek or take my hand. When Reagan narrowed her sharp thirteen-year-old eyes on us, I pretended not to notice her scrutiny. Carter, of course, leered and flirted with me outrageously, trying to make me laugh and piss his brother off. He succeeded on both counts while their parents discerned nothing.

Not touching except for the press of his leg against mine, Kennedy and I sat side-by-side through a football game on the wall-sized flat screen that made Carter so furious he stood up and cursed at the screen a couple of times, for which his entire family—all four of them—calmly rebuked him. The second time, he stomped from the room and was gone for several minutes. From the way he flexed his hand when he returned, I got the feeling he went to his bedroom and hit something.

As soon as Kennedy pulled into my driveway to drop me off, I hopped out of the car, thanking him for inviting me and making it clear that I was going inside alone. He smiled tightly. "We should hang out Saturday. I'll give you a call." Thankfully, he made no move to exit the car.

As though he hadn't suggested anything, I thanked him again and said good-bye. Once inside, I watched him from a curtained window. He stared pensively at the closed front door for a minute before pulling out his phone and calling someone as he backed out of the drive.

• • • • • • • • • •

After making Friday night plans with Dahlia and Jillian, I practiced my bass in the living room until the timer-set lamp clicked off just before eleven p.m. Chuckling into the darkness, I propped my instrument against the wall by feel and placed the bow on a shelf of a nearby bookcase. My phone lit up on the plant stand, signaling a message, and I stood in the dark, reading and answering.

Lucas: When will you be back on campus?

Me: Probably Sunday. You?

Lucas: Saturday.

Me: Family drama?

Lucas: No. My ride needs to go back then. Let me know if you're back early. I want to see you. I need to sketch you again.

Me: Oh?

Lucas: I've done a couple from memory but they aren't the same. Can't quite get the shape of your jaw. The line of your neck. And your lips. I need to spend more time staring at them and less time tasting them.

Me: I can't say I agree with that notion.

Lucas: More of both, then. Text me when you get back.

Okay, so sleeping was out.

I reread the text while stealthy recollections of his lips on mine curled through me, igniting small flames of desire that grew and fused as my memories of Saturday night replayed in graphic detail. Standing in the dark, I closed my eyes.

I should be fuming or at least distrustful where Lucas/Landon was concerned, but having tried to work up some outrage over his sin of omission, I simply couldn't. I reasoned that I was on resentment overload between Kennedy and Buck, and in comparison, Lucas seemed more a riddle than a risk. My plan for him, after all, had been to use him as a rebound—Operation Bad Boy Phase—and it wasn't like I'd been fully forthcoming about *that*.

Attempting to get a handle on my volatile musings, I grabbed a bottle of water from the fridge and walked upstairs to my bedroom, the only room still lit in the whole house.

When I checked my email, I saw there was one from LMaxfield amid the credit offers and listserv info, and my heart rate jumped. He'd sent it this afternoon, hours before our text exchange. Away from school, I was beginning to connect my tutor with Lucas—the Lucas who spoke to me from behind this Landon alias. I wanted to know why, but I didn't want to ask—I wanted him to tell me.

Jacqueline,

I discovered that the Bait & Tackle has added coffee and Wi-Fi, along with a new name promoting these innovative features. Joe (the proprietor) didn't bother to make up a whole new sign—he just affixed a whitewashed board to the ancient original. Now the hand-painted sign(s) read(s): Bait & Tackle & Coffee, and under "Coffee" it says "& Wi-Fi."

They have three tiny tables and a couple of lumpy, overstuffed floral chairs—like a Starbucks, if it had been decorated with yard sale furniture from someone's grandmother. It's the only place in town that's open today, so it's packed. The coffee's actually not horrible, but that's the best recommendation I can honestly give it. And predictably, the whole place smells like fish, which sort of detracts from the intended bistro ambiance.

Did your day go as planned?

You're locking and alarming your house every night, right? I don't mean to be insulting, but you said you were going to be home alone.

LM

Landon,

Yes, I'm amply skilled in locking up at night. The state-of-the-art alarm system is fully engaged. (And I'm not insulted. I appreciate the concern.)

I spent the day at my ex's. His parents have no idea we're broken up—he never told them, for some reason. It was awkward. I don't know why I let him talk me into going. He wants to see me Saturday to "talk."

I may go back to campus early. I haven't decided yet.

I'm seeing friends tomorrow, so that should be more fun.

What about your family? What did you do?

JW

I couldn't be sure when he'd get my answer, since he'd need the Bait & Tackle & Coffee's Wi-Fi to sign on. After a restless night—one that crawled by, leaving me more exhausted than I started—I made coffee and signed into to my school email. Unsurprisingly, there was nothing new from LMaxfield in my inbox. I thought about texting Lucas, but what would I say? That I'd tossed and turned all night, thinking of his hands on me?

chapter *Fifteen*

When I stopped for gas halfway back to campus, I sent Kennedy a text telling him I'd decided to go back early.

My phone rang before I even pulled back onto the interstate. Kennedy. I took a deep breath and switched off the stereo before answering.

"You've already left? I thought you were leaving tomorrow. I thought we were going to talk tonight."

I sighed, wanting to bang my head on the steering wheel, which wasn't the best idea while driving seventy miles an hour. "I don't understand what it is you want to talk about, Kennedy." I wondered if he'd been blind to how many times I'd been ready and willing to talk, and the multitude of chances he'd carelessly ignored.

"I think I made a mistake, Jackie." Misinterpreting my stunned silence, he added, "I mean Jacqueline. Sorry, I think that's going to take me a while—"

"What do you mean, you made a mistake?"

"Us. Breaking up."

I was silent again, the words sticking as I tried to take them in, gulp them down. I'd avoided campus gossip as much as possible, but I'd heard and seen enough to know that Kennedy had been no saint in the weeks we'd spent apart. He'd also had no shortage of willing participants. But girls willing to share your bed don't equal girls willing to put up with your random crap moods, listen to your exhaustive legal opinions, or support your life's goals the way someone who loves you would. No—that had been my role. And I'd been dismissed from it.

"Why?"

He sighed and I imagined what I knew he was doing—staring up at the ceiling, combing his hair back from his forehead, and leaving his hand there, elbow bent. He couldn't hide habitual mannerisms from me, even on the phone. "Why did I make a mistake, or why do I think it was a mistake?" I knew, too, that answering a question with a question was his way of buying time while he reasoned his way out of a problematic situation. "This conversation would have been easier in person—"

"We were together almost three *years*, and you just broke up with me—without even—there wasn't—" I was sputtering. I stopped and took a deep breath. "Maybe it wasn't a mistake."

"How can you say that?" He had the nerve to sound hurt.

"Oh, I don't know," I snapped. "Maybe the same way you so easily broke it off in the first place."

"Jackie—"

My teeth ground together. "Don't. Call. Me. *That*."

He was silent, and all I heard was road noise as my truck ate the miles of nothing between the last town and the next. Most of the fields on either side of the road were inactive, given the time of year, but a huge green picker was making its way through one cotton field, and I stared at it. No matter what happened to any individual person, life was going on elsewhere. The first time Kennedy kissed me, it stood to reason that at the same time, other people were splitting up. And the night Kennedy broke my heart, somewhere—maybe right there in my dorm—other people were falling in love.

"Jacqueline. I don't know what you want me to say."

In a matter of seconds, I'd passed through a town that boasted a sizable outlet mall and little else. Every mile took me farther from Kennedy. Closer to Lucas. I was unsettled by the notion that Lucas was someone to go *to*, before realizing that he'd been that safety zone for me from the moment we met.

"Nothing," I replied. "I don't want you to say anything."

My ex had the sense to know when he'd reached a deadlock. He thanked me for coming Thursday and said he'd be in touch once he got back to campus, which I didn't acknowledge.

• • • • • • • • • • •

Jacqueline,

It sounds like he wants you back, or at least, he wants something more than friendship. The question is, what do *you* want?

My family is just my dad and me. We had old friends over for Thanksgiving Day, so he was more conversational than he would have been otherwise. When it's just the two of us in that house, we tend to go hours without speaking. If you don't count "excuse me" and "pass the salt" sorts of things, the silence can encompass whole days.

Dad owns a charter fishing boat. Not much going on this time of year in the bay, though he arranges deep-sea fishing trips or native birdwatching tours over the winter. He'd scheduled one for today, so we said our good-byes at 5 a.m., and here I am, back at my place just after noon.

LM

Lucas was ten minutes from me. I wrestled with the urge to text him and tell him I was back, too. I knew I wouldn't win this battle for long.

I unpacked a week's worth of clean clothes, garden-scented and soft from Mom's Downy, which I usually skipped in the dorm's machines. I was relieved I wouldn't have to discreetly time laundry room use this week. Avoiding the stairwell altogether had become one of my quirks. I wouldn't go into it at all, even in a group. My subterfuge worked with everyone but Erin, who eyed me closely the second time I used, "I forgot something in my room—I'll meet you downstairs."

One night, she asked me outright, "You're afraid to go into the stairwell, aren't you?"

I was painting my toenails blood red, and I stared at the tiny brush and tried to keep my hand from shaking. *Start at the cuticle, sweep up. Start at the cuticle, sweep up*. "Wouldn't you be?"

"Yes," she answered.

The next time, it was Erin saying, "Oh crap, I left my purse in my room. J, come let me in, would ya?" Turning to the others, she said, "Hey, we'll meet y'all downstairs in five."

Me: I'm back.

Lucas: I didn't think you were coming back until tomorrow.

Me: I changed my mind.

Lucas: So I see. Free tonight?

Me: Yes.

Lucas: Dinner?

Me: Yes.

Lucas: I'll pick you up at 7.

• • • • • • • • • • •

"I've never had a guy cook for me before."

He smiled from the other side of the counter, chopping raw vegetables and drizzling something he'd just mixed up over them. "Good. That should effectively lower your expectations." He emptied the ingredients onto a piece of foil, rolled it up, and put it into the oven with the rest of dinner.

I inhaled through my nose. "Mmm, no, it smells good. And you look like you know what you're doing back there. I'm afraid my expectations are abnormally high."

He set a timer, washed and dried his hands, and came around the corner, taking my hand and leading me to the sofa. "We've got fifteen minutes."

We sat side-by-side, and he examined my hand, the pads of his fingers cool as he traced the short nails that wouldn't interfere with my bass playing, his thumb stroking over the back of my hand. Rotating it gently, his index finger traced up and down, inside the sensitive valleys between my fingers. He drew a spiral on my palm, slowly moving to center, and I was mesmerized, watching and feeling him touch me so softly.

His fingers slid between mine, palm to palm, and he reached to pull me onto his lap, his lips at the base of my throat. When the timer sounded minutes later, I was beyond being able to hear it.

The meal he'd prepared was enclosed in individual foil packets—veggies, baked potatoes, and red snapper he'd caught two days ago. Francis meowed like a fire alarm until given his own portion of the latter. "So I guess you're used to cooking for one?" I asked as we moved to the tiny table pushed against the only blank wall.

He nodded. "For the last three years or so. Before that, cooking for two."

"You cooked? Not your mom or dad?"

He cleared his throat, picking at his potato with his fork. "My mom died when I was thirteen. Before that, yeah, she cooked. After . . . well, it was either learn to cook or live on toast and fish—which I suspect Dad does when I'm not home, though I try to get him to buy fruit or something green occasionally."

Oh. His story lined up with Landon's—living with his father, no siblings—and he must have been conscious of that. He'd also been a boy who'd lost his mother, and I was too aware of that to call him out for duplicity just then.

"I'm sorry."

He nodded once, but didn't offer anything further.

After we ate, he let the cat outside, came back to the table and took my hand, and led me to his bedroom. We lay on our sides in the center of his bed, facing each other, saying nothing. His touch was almost unbearably light, whispering over my jaw, trailing down the side of my neck before releasing the buttons of the white shirt I'd chosen, one by one. Sliding it from my shoulder, he touched his lips to the bare skin, and I closed my eyes and sighed. My hands pushed under his shirt until he sat up, yanked it over his head, and flung it off in one movement, lying over me and kissing me.

His mouth was demanding, his lips parting mine, tongue driving into my mouth. I thought I felt a tremor move through him when my hand gripped the place on his side where the words were inscribed. He rolled me above him and pushed the shirt from my opposite shoulder, left it there, half-removed, while he moved his attention to the bare skin above the flesh-toned bra, my entire body straining toward his like a static charge that drew me in.

Without question or explanation, he stopped at the line I'd drawn last week. Talking was limited to *there* and *God* and *oh*. And then nothing but hums and moans and unintelligible sounds that could only be interpreted as *yes, yes, yes*.

"I should get you back." His voice was gruff. We hadn't spoken in at least an hour. The clock on his desk showed that the time had crept close to midnight.

He handed me the discarded bra and pulled his shirt back over his head. When I stood, he held my shirt as I slid my arms into the sleeves, and then he turned me, buttoning the buttons and leaning down to kiss me when he was done, his hands framing my face.

Standing by his bike, I was pulling on my gloves when the back door of the house across the yard opened and a man emerged, holding a full kitchen trash bag. He opened the wheeled garbage bin and tossed it in. As he turned to go inside, I noticed Lucas was stock-still, frozen, watching him. As though he felt our eyes on him, the man turned under the back door floodlight. He was Dr. Heller.

"Landon?" he said, and neither of us moved or responded. "Jacqueline?" he added, confused. All at once, he appeared to register what time it was, and the fact that the two of us had just exited his tenant's apartment. There could be no tutoring excuse—not that it was appropriate for us to meet in the apartment for tutoring, no matter the time of day.

No one spoke for one long moment, and then Dr. Heller's shoulders sagged. He sighed before pinning Lucas with a resolute expression. "I'll need you to meet me in the kitchen when you return. No more than thirty minutes, please."

Lucas's hands were tight around the helmet. He gave Dr. Heller one sharp nod before putting it on. When he turned to make sure I'd strapped mine correctly, our eyes met once but he didn't speak and neither did I. During the ten-minute ride back, no clarity rushed in. No magic words, no exoneration for his lies. I couldn't think of anything to say or do other than wait for him to tell me why.

We arrived and I climbed down from behind him, awkwardly removing the helmet and the hair tie with my gloved fingers. Still straddling the bike, he removed his helmet, too, and stored them both away as though he had no plans to put his back on. When I faced him, he was staring at his hands, tight on the wide handlebars. "You already knew, didn't you?" His voice was low, but I couldn't tell his frame of mind.

"Yes."

He looked up at me, frowning and searching my eyes. "Why didn't you say anything?"

"Why didn't you?" I returned. I didn't want to answer questions. I wanted my questions answered, and I was ticked off that he was going to make me ask them. "So your name is Landon? But Chief Watts calls you Lucas. And that girl—other people call you Lucas. So which is it?"

His gaze returned to his hands for a moment, and my anger expanded like a balloon inflating beneath my ribs. He seemed to be deciding what to tell me and what to withhold. The Harley rumbled softly, ready to rocket away at a second's notice.

"It's both. Landon is my first name, Lucas the middle. I go by Lucas . . . now. But Charles—Dr. Heller—has known me a long time. He still calls me Landon." His eyes swung up to mine. "You know, I think, how difficult it is to get some people to stop calling you what they've always called you."

Very logical. All of it. Except the part where he pretended to be two different guys with me. "You could have told me. You didn't. You *lied* to me."

He turned the bike off and swung his leg over, standing in front of me and gripping my shoulders. "I never lied to you. You made assumptions—based on what Ch—Dr. Heller called me. Look through our emails. I never called myself Landon."

I shrugged from his grasp. "But you let me call you Landon."

His hands dropped but he stared down at me, keeping me from moving. "You're right, this was my fault. And I'm sorry. I wanted you, and this couldn't happen as Landon. Anything between us is against the rules, and I broke them."

I swallowed thickly, combating choking up. I heard what he hadn't said yet. He was telling me it was over, just like that. The awful reality of desertion that Kennedy had begun weeks before came rushing back as though a dam had broken, and with no notice I was drowning in it. My parents had deserted me, Kennedy had deserted me, my friends, except for Erin and Maggie, had deserted me. And now Lucas—and Landon. Two different relationships, both of which had become significant.

"So it's just over."

He stared, and I couldn't have felt it more if his fingers roamed over my face. "Your grade could be at stake otherwise. I'll take responsibility for this, tonight, when I get back; Dr. Heller won't hold you accountable."

"So it's just over," I repeated.

"Yes," he said.

I turned and walked into the building, and didn't hear the engine of the Harley rumble to life until my foot was on the bottom stair.

chapter Sixteen

"Ms. Wallace, please see me for just a moment after class."

I glanced up to meet Dr. Heller's gaze at the end of the lecture Monday, and nodded my assent.

"Ooohhh," Benji said. "You little troublemaker." His smile fell when he saw my face. "What's the matter? You aren't actually in trouble are you?" He glanced to the back of the classroom, zeroing in on the only reason I could be in hot water with the professor. "Did he find out about—you know." He inclined his head in Lucas's direction.

"Yes."

His eyes widened and he lowered his voice. "Oh, *shit*, are you serious? How?"

I shook my head. "It doesn't matter. He found out, and it's over."

Pinning his lips together, he stuffed his notebook into his backpack and sighed. "Oh, man. I'm sorry." His hazel eyes were full of sympathy. "Anything I can do?"

I shook my head again, needing to redirect the conversation. "I'll be fine. How did the coming out go?"

Smiling broadly, he held his arms wide. "As you can see, I'm still in one piece, with all essential parts accounted for." He waggled his brows, tossing his backpack over his shoulder after I gave him a shove. "It was good. Getting everything out in the open was a relief—to both of us, I think."

"Good." I was happy for him, though I hadn't had the same experience with recent public revelations. I wouldn't glance back at Lucas. He'd stared at his sketchbook when I'd entered the classroom, resolutely against even looking at me.

"Hey, Jacqueline." Kennedy smiled as we passed in the aisle, as though he was proud of himself for finally remembering my name.

"Hi," I returned, slipping by him on my way down to the front of the lecture hall.

When I stopped on the lowest step, Dr. Heller glanced over the heads of the students clustered around him and requested that I come in during his afternoon office hours to pick up my paper. His unflinching expression said it wasn't an invitation as much as a directive. My face warm, I told him I would be there.

• • • • • • • • • •

"You haven't done anything wrong, so you have nothing to be worried about. Probably he just wants to make sure Lucas-Landon-Sideshow-Bob-whoever-the-hell-he-is didn't take advantage of you."

I appreciated Erin's reassurances, as mistaken as they might be.

Reclining on my bed, booted feet hanging off the end, I stared at the square of leaden sky visible from our single four-by-four window. Even in our overly warm room, I shivered. Erin and I discovered the previous winter that the ancient central heating would pump hot air into our little room until it was a sauna, only to click off and resume a slow slide back to frigid before rebooting back to sauna. It was a wonder we hadn't both ended up with pneumonia by February.

"*Landon* was the perfect tutor. What's between *Lucas* and me is no one's business."

"Except mine," Erin quipped.

I turned my head and half-smiled. "Except yours."

She added the finishing touches to a glitter-covered, sorority-themed poster. "What time are you supposed to be there?"

"Between three thirty and four thirty."

"You'd better scoot. I'm heading to work as soon as I finish this thing. Text me and let me know if I need to kick anyone's ass. Don't forget—tomorrow we're getting dresses for the Bash this weekend."

My roommate's ability to change subjects rapidly was legendary. "I remember."

• • • • • • • • • • •

Dr. Heller regarded me from the opposite side of his desk for the second time this semester, and I struggled not to squirm in the chair. I'd never been a kid who earned teachers' disapproval; finding myself in this position twice in a matter of weeks was unbelievable.

He hadn't looked at me since inviting me to have a seat. Rifling through a stack of folders and papers, he pulled out my research paper with a muttered, "Aha."

My hands clenched in my lap as he perused it, skimming through the stapled pages. I wondered if he'd already written a grade on it, or if what I said or didn't say in the coming minutes would influence it.

He cleared his throat and I flinched. "I've spoken with Mr. Maxfield, which I assume you know."

I took a nervous breath. "No, sir. We haven't spoken."

His eyebrows rose, eyes widening. "I see." He frowned as though he was confused. "Well. I'll ask you what I asked him, and I would appreciate your honesty, please. Did he assist you in producing this paper?"

I returned his perplexed frown, unsure what, exactly, he was asking. "He gave me some leads on research sources. And he read the completed paper and pointed out a few errors I needed to correct before turning it in. But the work is mine."

He nodded and sighed. "All right. There's also a matter of a quiz you may have been given some . . . let's say *notice* of . . . ahead of the other students?"

I swallowed. "He suggested that I do the worksheet he'd sent." Dr. Heller examined me with a direct look and one raised, bushy eyebrow, and I amended, "He suggested very *strongly* that I do it. But he never told me there was going to be a quiz, and frankly, I just thought he was being bossy—I didn't even pick up on any hint—" *Shit*.

"He's taken complete responsibility for his error in judgment, Ms. Wallace."

I couldn't breathe, my thoughts rioting. From the first moment I saw him—facing Buck in that parking lot after, I can only assume, pulling him off me—he'd been protecting me. Was he in danger of being fired from his job because of our relationship, whatever it had been?

I scooted closer, my hand on the desk. "Lucas didn't—he didn't take advantage of me in any way. He was very helpful as a tutor. I have another class during his group sessions, so I couldn't attend them, but he emailed the worksheets to me." Breathless, I stopped, not wanting to make this worse than it already was. I couldn't resemble some infatuated girl or my declarations wouldn't carry any weight at all. "He shouldn't be in trouble because of me."

My professor stared at my paper, still in his hands. If anything, he looked more concerned than he had moments ago. Forehead creased, he raised his eyes and stared at me a moment. "He also says that you weren't aware of the fact that the boy you were . . . seeing . . . was your tutor. That your academic relationship was carried out through email only."

I nodded, unwilling to contradict anything Lucas said.

He sighed again, sitting back in thought, one hand covering his mouth. Finally, he slid the paper across the desk to me. "Your research and the conclusions reached were impressive for an undergrad. Good job, Ms. Wallace. If you do well on the final, your grade in the course shouldn't suffer from the, um, emotional upheavals you faced mid-semester. A word of advice, though. This won't be the last time you have to deal with something in life that throws you off your game. In future courses, as well as in the real world—such as it is—professors and employers won't always be accommodating. We all have to—what's my daughter's terminology—suck it up and deal?"

I resisted flipping to the last page to check my grade. "Yes, sir." I knew I should stand up, thank him, and scramble out of his office while I was still on his good side. I couldn't do it. "And Lucas? Is he in trouble? Will he . . . will he lose his job?"

He shook his head. "There doesn't appear to have been any real harm done, although I've reminded Landon—er, Lucas—that sometimes, how a situation is perceived carries more weight than the reality of the matter. With that in mind, I suggested that he limit himself to appropriate tutoring interactions for the duration of the semester."

Lucas hadn't mentioned any possibility of future interactions. His answer to whether it was over had been conclusive, and he hadn't emailed or texted me to contradict it, nor had he looked my way in class today that I knew of.

"Thank you, Dr. Heller." I waited until I was outside to check the grade I'd received—a 94. Unquestionably better than I would have done on the midterm, had I been present for it.

• • • • • • • • • • •

I ignored Lucas on my way to my seat before class on Wednesday and Friday, and ignored him again as I left, especially as I found Kennedy waiting in the aisle to walk me out both days. On Wednesday, my ex asked me how the tutoring was going.

"What?" I stumbled on the next step and he caught my elbow.

"Was it two eighth-graders or two ninth-graders who had massive crushes on you?" He laughed, turning the heads of two girls we passed on the way outside; per typical Kennedy, he didn't seem to notice. "Or do they *all* have a crush on you by now?"

Ah—*bass* lessons, not *economics* tutoring. I tucked my chin into my fuzzy scarf and pulled my coat's zipper to my throat when we rounded the corner of the building and a blast of frigid air hit us, and he turned up his collar and shoved his bare hands into his coat pockets.

"I have no idea what they're thinking, most of the time. They're all a little surly."

He glanced at me and smiled, that dimple riveting my attention as it had since the first time I saw it, and from there, his beautiful green eyes. He bumped me lightly with his elbow. "Surliness is sound evidence that they're all crushing on you."

Scowling, I faced forward and picked up the pace. I couldn't imagine where he was going with that, but I wasn't following. "I'll see you later, Kennedy. I have to get to Spanish."

He caught my arm. "Maggie said you were coming to the Bash on Saturday?"

I nodded. Erin and I spent four hours shopping for dresses and shoes Tuesday night. She was going all out in her intention to make Chaz regret any decision he'd made that didn't include worshipping at her feet.

"What happened to 'I love the hunt'?" I'd asked as she discarded the tenth or eleventh not-quite-perfect cocktail dress before shimmying into a bit of silver fabric with a thigh-high split.

Smiling into the mirror with predatory resolve, she'd waited for me to zip her up and examined her body in the reflective dress that set off her red hair like she was on fire. "Oh, I'm *hunting* all right," she'd purred.

I split away from Kennedy without a backward glance, and he called, "See you later, Jacqueline."

I considered and rejected every excuse I could cook up for why I needed to bow out, belatedly wishing that I had never agreed to accompany Erin to the annual Bash. My normally sane roommate was determined to make her ex-boyfriend's life a living hell for at least one night. At dinner Friday, she said, "I have to do this. For closure." Maggie arched a brow at me from across the table. Between the Erin/Chaz drama, Kennedy's attempts to reverse our breakup, and the likely presence of Buck, Saturday night couldn't be over soon enough for me.

• • • • • • • • • • •

Avoiding eye contact during the self-defense class Saturday morning proved more difficult than dodging each other during economics, but Lucas and I managed it for the first hour. The oddest part of the past week was the worksheets he continued to send, but without any personal note. The entire email consisted of:

New worksheet attached, LM.

"Where a kick is more likely to be miscalculated by the victim or evaded by the perp, a knee-strike is close range and more easily executed, so we're going to focus on this defense first." Ralph's voice brought me back to the self-defense class. "And I assume you ladies know what you're aimin' for with that knee."

Dividing into two groups as we had two weeks ago, I went to stand in Don's group and Erin followed. He held a thick pad with straps for his muscular forearm to hold it in place, explaining knee-strike basics and asking for a volunteer to help demonstrate, which Erin readily answered. I was proud of her resounding *No!* as she grabbed Don's shoulders and slammed her knee into the pad. I recognized the move from Lucas having used it on Buck—though he'd struck him under the chin rather than the groin. Buck had gone straight to the ground. And stayed there.

When it was my turn, my self-conscious hesitation disappeared with my group's vocal encouragement and Don's "Again!" between each strike. Exhilarated, I walked back to Erin wide-eyed and shaking with adrenaline. She laughed and said, "I know, right?"

We progressed to kicks, and every time I landed one and heard Don's gratifying grunt, my fear that I could never replicate these in real life lessened. Vickie—the white-haired woman who'd unknowingly given me the courage to remain in the class two weeks ago—asked how, even if we hit the right place with enough force, we could win against a man his size.

Don reminded us that we didn't have to win a fight—we just had to get away. "Every second buys you time to run."

When Ralph announced a short break, I stole a look at Lucas. Over the heads of two girls, one of whom was talking to him, his eyes were on me, their icy gray-blue almost colorless from across the bright room. After the physical activity of the morning, my response was overwhelming. My breath went shallow and quick, neither of us turning away until Erin hooked her arm through mine and tugged.

"C'mon, lovergirl," she murmured, inaudible to anyone but me.

I flushed as I let her lead me into the hallway, toward the locker room. Leaning over the sink, I splashed water on my face and stared into the mirror, wondering what Lucas saw when he looked at me. What Kennedy saw. What Buck saw.

"Got it bad, don'tcha?" Erin handed me a paper towel and pursed her lips, angling her head as she examined my face in the mirror, too. Her dark eyes met mine. "I should have known that hookup therapy wouldn't work for you. If it makes you feel any better, he doesn't look any less strung out than you do."

I rolled my eyes, patting the water from my cheeks. "Believe it or not, that doesn't make me feel better."

She arched a brow, her gaze moving to her own reflection as she smoothed an imaginary imperfection on her lip and adjusted her wild ponytail. "Mmm-hmm."

• • • • • • • • • • •

"We're ready to learn the last few moves over the next hour or so—defense against holds and chokes. Next week, we'll integrate everything you've learned into potential scenarios." Clapping his hands together, Ralph added, "Divide up and let's get started."

After the twelve of us had automatically separated into our previous groups, Ralph addressed the men, who were partially padded up, including headgear. "Don, Lucas, let's have you two switch off for this part. Mix up the attacker tactics a bit."

Oh, God. So much for avoiding each other.

Though I knew there was no avoiding this, my brain cast about for any way out of having Lucas's arms locked around me in front of everyone. The first attack was called the bear hug, and the intrepid, white-haired Vickie volunteered to help demonstrate the slow-motion defense against it. I watched with Erin and the other three ladies in my group, my breathing erratic and my heart thudding like it was trying to break out of my ribcage. He hadn't even touched me yet.

The need for headgear became obvious when he explained the use of headbutts—the back of the victim's head smashing into the mouth or nose of the assailant. There was also instep stomping (everyone laughed when Lucas requested that we refrain from actual stomping of his unpadded foot—he would gladly react as though we'd done it forcefully), elbow to the midsection, and a move termed *the lawnmower* by Ralph, who came over to check on our progress.

Moving to stand in front of Lucas, he said, "This'll be another move that we'd prefer no one tries in earnest on our brave instructors." He turned and clapped Lucas's shoulder. "We don't wanna render our boys incapable of fatherhood." As the ladies chuckled, Lucas flushed slightly pink and stared at the floor, his lips screwed into a discomfited smirk. "In a real life attack, if you have a hand free and low, you will reach back and grab the goods, twisting and pulling straight out like you're startin' a lawnmower."

He demonstrated, complete with a lawnmower-starting sound

effect, and even Don's group was watching and laughing. Lucas bit his lip and shook his head.

One by one, the six of us went to stand in front of him, facing the group, waiting for him to grab them so they could practice the techniques. The lawnmower was a favorite of the older ladies, and they all used it, along with the sound effect. Eyes sparkling, Erin used every single defense we'd just learned, one after the other—headbutt, foot-stomp, shin-scrape, elbow to the abdomen with one arm and lawnmower-starting with the other. The ladies in our group cheered and Lucas said, "Good job. He'll be on the ground begging you to run away at this point."

"Should I kick him first?" she asked, completely serious.

"Uh . . . if he's not making a move toward you, then *run*. You don't want him to grab your foot and pull you down." Erin nodded and walked back to me, squeezing my hand when she reached my side.

He looked into my eyes as I approached. I stared back, turning my back to him as I reached him, trying to concentrate on what I was supposed to do next.

Suddenly, his arms were around me like bands, but gentler than any assailant would ever be. His muscled arms were solid and unyielding. Unnerved, I forgot every defense I'd just learned and struggled ineffectively against his strength.

"Hit me, Jacqueline," he said in my ear. "Elbow."

I elbowed his pad-covered abdomen and he grunted.

"Good. Foot stomp."

I acted it out, carefully.

"Headbutt."

The top of my head barely reached his padded chin, but I butted it.

"Lawnmower." His voice was soft, breathy, and I could not, even drawing on every bit of imagination I possessed, picture touching him there to harm him.

I did the move, without the sound effect, blushing full-on, and he let go. Stumbling toward Erin, I would have felt foolish but for the fact that every woman in the room was doing exactly what I'd just done. Except not with a guy whose touch made her insides go hot and liquid. Not with a guy who made her want to turn and be wrapped up in those arms.

My group smiled and patted my shoulders and commended me as if I hadn't completely frozen in the beginning.

The front bear hug was worse, but for the way Lucas's eyes dilated slightly when I looked up at him, my chest pressed against his. Like Erin said, he was not unaffected—a knowledge that made me feel both better and worse.

The chokeholds were easier, and I did them without his verbal cues.

And then the class was over, with Ralph encouraging us to practice—carefully—over the coming week. "Next week the guys will be in full body gear, and you'll be able to clobber the daylights out of 'em, no holds barred."

Erin and Vickie high-fived, and Ralph beamed at them both, rubbing his palms together. "Bloodthirsty and ruthless. Exactly what I wanna see."

chapter *Seventeen*

I hadn't attended any Greek events since the Halloween party, and had seen Buck only in passing since the stairwell incident—always within a group, and always in public. When he moved closer, I moved away, as though his very being repelled me, which was true. The mere thought of him still made my mouth go dry and my stomach knot.

In our room, Erin turned after her final mirror check. "He'd better stay the hell away from you or I will whip out the *lawnmower* on his ass," she declared.

"That move's not for ass use," I joked, hating the tremor that lanced through me at the thought of Buck with his arms banded around me. I hoped Erin was ready to have a shadow, because I didn't intend to leave her side.

Her arm encircling my shoulders, she turned us both to face the full-length mirror. "We look *hot*, girlfriend." Her eyes met mine in the reflection. "Thanks for doing this. The girls have been real supportive, but they're not you. I feel stronger knowing you'll be with me."

I smiled and hugged her to my side. We did look hot. In the shimmery silver dress, with her silver strappy heels, Erin was her own disco ball. My blue sheath—simply cut in front and the exact shade of my eyes—looked basic if not dull next to Erin, until I turned around. The combination of bass playing and yoga had given me a toned back, and the dress showed it off with a V cut almost to the waist. The nosebleed-level black patent slingbacks on my feet negated *dull* quite a bit all on their own.

Erin did a couple of dance moves. "Let's go make Chaz wish he was never born."

I rolled my eyes and laughed. "Oh, Erin. I'm so glad you're on my side."

"Damn right, bitch." She slapped my butt and we grabbed our coats.

In unspoken agreement, we passed the stairwell door and walked down the wide open front staircase to meet our ride. Everyone we passed gawked—one scrawny freshman tripping on a step, his eyes moving between Erin and me. Luckily, he was going up, so he landed on both hands, practically at Erin's feet. "Whoa," he breathed taking her in.

She patted his head as she passed him, crooning, "Aww, how sweet," like he was a puppy. His adoring expression at her touch indicated that *here* was a guy willing to put her on a pedestal and treat her like a goddess. I suspected that Erin didn't want that from a guy nearly as much as she insisted she did.

• • • • • • • • • • •

The men of Chaz's fraternity had gone all out, hanging an actual disco ball and hiring a band. Outfitted in suits, ties, and a hazardous level of confidence, they all looked hotter than hell and every one of them knew it. Two guys from the pledge class were at the door, one hanging coats, the other taking the plus-one invitation Erin handed over and giving us each a strip of tickets for the bar set up in the kitchen and a raffle ticket for the table of prizes another pledge watched over.

The prizes were mostly electronic provisions—from iPods to game systems to a forty-two-inch flat screen. "*Boys*," Erin scoffed. "Where's a spa day? Or a Victoria's Secret shopping spree?" The table guard's eyes widened in obvious approval of the latter idea.

"Hello, Erin," a deep voice said. We turned, and there was Chaz, looking amazing in a perfectly cut charcoal gray suit and red tie that somehow blended perfectly with Erin's hair. He glanced at me, his eyes warm and friendly. "Hi, Jacqueline." I sensed no reproach over the fact that their relationship had detonated over Erin standing up for me.

"Hi, Chaz. The place looks awesome," I answered for both of us while Erin swayed to the music and waved at friends, as though her ex didn't exist. The theme of the Bash this year was *Saturday Night Fever*. The band shifted from playing a Keith Urban cover to a Bee Gees song—something popular when my parents were in grade school, maybe.

Chaz glanced around perfunctorily, his eyes returning to me. "Thanks," he said, and then he only had eyes for Erin. Watching the people already dancing, she snagged a full red cup from a passing guy with a handful of them. He started to protest, but Chaz glared, daring him to say a word to her. He buttoned his lip and kept moving.

While she sipped and pretended to be oblivious to his presence, he stared at her. It was obvious where he wanted this to go, and the fact that Erin was conspicuously gazing anywhere but at him told me she was anything but immune. They didn't move from each other's orbits the rest of the night, but he didn't attempt to speak to her again either.

I knew Chaz was a good guy, if misguided and gullible. He'd swallowed Buck's side of what happened between us, had argued with Erin that maybe I was drunk that night and didn't remember everything clearly. He was probably one of those boys to whom rapists were ugly men who jumped out of bushes, assaulting random girls. Rapists weren't your nice-guy coworker, or your frat brother, or your best friend.

Maybe it never occurred to him that his best friend was capable of ripping a girl's self-confidence away in the span of five minutes. That he could hurt someone innocent to wound a rival. That he could violate her in a twisted attempt to obliterate his own powerlessness. That he could make her feel constantly threatened, and not give a shit.

The only time I felt completely safe was when I was with Lucas.

Damn.

Ten minutes later, I was watching Buck dance with a senior from Erin's sorority. He smiled and laughed, and so did she. He looked so . . . normal. For the first time, I wondered if I was the only girl he'd ever terrorized, and if so, why. I jumped when I heard Kennedy's voice in my ear. "You look stunning, Jacqueline." My drink sloshed over the cup's rim onto my hand, luckily missing my dress. He took the cup from my hand. "Ah, I'm sorry—didn't mean to startle you. C'mon, let me get you a towel."

I was disconcerted enough from his arm steering me through the crowd, his hand on my bare back, that I wasn't aware of the separation from Erin until we were in the kitchen with my arm over the sink as though I had a mortal injury rather than a beer-soaked hand. He rinsed and patted my hand dry, and I withdrew it from his grasp when he didn't let go right away.

He ignored my withdrawal, smiling down at me. "As I was trying to say before—you look beautiful tonight. I'm glad you came."

The music was loud, and conversation required us to stand closer than I wanted to be. "I came for Erin, Kennedy."

"I know. But that doesn't diminish my satisfaction that you're here."

He was wearing his usual Lacoste cologne, but it no longer made me want to lean against him and inhale. Once again, he stood in direct contrast to Lucas, whose scent wasn't any one thing—it was his leather jacket and his barely there aftershave, the meal he'd cooked for me and the subtle yet sharp smell of graphite on his fingers after he'd been drawing, the exhaust of his Harley and the minty shampoo smell of his pillow.

One brow cocked, Kennedy looked at me closely, and I realized he'd probably said or asked something.

"I'm sorry, what?" I leaned my ear toward him so I could take a second to push Lucas from my mind.

"I said, 'Let's dance.'"

Unable to shake my errant thoughts, I agreed and let my ex lead me to the designated dance floor, right in front of the band. An area had been cleared of furniture just under the motorized disco ball, which hung dangerously low for some of the taller guys. Rotating slowly, its mirrored surface threw flashes of light in waves around the room, illuminating faces and gyrating bodies, and glinting off any reflective surface from doorknobs to jewelry to Erin's silver dress. Her hands were locked behind the neck of a Pi Kappa Alpha senior, an empty cup hanging from her fingertips. Her dance partner was unknowingly at the receiving end of a death glare from Chaz. Erin had noticed, though, and she pressed closer to him, staring up into his eyes with rapt attention.

Poor Chaz. I should be angry with him, too, but he was clearly miserable.

"I heard about Chaz and Erin. What happened?" Kennedy had followed my gaze.

"You should ask him." I wondered what Kennedy would make of Buck's behavior. They were civil with each other, but that competitive fixation had been between them from day one.

"I did, sort of. He didn't seem to want to talk about it. Said they'd had a big fight, she was being unreasonable, blah blah—you know, the stupid stuff guys say when we fuck up something good."

Just then, the music changed to something fast, allowing me to reinstate my bubble of personal space and fortunately axing the conversation about breakups and fuckups. I was so relieved to end that exchange that I failed to pay attention to where Erin was. I failed to pay attention to where Buck was.

In a lull between songs, he walked up behind me. "Hey, Jacqueline" he said, and I jumped for the second time that night. "Are you done dancing with this loser? Come dance with me."

The hair on my arms stood on end, every nerve in my body on full alert, and I moved closer to Kennedy, who put his arm around my shoulders. I didn't want his arm on me, but given the choice between them, there was no choice.

Smiling, Buck held out a hand.

I stared at it, incredulous and cringing closer to Kennedy, whose body became rigid, aligned with mine. "No."

With his usual indolent smirk, Buck gazed down at me as though my ex wasn't there. Like we were alone. "All right then, maybe later."

I shook my head and focused on the word I'd said over and over that morning. The word that preceded every kick. "I said *no*. Don't you understand *no*?" From the corner of my eye, I saw Kennedy's gaze snap to my face.

Buck's eyes narrowed and his mask of indifference slipped for a split second. And then he recovered and the guise was back in place. I knew in that moment that he wasn't giving up. He was merely biding his time. "Sure. I hear you. *Jacqueline*." His eyes shifted to Kennedy, whose guarded expression was at odds with the piqued rigidity of his body. "Kennedy." He nodded and Kennedy responded in kind, and then he walked away.

I slumped against my ex, and then moved out of his grasp, my eyes searching for Erin's silver dress among the crush of people in the little house.

"Jacqueline, what's going on between you and Buck?"

I ignored his question. "I need Erin. I need to find Erin." I started in the opposite direction Buck had gone and Kennedy grabbed my upper arm to pull me back. I wrenched it away, and then realized people were staring.

He moved closer, without touching me. "Jacqueline, what's going on? I'll help you find Erin." His voice was low, for my ears only. "But first, tell me. Why are you so angry at Buck?"

I looked up at him and my eyes stung. "Not here."

He compressed his lips. "Come with me? To my room?" When I hesitated, he added, "Jacqueline, you're freaking out. Come talk to me."

I nodded and he led me up the stairs.

He shut the door and we sat on his bed. His room, as usual, was neat and organized, though the bed wasn't made, and there were jeans and shirts tossed over his desk chair. I recognized the sheets and duvet cover we'd chosen before coming back to campus this fall, because he wanted something new. I recognized his bookcase and his favorite novels, his law books, his collection of presidential biographies. The contents of this room were familiar. He was familiar.

"What's going on?" His concern was genuine.

I cleared my throat and told him what happened the night of the Halloween party, leaving Lucas out of the story. Listening silently, he got up and paced, taking deep breaths, his fists knotted. When I was done, he stopped and sat, hard. "You said you got away. So he didn't . . . ?"

I shook my head. "No."

A breath whooshed out of him. "*Goddammit*." He pulled his tie loose and unbuttoned the top button of his white dress shirt. His teeth were clamped so tightly that the cords of his neck popped out under his skin like pipes running from his jaw down. He shook his head and smashed a fist on his thigh. "*Motherfucker*."

Kennedy wasn't usually much of a curser—certainly neither of these words was part of his standard vocabulary. He peered at me closely. "I will handle this."

"It's already been—it's over, Kennedy. I just . . . I just want him to leave me alone." I was curiously without tears, which was odd. I felt like I'd gained strength from telling him, just like I felt stronger after telling Erin.

His jaw clenched again. "He will." He took my face in his hands and repeated, "He will leave you alone. I'll make sure of it." And then he kissed me.

The feel of his mouth was as familiar as the items I'd catalogued when I walked into his room. The books on the bookshelf. The comforter under my hand. The rock-climbing equipment in the corner. The hoodie I used to borrow. The smell of his cologne.

Unwittingly, I registered the feel of his lips, moving a little too roughly. I reasoned that his anger at Buck made his kiss less tender, but I knew better. Because this, too, was familiar. This kiss—it was how he'd always kissed me. His tongue snaked into my mouth, possessively, and it was familiar and fine and not Lucas.

I jerked back.

His hands dropped. "God, Jackie, I'm sorry—that was so inappropriate—"

I ignored his slip. "No. It's okay, I just . . . I don't . . ." I cast about in my head, trying to define what I didn't want. We'd been broken up for seven weeks. Seven weeks, and I was done. I stared at my palm, turned up on my lap; the realization and the finality were something of a shock.

"I understand. You still need time." He stood, and I stood, wanting out of this familiar room and this conversation.

Time would not change what I was feeling—or not feeling. I'd had time, and though the ache from his desertion hadn't disappeared, it was decreasing. My future was blurry, yes, but I was beginning to imagine a future when I would no longer miss him at all.

"Let's go find Erin for you. And I'm going to have a talk with Buck."

I froze, halfway to the door. "Kennedy, I don't expect you to—"

He turned. "I know. Doesn't matter. I'm handling this. Handling *him*."

I took a deep breath and followed him from the room, hoping his intentions sprung from a determination to do the right thing, and not just because he wanted to win me back.

• • • • • • • • • • •

Erin and I watched from the window as Buck and Kennedy faced off in the lot behind the house. It was too cold for anyone to party outside, so they were alone. We couldn't hear the words, but the body language was unmistakable. Buck was taller and bigger, but my ex possessed an innate superiority that refused to cede control to anyone he deemed unworthy of it. Buck's face was a veneer of annoyance overlaying absolute fury as Kennedy spoke, stabbing a finger at him one, two, three times, never touching him but showing no fear.

I envied him that ability. I always had.

We turned away from the window when Kennedy spun to come back into the house, but not before Buck glanced at the window and fixed me with a look of pure hatred.

"Jesus H. Christ," Erin murmured, taking my arm. "Time for a *drink*."

We found Maggie in a group of people playing quarters. "Errrrrrin!" she slurred. "Come be on my team!"

Erin crooked a brow. "We're playing teams?"

"Yes." She grabbed Erin's arm and pulled her onto her lap. "J, you be partners with Mindi here! Erin and me are gonna kick y'all's asses." Mindi was a petite blonde pledge. She smiled and blinked big green eyes, unable to focus on me.

"Your name is Jay?" Her drawl was very pronounced and her lashes fluttered up and down like a cartoon character, making her seem younger and more vulnerable than eighteen. She was the reverse of Maggie's sarcastic demeanor and dark pixie looks. "Like a boy's name, Jay?"

The guys across the table chuckled and Maggie rolled her eyes disgustedly. It was clear why she wanted me to take her partner. "Um, no. J as in Jacqueline." One of the boys grabbed two folding chairs from against the wall, wedging them on either side of Mindi and Maggie. I took the one next to Mindi and Erin slid into the other.

"Oh." Mindi frowned and blinked. "So can I just call you Jacqueline?" My name was almost unrecognizable between the accent and the drunken slurring.

Maggie started to mumble under her breath so I said, "Sure, that's great," and looked around the table. "So, are we winning?"

The boys on the other side grinned. We definitely weren't winning.

chapter *Eighteen*

By the time our designated driver dropped us back at the dorm, Erin and I had quartered and beer-ponged our way to a night of spinning walls at best and toilet-hugging at worst. Neither of us spoke above a whisper until after three o'clock Sunday afternoon. There was a scheduled sorority meeting four hours later, and Erin cursed the lineage of whoever put that on the calendar the day after the Brotherhood Bash.

"We won't get a damned thing decided—and at least half of us will kill the first person to bang that gavel." We were still conversing at half-volume.

I watched her wind a purple scarf around her neck and pull on matching gloves while waiting for my laptop to boot up. "At least your misery will have company."

"Yea." She pulled a purple cap over her wild red hair and shrugged into her coat. "See you in a couple of miserable hours."

Lucas had already sent Monday's worksheet. Still no personal note.

I understood why he couldn't see me, and maybe why whatever we had been doing was over. But I didn't understand why our emails had to stop, too. I missed them, and wondered what he'd do if I emailed him back. I wanted to tell him about last night and

Buck, about saying no and feeling scared to death and tough at the same time.

One week of class remained, followed by a week of finals, and then the semester would be over. I had no idea if it would make any difference to him.

I did the least brain-pounding homework I could do—labeling a constellation chart due tomorrow in astronomy lab. I'd missed my bass practice times all weekend in addition to the ensemble rehearsal, so I would be scrambling to complete additional hours of practice during the week.

By the time Erin returned, I was seriously considering just going to bed and sleeping off the lingering remains of my hangover. Yawning, I turned toward the door, "I was thinking about crashing early—"

Erin wasn't alone. Under her arm was Mindi, my quarters partner from the previous night. At first, I thought she was just way more hungover than I was; then I noticed Erin's grim expression, and I took in Mindi's red-rimmed, bloodshot eyes. She didn't just feel like shit from too much alcohol. She'd been crying. A lot. I swung my legs off the side of the bed.

"Erin?"

"J, we have a problem." The door shut behind them and Erin tugged Mindi to sit on her bed. "Last night, after you and I left, Mindi danced with Buck." Mindi flinched and closed her eyes, and tears started streaming down her face.

My heart began to race. I imagined everything Erin could say next, and none of it was good. I hadn't prayed in a long time, but

I found myself begging. *Please God let it not have gone further than what happened to me. Please. Please.*

"He talked her into going to his room." At this, Mindi's hands flew up to cover her face and she crumpled face-first into Erin's shoulder like a child. "Shh, shh," Erin crooned, fitting both arms around her. We stared at each other over Mindi's head, and I knew there'd been no Lucas for her.

"J, we have to tell. We have to tell this time."

"No one will believe me!" Mindi rasped. She was hoarse, and I imagined her doing what I'd done—begging him to stop. I imagined her crying all night, and half the day, and I was more pissed than I'd ever been, and scared. "I'm not . . ." Her voice lowered to a whisper. "I wasn't a virgin."

"That doesn't matter," Erin said firmly.

I gulped at the knot in my throat and it slid down, but not without a fight. "They'll believe you. He tried to—he tried with me, a month ago."

Mindi gasped, her blotchy face and wide eyes turning to me. "He raped you, too?"

I shook my head as chills spiked up in a wave from my neck to my ankles. "Someone stopped him. I got lucky." I had no idea how lucky until this moment. I thought I knew, but I didn't.

"Oh." Her voice warbled softly, and she hadn't quit crying. "Will that count?"

Erin coaxed Mindi to lie down, flapping a blanket over her. "It'll count." She sat next to Mindi and held her hand. "Will Lucas corroborate your story, J? I mean, I'm guessing, with what we know about him, that he will."

Lucas had been irate that I'd not let him call the police that night. It hadn't occurred to me that by not reporting what had happened, I let Buck think he was untouchable. That he'd do it again. I'd assumed that what Lucas had done to Buck was deterrent enough. Not that it had prevented him from what he did in the stairwell . . . or his implied threats during the party, right in front of Kennedy.

I nodded. "He will."

Erin took a shaky breath and looked down at Mindi. "We need to call the police or go to the hospital or something, right? I have no idea what to do first."

"The hospital?" Mindi was afraid, and I couldn't blame her.

"They'll probably need to do . . . an exam, or something." Erin gentled her voice, but at the word *exam*, Mindi's eyes widened and filled with tears again.

Her knuckles blanched, gripping the blanket. "I don't want an exam! I don't want to go to the hospital!"

How could I blame her, when reporting would bring more pain and humiliation?

"We'll go with you. You can do this." Erin turned to me. "What should we do first?"

I shook my head, thinking of the campus police. Some, like Don, would probably do well with this situation. Some might not. We could go straight to the hospital, but I wasn't sure what the steps were. I picked up my phone and dialed.

"Hello?" Lucas's voice was wary, and I realized I'd never called him before.

"I need you." It had been over a week since we'd communicated outside of the worksheets he'd sent and the self-defense class yesterday morning.

"Where are you?"

"In my room." I expected him to ask what I wanted. He didn't.

"Be there in ten minutes."

I closed my eyes. "Thank you."

He hung up, and I put the phone down, and we waited.

• • • • • • • • • •

Lucas squatted on his heels just below Mindi's eye level. "If you don't report it, he's going to do it again. To someone else." His voice hummed through me, barely audible from across the room. "Your friends will stay with you."

Erin sat on the bed, holding her hand. I barely knew this girl, but thanks to Buck, we were now allies, associated in a way no one ever wants to be linked.

"Will you be there?" Her voice was a whisper.

"If you want," he answered.

She nodded, and I tamped down a trace of jealousy. There was nothing to envy in this situation.

• • • • • • • • • •

The television in the ER waiting room was set at an earsplitting volume that was no help to my aching head. I wanted to turn it off, or down, but an elderly man was planted in a chair ten feet from it, arms crossed over his chest, staring up at the sitcom repeat. If that noise was distracting him from his reason for being here, who was I to take that diversion away?

Lucas sat next to me, his bent knee angled toward me, brushing my thigh. His hand was so close to mine I could have reached my pinky finger out to stroke his. I didn't.

"Got something against that show?"

His silly question broke my scowl. "No, but I think I could hear it from across the street." He was wearing that ghost smile, and I wanted to melt into it.

"Hmm," he said, staring at the boot on his knee. "Are you a little hungover, too?" When Erin and Mindi filled him in on the details of last night, he'd quickly figured out that I'd gone with Erin to the Greek event.

"Maybe a little." I wondered if he would think I'd senselessly put myself in danger by attending a party where Buck would obviously be present. His reprimand the night we met—*real responsible*—still stung, mostly because it was true.

"So did he talk to you? Last night?" He was still staring at his boot.

"Yeah. He asked me to dance."

A muscle worked in his jaw, and his eyes were cold when he raised them to mine.

"I said no." I heard the defensiveness in my tone.

He took a deep breath and turned more fully toward me, his voice low and menacing. "Jacqueline, it's taking everything I've got right now to sit here and wait for law-abiding justice to take care of this, instead of hunting him down myself and beating the *fucking shit* out of him. I'm not blaming you—or her. Neither of you asked for what he did—there's no such thing as asking for it. That's a fucking lie argued by psychopaths and dumbasses. Okay?"

I nodded, breathless at his declaration.

His eyes narrowed. "Did he accept your *no*?" What I heard at the end of his sentence: *this time*?

I nodded again. "Kennedy was with me. He noticed how weird I acted with Buck, so I told him what happened. I didn't say anything about you, or the fight. I just told him I got away."

A small crease appeared between his brows. "How'd he take it?"

I remembered Kennedy's uncharacteristic cursing outburst. "He was angrier than I've ever seen him. He took Buck outside and talked to him, told him to stay away from me . . . which probably made Buck feel weak, and that's why . . ." That's why he raped Mindi.

"What did I just say? This is not your fault."

I nodded, staring into my lap, tears stinging my eyes. I wanted to believe it wasn't my fault, but Mindi was hurt after Kennedy had chewed him out. For me. It felt like my fault. I knew better, but I couldn't help connecting the dots.

Lucas's fingers brushed under my chin and turned my face to his. "Not. Your. Fault."

I nodded again, holding onto his words like they were redemption.

• • • • • • • • • •

I parked in front of a neighbor's house, snapping the truck door shut as quietly as possible and tiptoeing down the sparsely lit driveway toward the detached garage. It was late—hopefully late enough that no one would be peering out a window at a girl sneaking up to a guy's apartment.

Lucas's motorcycle was parked under the open steps. I stood at the bottom with my hand on the rail, heart hammering, and looked back at Dr. Heller's house. I couldn't see any movement within, though there were lights on inside. Taking a deep breath, I climbed the steps and knocked lightly.

There was a peephole in the door, so I was sure he'd seen me standing under the porch light by the puzzled expression on his face when he yanked the door open. An hour ago, he'd left me at the dorm with Erin and Mindi, and after he'd gone, I realized I hadn't said what I wanted to say. And most of what I wanted to say included a need to see him while I said it.

"Jacqueline? Why—?" He cut himself off at the look on my face, pulling me inside and shutting the door behind me. "What's wrong?" His hands gripped my elbows as I stared up at him. He was wearing drawstring pajama bottoms and a dark T-shirt, the sexy lines of his tattoos spilling from his sleeves to his wrists. He also wore thin, black-framed glasses that accentuated the blue in his eyes and his dark lashes.

I took a breath and blurted everything out before I was too chickenshit to say any of it. "I wanted to tell you that I just—I miss you. And maybe that sounds ridiculous—like we barely know each other, but between the emails and texts and . . . everything else, I felt like we did. Like we do. And

I miss—I don't know how else to say it—I miss both of you."

He swallowed, closing his eyes and inhaling slowly. I knew he would be all rational and do-the-right-thing and he would push me away again, and I was determined not to give him that chance. But then his eyes flashed open and he said, "Fuck it," pushing me against the door, slamming his forearms on either side of my head and kissing me more forcefully than I'd ever been kissed, so firmly that I could feel the ring at the edge of his mouth scoring into the surface of my lip.

He pressed his hard body against mine and I pressed back, grabbing handfuls of his T-shirt and fitting myself to him while his tongue stroked the interior of my mouth. When he drew back a fraction, I protested with an embarrassingly inarticulate sound and he chuckled softly, but he was just removing my coat and towing me to the sofa. Sitting, he dragged me astride his lap, cradling my head in one palm and crushing me closer with the other.

We parted, breathless, and he tossed his glasses on the side table and tore his T-shirt over his head, and then removed mine more gently. His warm hands spanned my sides and held me tighter as our lips moved together, his tongue making languid, sweeping passes across mine. I wound my arms around his neck, opening my mouth and taking him in. When he kissed the corner of my mouth and dipped his lips to the hollow at the base of my throat, my head fell back. I couldn't stop the soft keening moan his light, sucking kisses triggered.

"You have a freckle here," he whispered, sweeping his tongue over a spot just under my jaw. "It drives me crazy every time you're above me. I just want to do this . . ." The gentle draw of his mouth pushed me over the edge, and my knees tightened around his hips as I rocked against him.

Light eyes smoldering, he removed my bra, outlining concentric rings with his fingertips, touching me so softly that I grew dizzy wanting more. His hands cupped my breasts, thumbs brushing the undersides, and I leaned my face down to his and sucked his tongue into my mouth, sliding my hand down his taut abdomen and lower over the front of the soft flannel pants. I tugged on one of the strings.

"God, Jacqueline," he gasped, straining against my hand while his arms snaked around me, fingers stealing into my hair at the nape as our mouths devoured each other. Breaking the kiss, he pressed his forehead to my shoulder and groaned, his teeth clamped shut. "Tell me to stop."

Confused, I shook my head, though I had no idea if the action was fervent or imperceptible. His breath fanned over my breasts and I bent to his ear, my voice a murmur. "I don't want you to stop."

Wordlessly rolling us down and onto our sides, he unzipped my jeans and slipped his hand between the fabric of my underwear and my skin, his fingers searching for and finding the place he sought as he kissed me. I gasped his name into his mouth, my fingers digging into his bicep, and his voice was a low growl in my ear. "Jacqueline. Say stop."

I shook my head once, my palm sliding down to press against the evidence of what his body wanted from me. "Don't stop," I breathed, telling him that I wanted what he wanted, unconditionally. I kissed him back, sure in the knowledge that my actions and words were all the confirmation he needed to continue.

I was wrong. "Say stop, please. *Please*." The last whispered word was a plea I couldn't deny, even if I didn't understand the reason for it.

"Stop," I whispered, not meaning it, not wanting it, and he shuddered and removed his hand from me. Curling my hands between our chests, I didn't move away, didn't speak. I just lay in his arms for long minutes, until his breathing slowed, finally becoming deep and even.

Landon Lucas Maxfield was asleep on his sofa. With me.

• • • • • • • • • •

I woke to the muffled sound of Francis yowling to be let inside. Disentangling myself from Lucas cautiously, I slid from the sofa and went to let him in, grabbing my bra and long-sleeved T-shirt and pulling them back on. A gust of chilly air entered with Lucas's cat, and I shut the door as soon as he fully cleared the doorway. After wrapping his tail around my leg for the span of two seconds, he stalked off to the bedroom, and I supposed that was as thankful as he ever got.

I returned to the sofa, but I sank to the floor and examined Lucas instead of waking him or snuggling back into his embrace. With the planes of his face partially obscured by his dark hair, his full lips slightly parted and thick lashes combined in sleep, I could see the boy inside the man more clearly than I had before. I didn't understand what happened earlier, why he made me stop him or why he held himself apart from everyone, from *me*, but I wanted to understand.

I guessed that the rose tattoo was a possible clue, given its placement over his heart. Most of the ink on his arms consisted of symbols and intricate motifs, and I wondered if any these were his own design. He shifted onto his back then, and I could finally read the words on his left side:

Love is not the absence of logic
but logic examined and recalculated
heated and curved to fit
inside the contours of the heart

I needed no more proof to know that somewhere in his possibly not-so-distant past, Lucas had loved someone, deeply. Someone he must have lost, because she didn't appear to be around. And then I looked more closely at the tattoo banding the upturned wrist that lay near his face. Within the inky pattern, masquerading as normal pink skin within the design, was a thin but jagged scar. It ran from one side to the other—all the way across, contained by the black tattooed lines like hidden code.

His right wrist was circled with the same banded design, and watching his face for signs of wakefulness, I lifted it from his chest and gently turned it to check. It, too, was scarred from one side to the other—the scar hidden skillfully by the tattoo artist.

Stunned, I sat on the floor, watching him sleep. I had no idea if this was something I could ever bring up with him—if it was something he'd ever willingly tell me. Even having spent my fair share of days and nights miserable over the breakup with Kennedy, I was never depressed enough to consider suicide. I had no idea what it would take to get to that hopeless point. Not really.

It was late, and I needed to get back to my dorm. Our class—my class—began in only eight hours. On the kitchen counter, I found a discarded envelope and I scribbled a note letting him know I'd gone back to the dorm and would see him tomorrow.

"Wait." Lucas's voice stopped me with my hand on the doorknob. He sat up, slightly disoriented from sleep.

"I didn't want to wake you, so I left a note." I picked it up from the end table, folding it and shoving it into my pocket. I was so overfull of words to say and questions to ask that none would come out.

He rubbed his eyes and stood, stretching his neck to the side, extending his arms back, eyes closed. His biceps and pecs flexed from the movement, and I wanted to stop staring, but couldn't until his eyes flashed open. "I'll walk you out to your truck."

He turned to grab his T-shirt and pull it back on, and I was able to ogle him shamelessly again. Across the top of his defined shoulders and back were more inked designs and scripted words, but the T-shirt covered them much too abruptly. He disappeared into his bedroom and came out wearing his hoodie and a very beat-up pair of Sperrys I'd never seen him wear. Boots were his standard footwear.

"Francis is on the bed? Unless he's developed opposable thumbs, I guess you let him in." Crossing the room to me, he smiled.

I nodded as he neared, and his smile ebbed. I knew he was thinking about what happened before we fell asleep wrapped up in each other, wondering what I thought about him pleading with me to say *stop* when I'd made it clear that I didn't want to. If he only knew—my confusion over his strange rejection was nothing to the apprehension over what had caused the scars on his wrists.

chapter Nineteen

After a week of Lucas ignoring my existence while we were in class, I wasn't sure what to expect Monday morning. The alteration was minor, but undeniable. When I entered the classroom, his eyes met mine, the barest suggestion of a smile playing on his mouth. Everything about him had grown familiar. The night I danced with him, his features had merged into an exceptionally crush-worthy guy. Now, he was all sharp angled jaw and strong chin, his nose with the slightest hint of a prior break. A crescent-shaped scar sat high on one cheekbone, and his colorless eyes were sometimes a little eerie. The fringes of his bedhead hair were just long enough to soften the whole; if he ever cut it short, he would look like a completely different guy.

He returned his attention to the ever-present sketchbook, and I pulled my gaze forward in an effort to keep from pitching down the steps. Just hours before, he'd held my face in his hands, pressed me against the door to my truck, and kissed me as though we'd done what I'd wanted to do. I'd driven back to my dorm in a state of bewildered lust.

Sliding into my seat next to Benji, I withstood the temptation to look over my shoulder. If he wasn't watching me, I'd be disappointed. If he was, I'd be caught.

The girl on my right was giving her usual Monday morning weekend recap to her neighbor . . . and the two or three dozen other people who could hear her. Benji pantomimed her perfectly, and I pretended a coughing fit to hide my laughter. Unfortunately, the coughing drew her attention.

"Are you *dying* or something?" she asked, affecting a pointed sneer as I shook my head. "Well, hacking up a lung out in public isn't all that attractive—just sayin'."

My face flamed, but then Benji leaned up and spoke around me. "Um, giving half the class an exhaustive summary every Monday morning—in lurid detail—of how much of an alcoholic skank you are? *Isn't all that attractive, either*. Just sayin'."

She gasped as nearby people snickered, and I caught my lower lip between my teeth while trying to stare straight ahead. Thankfully, Dr. Heller entered then, and class started, and I went back to fifty long minutes of attempting to forget Lucas's presence three rows back and five seats over.

"So . . . nine days till the final." Benji stuffed his backpack and smirked at me while I packed mine.

"Mmm-hmm."

"Nine days until no more . . . *restrictions*." I rolled my eyes directly at him as his brows danced up and down. "Eh? Eh?"

I couldn't help checking to see if Lucas was still in the room. He was talking to the Zeta girl he'd spoken to before—but he was watching me over her head.

Benji sidled by on his way to the aisle, a grin splitting his face. "I'll take Hot Tutors for two hundred, Alex," he said in an unnaturally feminine voice before he began humming the *Jeopardy!*

theme song. He was *still* humming it when he smiled at Lucas just before exiting.

I hoped I wasn't blushing as Lucas fell into step with me, but neither of us spoke until we were outside. Clearing his throat, he gestured toward Benji's retreating back with one shoulder. "Does he, um, does he know? About . . . ?"

He worried his bottom lip and the small silver ring, a slight frown on his face.

"He's actually how I figured out . . . who you were."

"Oh?" He walked with me toward my Spanish class, as he had once before.

"He'd noticed us . . . looking at each other," I shrugged, "and he asked me if I went to your tutoring sessions."

Closing his eyes for a beat, he took a breath. "God. I'm so sorry." I waited, hoping he would finally tell me the reason for the Landon/Lucas charade. We hiked across the hilly campus in silence for a minute or two, every step taking us nearer to my class. Without a single cloud in the sky, the sun warmed us in direct patches of light while we froze in the shade cast by trees and buildings.

"I noticed you the first week." His voice was soft. "Not just because of how pretty you are, though of course, that played into it." I smiled, watching our feet as we matched our steps. "It was the way you lean onto your elbows when you're listening in class, when something catches your interest. And when you laugh, it's never to get attention, it's just—laughter. The way you obsessively tuck your hair behind your ear on the left side, but let the right side fall down like a screen. And when you're bored, you tap your foot soundlessly and move your fingers on the desktop like you're playing an instrument. I wanted to sketch you."

We stopped and stood in a square of sun, well away from the shadowed entrance to the language arts building. "Almost every time I saw you, you were with *him*. But one day, you walked up to the building alone. I was holding the door for several girls in front of you, and I waited for you to catch up. When you reached me, you look pleased, and a little surprised. Unlike the others, you didn't expect the door to be held for you by some random guy. You smiled up at me and said, 'Thank you.' That was the last straw. I prayed you'd never come to a session, and not with him. I didn't want you to know I was the tutor.

"He took you for granted, even when you stood next to him, holding his hand. Like you were an accessory." He frowned, and I remembered feeling exactly like that with Kennedy. Often. "I never wanted you to get hurt, but I wanted to take you from him. I had to constantly remind myself that it didn't matter if you were his or not, because you were on the other side of a line I couldn't cross. And then you didn't show up the day of the midterm—or the next, or the next. I worried that something had happened to you. He was kind of reserved the first couple of days. By the end of the week, girls were flirting with him before class, and the way he responded told me what had happened.

"I was sure you'd dropped the class, which made me selfishly ecstatic. Without even knowing I was doing it, I started looking for you on campus." He stared into my eyes and lowered his voice even further. "And then, the Halloween party."

I couldn't breathe. "You were there? At the party?"

He nodded.

"How? You aren't Greek, are you?"

He shook his head. "I'd fixed the house's AC the night before. Maintenance doesn't do nonemergency stuff on evenings or weekends, but I'm contract labor, so I agreed to do it. When I wouldn't take a tip, a couple of the guys invited me to the party. I only said yes because I was hoping you might be there. It had been two weeks, and this campus is so huge I was starting to think I'd never run into you." He chuckled softly and rubbed a hand at the back of his neck. "Wow, that sounds total stalker."

Or totally hot. *God*. "Why didn't you talk to me that night? Before . . ."

He shook his head. "You were so withdrawn and miserable. Almost every guy who approached you was rejected without a second glance. There was no way I was going to become one of them. You danced with a handful of guys you already knew—and *he* was one of those."

"Buck."

"Yes. When you left, he followed, and I thought maybe . . . maybe you two had decided to leave early together, without everyone knowing. Meet outside or something."

I watched a trio of my classmates enter the building. "He's my roommate's boyfriend's best friend. Well, her *ex's* best friend, now. He was a known entity. A friend, I thought. Boy, was I wrong."

He nodded, frowning. "I was about to leave—my bike was parked out front. Something didn't feel right, but I was struggling with the same desire to take him out that I'd felt for half the semester with your boyfriend, so I questioned my own motives. I lost a minute arguing with myself, and I'm sorry about that. I finally decided if you two were hooking up, I'd just go around front, rev up the Harley, and be done with it. With you."

"But that's not what happened."

"No."

Suddenly aware of the lack of people bustling around us, I pulled out my phone. It was two minutes past ten. "Crap. I'm late."

"Uh-oh. Isn't this the professor who makes an example of you if you're late?"

Impressive. "You remembered." Groaning, I pushed my phone into my bag. "I sorta feel like skipping now."

His mouth turned up on one side. "What kind of university employee would I be, to encourage you to skip class the last week of the semester?"

"We're just reviewing. I have an A. I don't really need the review."

We stared at each other.

I angled my head and looked directly into his clear eyes. "You don't have a class?"

"Not until eleven." Not for the first time, the feel of his gaze drifting over my face was like a soft breeze, or the lightest possible touch. He stopped on my mouth.

Lips parted, my breathing slowed as my heart rate sped. "You never did sketch me again."

His eyes darted to mine, but he didn't answer, so I thought maybe he didn't remember his texted request.

"You said you were having a hard time doing it from memory. My jaw. My neck . . ."

He nodded. "And your lips. I said I needed more time staring at them and less time tasting them."

I nodded. Good God, what did he *not* remember?

"A very foolish thing for me to say, I think." He was staring at my mouth again.

My lips tingled from his focused perusal. I wanted to rub my fingers across them. Or graze them with my teeth to stop the tickling sensation. When I wet them with my tongue, he sucked in a breath. "Coffee. Let's go get coffee."

I nodded, and without another word, we walked toward the student center, the busiest place on campus at this time of day.

"So you wear glasses, huh?" We'd been sitting at a tiny table, sipping our coffees and enduring a decidedly uncomfortable silence, so I'd blurted the first viable thing that entered my brain.

"Um. Yeah."

Great. I'd just brought up *that night*. But shouldn't I bring up *that night*? Shouldn't we talk about it? Shouldn't I ask him if he was pushing me away because he was the class tutor, or because of those scars on his wrists?

"I wear contacts. But my eyes get tired of them by the end of the day."

Cue the mental picture of Lucas pulling his door open, the apprehension on his face, the glasses transforming him into someone official while the pajamas produced a contrary effect. I cleared my throat. "They look really good on you. The glasses. I mean, you could wear them all the time, if you wanted to."

"They're kind of a pain with the motorcycle helmet. And taekwondo."

"Oh. Yeah, I can imagine."

We were quiet again, with forty minutes until his class and my rescheduled bass practice time. "I could sketch you now," he said.

For no good reason, my face flamed.

Luckily, he was reaching into his backpack, withdrawing his sketchpad, and turning to a blank page. He took the pencil from behind his ear before looking across the table at me. If he noticed my heightened color, he didn't mention it. Without a word, he leaned back in his chair, the pad on his knee, and started drawing, his pencil making the effortless, sweeping arches of someone who knows what he's doing. His eyes moved from the pad to me and back, over and over, and I sat silently sipping, watching his face. Watching his hands.

There was something intimate about modeling for someone. I'd volunteered as a model once in my junior year art class, for extra credit. Severely lacking in drawing skill, I'd jumped at the extra two points without stopping to consider that I would be sitting on top of a table for an entire class period. Giving a classroom of teenaged boys free rein to stare at me for an hour was a whole new sort of awkward. Especially when Jillian's boyfriend, Zeke, started his portrait with my chest. He stared unabashedly, showing off his artistic efforts to his tablemates while I flushed and pretended I couldn't hear his wisecracks about nips and cleavage and how he wished I'd just lose the shirt altogether—or at least unbutton it.

"Most artists begin with the head," Ms. Wachowski said as she looked over his shoulder. Zeke and the other boys at the table snorted with laughter while I burned with humiliation and the entire class looked on.

"What are you thinking about?"

I wasn't relaying *that* story. "High school."

The hair falling over his forehead obscured the crease I knew was there, but his lips pressed tight.

"What?" I asked, wondering at the change those two words brought.

Surrounded by conversations, music, and mechanical sounds, the scratch of the lead across the paper was inaudible in the coffee shop. I watched the pencil dance in his hand, wondering what part of me he was sketching, and what parts he might want to sketch. What was he like as a sixteen-year-old boy? Did he draw then? Hang out with other boys his age? Had he fallen in love? Had his heart broken by some callous girl?

Had he already put those scars on his wrists, or was that yet to come?

"You said you'd been with him for three years." He spoke just loud enough for me to hear him, staring down at the pad as the pencil worked back and forth. There was no question in his voice. He assumed I was thinking about Kennedy.

"I wasn't thinking about him."

His jaw flexed, lips compressed again. Jealousy? Guilt crept in when I realized I *wanted* him to feel jealous.

"What was high school like for you?" I asked and then wanted to take it back. His eyes flashed to mine and his hand stilled.

"A lot different than it was for you, I imagine." His eyes

still roved over my face, but he was no longer drawing, and his expression was tense.

"Oh? How?" I smiled, hoping to either bring us back from this ledge-clinging position, or shove us over the edge.

He lifted his gaze to me then and stared. "For one, I never had a girlfriend."

I thought of the rose over his heart, and the poem inscribed on his left side. I didn't want that love to be recent. "Really? Not one?"

He shook his head. "I was . . . unsettled, you could say. I hooked up with girls. No relationships. Skipped class as much as I bothered to show up. Partied with the locals and the beach tourists. Got into fights often, in school and out. Got suspended or expelled so frequently I was never quite sure when I woke up in the morning whether I was supposed to go or not."

"What happened?"

His face went blank. "What?"

"I mean, how did you get into college and become this"—I gestured at him and shrugged—"serious student?"

He stared at the pencil in his hand, his thumbnail scraping over the lead, sharpening it. "I was seventeen, about to flunk out for the last time, prepared to work the boat with Dad the rest of my life. One night, I was partying with some friends. We made a bonfire on the beach, which always drew the tourist kids in—and they always wanted to be hooked up. One of my friends was a dealer. Not big stuff—just party drugs. He'd sell high, so we could skim some off without having to pay his distributor for it.

"His sister tagged along that night. She had a crush on me,

but she was fourteen. Totally innocent. Not my type. She didn't take the dismissal well, and started flirting with the guys who financed our night, so to speak. Her dumbass brother was so high he wasn't watching her at all. My head wasn't much clearer, but when the guy she was dancing with pulled her down the beach, she looked like she was trying to yank away from him.

"I remember going after them, but everything after that is murky. I was told I broke the guy's jaw. Got arrested, charges filed. I probably would have ended up in prison, but the Hellers were visiting that week, and Charles did something to make it all go away.

"He and my dad had words. Next thing I knew I was signed up for martial arts classes. I was stupid enough to see the wrong-minded benefit of being able to beat the shit outta people even better than I already could, so I didn't object. What I didn't see coming was how it would center me for the first time in a long time. Before he left, Charles lectured me like Dad never had. I didn't like disappointing him." He looked at me closely. "Still don't."

We sipped our coffees and I waited, holding my tongue, knowing there was more.

"He told me I was throwing my future away, that I was better than drugs and fights. He said my mother was watching, and asked if I wanted her to be proud or ashamed. Then, he promised he'd help me get into the university, pull every string he could pull, if I'd just try. He knew I was looking for an escape, and he gave me one second chance."

A chill moved down my back at his words.

"He's good at offering those."

He smiled, just barely. "Yes. He is. I took it. My senior year looked good, but I'd all but killed my overall GPA before that. I don't know how he got me accepted, even conditionally. Dad can't pay for it, of course, so that's why all the odd jobs. I pay rent for the apartment, but I couldn't get a cot in somebody's garage for what he charges me."

"He's like a guardian angel for you."

Raising his light, unnerving eyes to mine, he said, "You don't even know."

chapter *Twenty*

I blinked at Erin, confused. "What do you mean, she's probably not testifying?"

My roommate slammed her phone onto her desk. Slammed the door of our mini-fridge after grabbing a bottle of water from it. Kicked her shoes off and then threw one of them across the room where it bounced off the wall over her bed and landed in the center. "They got to her. Kennedy, D.J., and Dean. Convinced her—or have almost convinced her—that they'll *handle* Buck. That she'll take down the frat and maybe the whole Greek system if she testifies."

"*What?*" Kennedy, along with the V.P. and the president of his frat, had persuaded Mindi not to testify?

"They're making *her* feel guilty. For being raped!" I'd never seen Erin so enraged. "This is total fucking crap. I'm calling Katie."

I got up and crossed the room, holding her forearm to keep her from dialing. "Erin, you can't tell if Mindi doesn't want you to tell."

She looked at me closely. "J, you know how the Greeks work. Everyone already knows."

"Oh. Right."

She dialed, and I listened as she told her sorority president what she thought of the proposed cover-up. "Okay, I'll be there in an hour, with Mindi." She put the phone down, her expression calmer and more calculating. Sitting on my bed, she took my hand. "You have to go with us, J. You have to tell them what he did to you."

Somehow, testifying to a bunch of sorority girls was more terrifying than the thought of reporting Buck to the cops or giving a deposition to the district attorney. "W-why?" I sputtered. "I'm not one of you guys, Erin. They don't care—"

"It shows precedent."

How many times had I heard Kennedy use this legal jargon—one of his favorites. "Are you sure a failed attempt with me shows a pattern? It's only twice . . ."

Her eyes flared. "Jacqueline—"

"You're right, you're right . . . God, what am I saying?" My hands trembled, sliding over my face, and Erin pulled them down gently.

"We have to make sure he doesn't do this again."

I nodded, knowing she was right, and she tapped out a text to Mindi.

Erin had just unlocked the Volvo when I heard my name and turned to find Kennedy jogging across the dorm lot. "Hey, Jacqueline. Erin." When he gave her a tight, serious smile, she scowled at him. He turned back to me. "We need to talk."

I glared at him. "About what? About you helping them talk Mindi out of pressing charges, when you know what he did to me?"

He huffed a tired sigh. "It's not like that—"

"Oh? What's it like?"

"Can we speak privately? Please?"

I glanced at Erin and she pursed her lips and gave my ex a cynical once-over before turning her attention back to me. "I'm picking Mindi up, and I'll meet you at the house?" She was worried that I'd let him talk me out of this, as ill at ease as I already was.

I peered at Kennedy, and I knew that convincing me to abandon the allegation against Buck was his agenda. "You'll drive me over? Now? That's the only way this talk is happening."

Frustrated and maybe a little confused by my counter, he agreed. "Sure. I'll take you over, if you'll talk to me on the way."

I stared across the top of the sedan at Erin. "I'll meet you there."

She nodded, unwavering hope in her eyes, and I followed Kennedy to his car.

After adjusting the stereo to backdrop level, he drove slowly, with one wrist draped over the top of the leather-wrapped steering wheel. "Thanks for agreeing to talk to me." He glanced across, his eyes skittering away from mine and back to the road. "I want you to know that I believe, one hundred percent, everything you told me Saturday night. I know Buck's a scumbag—I just didn't know how much of one. We've started proceedings to expel him."

"Expel him—from the frat? Like *that's* punishment?" Closing my eyes, I shook my head to clear it.

"Buck came to this campus thinking he was going to make pledge class president, thinking he'd move up in the ranks, run the whole frat and maybe the council by senior year, and now he's about to be out on his ass, daddy or no daddy. Damn right it's punishment."

I gasped. "Kennedy, *he raped a girl*."

He had the grace to flinch. "I understand that, but—"

"There's no *but*! There's no fucking *but*!" My chest heaved with the effort to lock my hands in my lap instead of pummeling his smug face. "He deserves prison time, and I'm going to do everything I can to see he gets it." I couldn't help thinking that if Kennedy had been sent to keep me from testifying, then this discussion had produced the reverse effect.

He pulled to a stop in front of the house and put the car in park. He gripped the wheel with both hands. "Jacqueline, you need to understand something. Buck's been talking shit about hooking up with you for weeks now. Others have corroborated his account. Everyone knows about it. No one else buys your *he-tried-to-rape-me-too* story now. It's kind of late for that."

My breath left me, my throat closing up, and pain shot down my arms to my fingertips. Closing my eyes momentarily, I fought dizziness and the welling of tears, and so much fury I literally saw red behind my closed lids.

"My . . . *story*?"

His green eyes met mine. "I told you, I believe you." I stared into his eyes, this boy I'd known so intimately for three years. I could see that he did believe me, but that belief conflicted with his compulsion to save face. He wasn't going to do the right thing.

"You believe me, yet here you sit, trying to talk me out of persuading anyone *else* to believe me."

"Jacqueline, it's more complicated than that—"

"The hell it is." I threw the door wide open and jumped out. Slamming the door on any further protest, I turned and stomped up the sidewalk to Erin and Mindi's sorority house. I was shaking with anger, and fear, and something else: resolve.

• • • • • • • • • • •

There were less than twenty girls in attendance at the meeting: Erin, Mindi, the sorority officers, and me.

As the president, Katie presided from the head of the long, polished table. Seated on either side of her were the senior officers; I recognized Olivia's older sister as one of them. She and Olivia could have been twins, they looked so much alike—right down to the bitchy sneer.

"Mindi, sweetie, no one's blaming you here," she said, her voice dripping with an insincerity that contradicted her words. "But the thing is, you did go to his room with him. I mean, the expectation was *there*, you know?"

Erin put her hand on my thigh when I sucked in a breath—a warning against replying yet. I exhaled through my nose and fumed silently. I was an outsider. I could be removed easily, and that would be no good for Mindi. She needed all the support she could get.

"You weren't like, a virgin, either, right?" another girl said.

"God, Taylor, that's not material," another said.

Taylor shrugged. "It would matter to *me*."

Mindi's face was pale and she looked like she was either going to vomit or pass out. Erin leaned closer to her and whispered, "Breathe, honey."

Several people said more stupid things, and others said more sensible things, and finally it seemed like everyone had spoken their minds except Katie, Erin, and the two people who ultimately held Buck's fate in their hands: Mindi and me. Finally, Katie banged the gavel lightly, stopping all conversation and turning every head in her direction. Her posture so perfect that she could have been a queen wearing a heavy crown, she fixed her eyes on me. "Jackie, I understand that you're alleging that Buck attempted to rape you on the night of the Halloween party?"

A couple of girls mumbled asides and one actually giggled. My hands tightening into fists in my lap, I ignored them, swallowed, and nodded. "Yes."

"Okay sorry, I don't see why she's even here," a junior class rep said. "If he didn't actually do it—"

"He had every intention of *doing* it," Erin said through gritted teeth. "He was just stopped before he *succeeded*."

The other girl tossed her hair over her shoulder. "But she didn't report it that night. Why not? And why *now*? I mean, how do we know this isn't a ploy for attention? Or some sort of vendetta against Buck?"

Erin growled next to me.

"He was stopped by a guy who saw the whole thing and is willing to make an official report with me." My voice wavered, and beneath the table, Erin took my right hand and held it tightly. "As far as why now instead of then . . . that was my bad judgment. It didn't occur to me that he'd do this to someone else." I glanced at Mindi, an apology in my eyes, and then Katie. "I thought it was just me."

"What guy? One of the brothers? Because dude, they're *not*

going to testify against Buck," Taylor said, and several girls nodded.

"No. Lucas Maxfield."

"Oh, I know him," Olivia's sister said. "He's yummy . . ."

"Is he the non-Greek guy who was at the Halloween party without a costume? Cowboy boots? Dark hair? Gorgeous eyes? Total hottie?" the girl next to her asked.

"Yeah, that's him."

"Mindi," Katie interrupted, "I understand that Dean and D.J. spoke with you yesterday?"

Mindi nodded, her still red-rimmed eyes wide. "They want me to drop the charges. They said they would handle it internally."

Heads pivoted back and forth between the sorority president and the freshman pledge as they volleyed questions and answers. "What are your plans now?"

"I don't know. I'm really confused."

Katie pinned her with a look. "Did Buck do what you said he did?"

Mindi's eyes filled with tears, and when she nodded, they spilled down her cheeks.

"Then what the hell is there to be confused about?"

Everyone sat in stunned silence for a moment, until the girl who'd pronounced Lucas a *total hottie* exclaimed, "Are you saying she should press charges?"

"Absolutely."

Gasps sounded around the table, and I was so dumbfounded I couldn't move.

"But this will look so bad for—"

"You know what looks bad?" Katie cut off her VP. "A bunch of women who don't support each other when a guy pulls some shit like this. I'm sick of it. Less than an hour ago, I told D.J. where he could stick his goddamned *fraternal reputation*." She stood up and leaned forward, her hands on the table. "Let me tell you girls a story, short and sweet. In high school, I was a junior varsity cheerleader dating a senior who was up for football scholarships. I'd slept with him several times willingly. One night I wasn't in the mood, but he was. So he held me down and forced me. The few people I told about it—including my best friend—pointed out what would happen to *him* if I told. They stressed the fact that I hadn't been a virgin, that we were dating, that we'd had sex before. So I kept quiet. I never even told my mother. That boy put bruises on my body. I was crying and begging him to stop and he didn't. That's called *rape*, ladies."

She drew herself up and crossed her arms over her chest. "So Buck can enjoy sitting in a cell contemplating how he blew up his life. That dickwad hurt two people *sitting at this table*. And you're worried about who'll look bad if they tell? Screw that. Dean and D.J. and Kennedy and every frat boy on this campus can all go *fuck* themselves. Are we sisters or *not*?"

•••••••••••

Jacqueline,

I've attached the review that I'll hand out on Thursday. I guess it's technically preferential for me to give it to you a couple of days early, but I did tell you that you were my favorite, after all.

LM (aka Lucas, aka Landon, aka Mr. Maxfield)

Mr. Landon Lucas Maxfield,

It feels odd to get economics email from you. Like you aren't really the same person. (I just remembered how I asked if you needed help in economics. I was all set to recommend you as a tutor to *yourself*. You must have thought I was so clueless.)

Thank you for the review worksheet. I won't even look at it until Thursday. That way you don't need to feel guilty about giving it to me early.

Mindi and I filed reports at the police station earlier. Erin drove us. It was the first time I actually gave anyone a detailed account of the whole thing. I was shaking and crying by the time I was done, and I felt weak and stupid all over again. Mindi was in even worse shape; the case worker said she may need to be treated for PTSD. She told us both to go to the school counseling office or a private therapist for treatment.

Mindi called her parents on the way back to campus, and they'll be on a flight here in the morning. It never even occurred to me to tell mine. I don't think I could deal with another I-told-you-so speech from my mother. Not about this.

I gave the detective your information, and she said they would call you when they want you to come in. I'm not sure what happens next.

JW (aka Jacqueline, aka J, aka Ms. Wallace, aka Jackie—but will apply self-defense training as needed if called such)

Ms. Jacqueline (not-Jackie) Wallace,

I never for one moment thought you were clueless. I got caught up in my own deception, and I felt increasingly rotten about it. I'm glad you found out, and I'm sorry I didn't tell you myself. If anyone was clueless, it was me.

I feel like such a jackass for ever saying anything to make you think that any part of that night was your fault. I was so amped and pissed—at him. If you hadn't made that sound in the truck, I think I might have killed him.

Did you both file a restraining order?

Lucas

Me: Can we switch to text?

Lucas: Sure np

Me: We got the paperwork to file a temporary RO tomorrow afternoon.

Lucas: Good. If you feel threatened, I want you to call me. Ok?

Me: Ok.

Lucas: Tomorrow is my last class day in econ. Dr. H will be doing a review on Friday.

Me: Obviously, you don't need that. I thought you were a bad slacker student. Sitting on the back row, drawing, not paying any attention to the lecture.

Lucas: I guess I did look that way. This is my third semester to tutor, and my fourth to sit through the class. I know the material pretty well.

Me: So, after Wednesday, we don't have class together? And after the final next Wednesday, then what?

Several minutes passed, and I knew I'd asked a question he either didn't know the answer to or didn't want to answer.

Lucas: Winter break. There are things you don't know about

me. I told myself I won't lie to you again, but I'm not ready to put everything out there. I don't know if I can. I'm sorry.

Winter break began a week from Friday—the last day of fall finals. I was required to leave the dorm over break, and the spring semester wouldn't begin for seven weeks. A lot could change in that space of time.

I fell out of a tree in sixth grade and broke my arm. I couldn't play my bass or braid my own hair for seven weeks. When I was fifteen, my best friend Dahlia went to summer camp for seven weeks. When she returned, she was best friends with Jillian. I remained friends with them both, but things were never the same between Dahlia and me. Seven weeks after fall semester started, Kennedy broke up with me, and seven weeks later, I realized I was getting over him.

Seven weeks could change everything.

Erin came in from work before I could formulate a reply to Lucas, if there even was one. Uncharacteristically quiet and wearing a distracted expression, she peeled off her work clothes carefully, dropping them into the laundry basket without her usual garment-flinging tendency.

"Erin? Is everything all right?"

She flopped onto her bed and stared at the ceiling. "Chaz was standing next to my car when I came out tonight. Holding flowers."

I didn't see any flowers, so I could only imagine what had happened to them. Probably nothing good. "What did he want?"

I knew exactly what he wanted. I knew what he'd wanted last Saturday. What he'd probably wanted ever since he'd been dumb enough to choose his dick of a best friend over his girlfriend.

"He apologized. He groveled. He said he'd apologize and grovel to *you* if I wanted him to. He swore he'd never thought Buck would resort to—*that*—to get a girl, because girls are always throwing themselves at him. I told him three weeks ago that it isn't about *sex*. It's about *dominance*." She raised up on her elbows to look at me. "He didn't listen to me then. And now, when Buck is about to be arrested and charged with rape—*now* he's listening."

I shrugged. "I guess that guys who'd never do something like that have a hard time believing some other guy would," I said, but I could see her point. Awareness and apologies were fine and good, but they could come too late.

chapter *Twenty-One*

Kennedy was waiting outside the classroom Wednesday morning. Avoiding eye contact, I intended to walk by him into class, but he reached out as I passed. "Jacqueline—come talk to me."

Allowing him to pull me a few feet to the left of the door, I faced the classroom so I could see when Lucas arrived.

He kept his voice low and leaned one shoulder on the smooth tile wall. "Chaz says you and Mindi filed police reports yesterday."

I expected anger or exasperation, but saw neither. "We did."

He rubbed a couple of fingers over his flawlessly stubbled chin—a habit that used to make me want to do the same. "You should know, Buck is claiming that the thing with Mindi was consensual, and the thing with you didn't happen at all the night you said it did."

My mouth fell open and snapped closed. "The 'thing' with Mindi? The 'thing' with me?"

Ignoring my indignation, he added, "He apparently forgot that he'd told Chaz and at least a dozen other guys that you and he had hooked up in your truck, right after the party, before he got jumped."

I knew Buck had spread rumors, but I hadn't heard the details. "Kennedy, you know I wouldn't do that."

He shrugged. "I didn't think so, but I wasn't sure how you were reacting to our breakup. I did a few, um, ill-advised things after . . . I figured you were entitled to the same."

I thought of OBBP, Erin and Maggie's solution to my after-breakup nosedive, and conceded—to myself—that he wasn't completely off the mark. Still, I wondered if he'd ever known me at all. "So you thought I might be so upset over losing you that I'd start screwing random guys in parking lots?"

He pinched the bridge of his nose. "Of course not. I mean, I mostly assumed that he was exaggerating. I had no idea that he'd . . ." His jaw clenched and his green eyes blazed. "It never occurred to me that he'd do *that*."

I was getting sick and tired of that sentiment.

I saw Lucas approaching at the same time he spotted me. Without pausing, he walked straight over and stood next to me. "You okay?"

I'd grown addicted to that sentence from him, and the way he said it, his voice like steel under velvet. I nodded. "I'm fine."

He nodded once at me and gave Kennedy a quick glance that promised lethal injury if he saw fit to inflict it.

Kennedy blinked and looked over his shoulder to watch Lucas enter the classroom. "That guy's in our class? And what the hell was that look for?" He turned back to examine my face more closely as I watched Lucas disappear through the door. "Chaz said some guy was in the parking lot that night. That he's the one who beat the shit outta Buck, not a couple of homeless guys like Buck said." He gestured with a thumb. "Is that who he was talking about?"

I nodded.

"Why did you tell me you just got away?"

"I don't want to talk about that night, Kennedy." *With you*, I added silently. I'd have to talk about it soon enough, when I had to give a deposition to the defense, and again when it went to trial.

"Fair enough. But you weren't exactly honest with me the other night."

"I was honest; I just wasn't completely forthcoming. I don't know why I even told you, especially after you asked me to drop the charges so the frat could save face—"

"That was a mistake. One that's been rectified—"

"Yes, by a bunch of sorority girls much braver than you. Mindi was about to cave to your pressure, and if she'd dropped her case, I wouldn't have had one at all. You of all people *know that*. So thanks, Kennedy, for your support." I sighed. "Look, I appreciate your talk with Buck, and for what it's worth, I know you genuinely didn't want him to hurt me. But he needs to go to jail, not just be dressed down by a peer and tossed out of his fraternity." I spun to enter the classroom and stopped when he called my name.

"Jacqueline—I'm sorry."

Erin was right. Apologies could come too late. I nodded, accepting his for the sake of everything we used to be, but nothing more.

Dr. Heller had begun the lecture, so I slipped into my seat, accepted Benji's smile of hello, and gave myself credit for becoming a survivor. I had survived Kennedy's decision to end our relationship. I had survived what Buck tried to do to me.

Twice. And I would survive if Lucas wouldn't—or couldn't—trust me with his personal demons.

• • • • • • • • • • •

The trees had transitioned from leafy to bare without my notice. The shift was always a quick thing here—never a lengthy, multihued transformation like it was farther north. Even so, I'd been too preoccupied to observe the alteration as it occurred. It seemed like one day the trees were thick and green, and the next, the leaves had vanished altogether, except in small, dead piles trapped in terraced corners and caught under border hedges.

The occasional warm days were gone as well. Lucas and I hunched into our coats, and my scarf was wound around my neck twice and encroaching on my face. I exhaled into it and savored the warmth that lasted about two seconds.

Lucas pulled his beanie lower. "Do you want me to come with you this afternoon? I can get someone to cover my shift at Starbucks."

I turned my head to look at him, but my scarf didn't turn with me. "No. Mindi's parents are here. They're going to make sure everything's taken care of for both of us. They even offered to get me a hotel room—they're keeping Mindi there with them for the next week, and then taking her directly back home after finals. Her dad's moving her stuff out of her dorm tonight. Erin says they may withdraw her permanently."

He frowned. "I guess it wouldn't do any good to point out that this could have happened anywhere."

I shook my head. "Maybe once they get over the shock of it. But Mindi might not want to come back *here*, even if that's true."

"Understandable," he mumbled, staring straight ahead as we walked.

We were silent until we got to the small building where my Spanish class was located. "I wish I could skip again today, but we have oral presentations that count as part of the final."

He smiled, reaching out to loosen a stubborn strand of hair that clung to my lip. I couldn't get it with my gloved fingers. His index finger was faintly gray, and I guessed that he'd been sketching in class today. "I'd like to see you, before you go home. Outside of Saturday's class, I mean." His finger trailed my jaw, dipping into the pool of scarf and tucking beneath my chin.

I felt my stomach drop to my feet. I'd become familiar with nonverbal farewells recently, and good-bye was in his eyes. I wasn't ready to see it. "I have a solo performance for a final grade tonight, a mandatory recital to attend on Friday, and my ensemble is performing Saturday. But I can come over tomorrow night, if you want."

He nodded, staring into my eyes, looking like he might kiss me. "I want." Students still hustled to their classes all around us. I wasn't late to class yet, this time. He pulled my scarf back into place over my chin and smiled. "You look like a partial mummy. Like someone was interrupted while winding you into your shroud."

A full smile from Lucas was so rare. Used to his ghost smile, dark scowls, and intense stares, I was so stunned that my breath faltered. And then I smiled back, and even if he couldn't quite see my mouth I knew the crinkles around my eyes replicated those around his, the darker blue of my eyes connecting with the his gray-blue. "Maybe I did a hammer-fist strike and bloodied his nose before he could do all that gruesome mummy stuff to me."

He laughed softly, holding the warm smile in place, and I leaned toward him like a flower to sunlight.

"You are fond of that hammer-fist strike."

"Maybe not as fond as Erin is of all things groin-strike related."

He laughed again and leaned to kiss my forehead, letting me go swiftly and glancing around. His smile faded, and I thought I'd probably be willing to do almost anything to bring it back. "Text me when you're done this afternoon?"

I nodded. "I will."

• • • • • • • • • • •

I wasn't sure what I would find when I Googled Lucas's name Wednesday night. I hoped for an obituary that would give me a starting point, which I found. Like many obits, the one for Rosemary Lucas Maxfield didn't give a clue to how she died. No "in lieu of flowers please send a donation to" with the name of some awful young-mother-killing illness at the end. I Googled her name, expecting nothing—but multiple articles popped up, all dated eight years ago. The titles knocked the breath from me. I chose one and clicked—my heart thumping so hard I could feel the individual beats—while I wished these commentaries were about someone else's mother. Someone I didn't know.

Two Dead in Murder-Suicide

Authorities have confirmed the horrific details of a murder-suicide that took place during an apparent home invasion in the early hours of the morning on Tuesday. Police say that Darren W. Smith, a local handyman, broke into the home of Raymond and Rosemary Maxfield through a back window around 4 a.m. Tuesday morning. Dr. Maxfield was away on business. After restraining her son in his room, Smith raped Rosemary Maxfield repeatedly before slashing her throat. Cause of death was massive blood loss from multiple sharp-force injuries. Smith then fatally shot himself. Weapons found at the scene included a seven-inch hunting knife and a 9 mm pistol.

Smith was one of a group of contractors working on the Maxfield home earlier this summer. There appears to have been no other connection between Smith and the Maxfields, despite surveillance-type photos of the family found yesterday by investigators at Smith's home. Police believe that Smith was aware of Dr. Maxfield's absence from home.

Unable to get in touch with his wife or son by Tuesday evening, Raymond Maxfield requested that family friends Charles and Cindy Heller check on them. At approximately 7 p.m., the couple discovered Rosemary Maxfield in her bedroom, covered in blood, with Smith near her, dead from a self-inflicted gunshot to the head. The minor child was taken to County Hospital and treated for dehydration, shock, and minor injuries relating to the restraints, but was otherwise unharmed.

Heller made a short statement earlier this evening, requesting that the press and the community allow Maxfield and his son privacy to process the shocking manner in which they lost their 38-year-old wife and mother. "I was in the army. Special Forces. I've seen some atrocious stuff. But this was the worst thing I've ever come across, and I'll always regret taking my wife with me that night," Heller said. The Hellers and Maxfields have been close friends for sixteen years. "Rose was an adoring wife and mother, a loving and wonderful friend. She'll be terribly missed."

• • • • • • • • • •

"Thank you for seeing me outside office hours." I took a deep breath and sat, hands knotted in my lap. "I need to talk to you about Lucas. There's something I need to know about him."

Dr. Heller's brows drew together. "I'm not sure what I can divulge. If it's of a personal nature, you should probably ask him."

I was afraid he'd say this, but I needed to know more before I saw Lucas again. I needed to know if that night had been the catalyst for the scars on his wrists, or if there was something more. "I can't ask him. It's about . . . what happened to his mother. To him."

Dr. Heller looked as though I'd sucker-punched him. "He told you about that?"

I shook my head. "No. I Googled his name, looking for her obituary. When it didn't give a clue how she died, I Googled her name. Yours was in the article I found."

He scowled. "Ms. Wallace, I'm not willing to talk about what happened to Rose Maxfield just to appease someone's morbid curiosity."

I took another shaky breath. "This isn't curiosity." I scooted to the edge of the chair. "His wrists—they're both scarred. I've never known anyone who tried . . . *that*, and I'm afraid to say the wrong thing. You've known him all of his life. I've only known him a few weeks, but I care about him. A lot."

He thought for a moment, and I knew he was weighing what to tell me, staring at me from under his bushy brows. It was hard to imagine that this soft-spoken, doughy man had once been a member of Special Forces. Hard to imagine he'd been the one to discover one of his closest friends savagely murdered.

He cleared his throat, and I didn't move. "I became good friends with Raymond Maxfield in grad school. We were both PhD-track, but while I planned to go the more typical teaching and researching route, Ray was bound for a more lucrative, nonacademic career.

"We attended a small gathering at the home of one of our professors, whose daughter was an undergrad, living at home. She was stunning—all dark hair and dark eyes—so when she passed through on her way to the kitchen, Ray got up with an excuse to get ice, and I followed. He was my best friend, but I wasn't letting him call dibs on a girl like that. It was every man for himself." He chuckled softly.

"Five minutes later, I was feeling damned sure of my chances. He'd asked her major, and when she'd answered 'Art,' Ray had blurted out, 'Your father is Dr. Lucas—one of the foremost minds in modern economics—and you're studying *art*? What the hell are you gonna do with a degree in *art*?' "

He smiled, his eyes unfocused, remembering. "She drew herself up to all five foot two, eyes flashing, and said, 'I'm going to make the world more beautiful. What are you going to do? Make money? I'm *so* impressed.' She whirled around and left the kitchen. For days, Ray was *furious* that he hadn't formulated a single retort while she was standing there.

"A week later, I ran into her in the coffee shop. She asked if I was as anti-art as my friend. I'm no dummy, so I exclaimed, 'No way—I know how essential art is in the expression of the human condition!' So she invited me to an exhibit she was having, and told me I could bring Ray. I immediately regretted telling him at all, because he was determined to impart those clever comebacks he'd been formulating since the night they met.

"The gallery was squeezed between a liquor store and a furniture rental place. As we walked to the door, Ray made a remark about the 'more beautiful world' she wasn't making, and I wanted to kick myself again for bringing him.

"Rose walked up wearing a gauzy dress, her hair twisted up—very art student. With her was a smartly dressed blonde—Ray's usual type—who she introduced as her best friend, and also a finance major. Ray barely noticed the other girl. 'Where's your stuff?' he asked Rose. His question seemed to take the bite out of her. She was fidgety as she led us to the wall showcasing her paintings—watercolors. We all waited, tense, for Ray to pronounce judgment.

"He examined each piece without comment, and then he looked down at her, and said, 'They're beautiful. I don't think you should ever do anything that isn't this.' She graduated three months later, and he had a ring on her finger that night. Once he finished his doctorate, they got married, and he started his career with a vengeance, as he'd always planned to do.

"Oddly enough, I ended up with the pretty finance major, and we married not long after they did. The four of us stayed close friends. Landon is like an older cousin to our three."

Dr. Heller stopped and took a deep, sad breath, and my uneasiness returned.

"Ray was working for the FDIC. Lots of travel. I was teaching at Georgetown; we lived maybe twenty minutes from each other. When he couldn't get in touch with them that night, Cindy and I drove over to check. We found Rose in her room, with Smith's body, and Landon in his room." Dr. Heller swallowed and I couldn't breathe. "He was so hoarse from screaming he couldn't speak, and his wrists were zip-tied to the bed post. He'd dragged that bed until it ran into other furniture and couldn't go any farther. His wrists were lacerated, trying to get loose from those ties to get to his mother. There was dried blood on his arms and the corner of the bed. That's where the scars came from. He'd been like that fifteen, sixteen hours."

My stomach heaved and tears streamed down my face, but Dr.

Heller's voice was flat. I sensed he was holding himself apart from the memory as much as he could. I felt cruel for making him relive such a horrible night.

"Rose was the emotional heart of the three of them. Ray adored her, and losing her that way, when he wasn't there to protect her . . . He shut down. He'd made tremendous strides in his career, but he quit it all. Moved the two of them to his dad's place on the coast, went back to the fishing boat he'd been so determined to never have any part of when he left home at eighteen. His father died a couple of years later, left him everything.

"Landon shut down in a different way. Cindy and I tried to tell Ray that he shouldn't be uprooted from everything he knew, that he surely needed therapy, but Ray was out of his mind with grief. He couldn't stand to be in that house or that city."

He looked up at me then, pulling a tissue box from a desk drawer when he took in my face. "I think you need to get the rest from Landon—I mean, Lucas. He changed his name to his middle name—his mother's maiden name—when he came here for college. Trying to reinvent himself, I guess. An eighteen-year habit is hard to break, and he hasn't called me on it enough in the past three years." He peered at me and exhaled. "I wish I'd never seen you leaving his apartment. As far as I'm concerned, any student/tutor restrictions are over. Just . . . so you know."

I dabbed a tissue under my eyes and thanked him.

University restrictions were the least of my worries.

chapter *Twenty-Two*

"You're a good cook." I grabbed the empty glasses and followed Lucas to the sink. He rinsed the bowls of pesto remains and turned to take the glasses from me.

"Pasta's easy—the college-version gold standard for impressing a date with your mad culinary skills."

"So this *is* a date?" Before he could do an about-face, I added, "And you made the pesto from scratch—I watched you. That was impressive all on its own. Besides, you've never lived in a dorm, where the pasta choices are usually Chef Boyardee from a can, or two-for-a-dollar ramen noodles. The occasional Lean Cuisine. Trust me, your skills are positively epicurean."

He laughed, treating me to the full smile I craved. "Oh, really?"

I returned the smile, but it felt counterfeit—as though someone else had shaped my mouth into a happier contour than I was capable of feeling. "Really."

Every minute, I battled a mounting dread over what I'd learned on the Internet the previous night and from Dr. Heller hours before. Lucas had been through such hell, and shared it with no one, as far as I knew. He'd said there were things I didn't know about him that he might never be able to reveal, and instead of respecting those secrets, I'd unearthed them. I wanted to be the one he let in, but my prying could easily be turned into an excuse to shut me out.

"I guess it would wreck my standing as a top chef if I told you I made brownies from a box for dessert." His expression was stern.

"Are you kidding?" I rolled my eyes. "I *love* brownies from a box. How'd you know?"

He was trying to maintain a severe demeanor and failing. "You're full of contradictions, Ms. Wallace."

I looked up at him and arched a brow. "I'm a girl. That's part of the job description, Mr. Maxfield."

He dried his hands on a dish towel and tossed it on the counter, pulling me closer. "I'm very aware of the fact that you're a girl." His fingers threaded through mine and he restrained both of my hands behind me, gently, pressing them into my lower back. My breathing quickened along with my heart rate as we stared at each other.

"How would you get out of this hold, Jacqueline?" His arms surrounded me and my body bowed into his.

"I wouldn't want to," I whispered. "I don't want to."

"But if you did want to. How would you?"

I closed my eyes and visualized. "I would knee you in the groin. I would stomp on your instep." I opened my eyes and calculated our relative heights. "You're too tall for me to headbutt, I think. Unless I jump up like they taught us to do in soccer camp."

One corner of his mouth turned up. "Good." He leaned down, our lips inches apart. "And if I kissed you, and you didn't want me to?"

I wanted him to so badly my head swam. "I—I would bite you."

"Oh, God," he breathed, his eyes closing. "Why does that sound so *good?*"

I leaned in and up, as close as I could get, but his lips were still out of reach, and my arms—trapped behind me—couldn't stretch to pull him down. "Kiss me and find out."

His lips were warm. He kissed me carefully, nibbling and sucking my lower lip. Drawing the tip of my tongue along the inner edge of his mouth, I swept it over the slim ring, lightly, and he groaned and pulled me in so tight I could barely breathe. My hands were suddenly freed and he grasped my hips, lifting me onto the counter so that our angles were reversed.

Thrusting my fingers into his hair, I pressed my tongue into his mouth, cautiously, tracing over the hard palate just behind his teeth while wrapping my arms and legs around him. He sucked my tongue into his mouth and I gasped. I'd never kissed anyone like that; I'd never been kissed like that. One hand at the back of my neck, directing me, the other balancing me on the edge of the counter, he coaxed me to do it again and when I did, he caressed my tongue with his own, grazing his teeth over the surface, biting it softly as I withdrew.

"Holy crap," I moaned before he drove his tongue into my mouth, finally, and I tightened my grip on him everywhere, wanting to cry from how right it felt.

Plucking me from the counter, he strode into his room and we fell onto his bed, my legs still locked around him. Braced over me, he kissed me deeply, stroking the interior of my mouth until I was writhing under him. He pulled me up and removed my sweater and I unbuttoned his shirt. Leaving it hanging open, he started to unzip my jeans, stopping to scan my face.

"Yes." There was no hesitation in my voice.

He pulled the zipper down slowly, watching me; I felt the pressure of it as I lay still, panting softly, staring up at him. One hand on my thigh and the other stilled at the base of the zipper, he murmured, "I haven't tried this with anyone . . . *significant* in a long time. It's never worked before."

I tried to rein in the disbelief all too evident in my tone. "You haven't had sex before?"

He closed his eyes and sighed, his hands moving to grip my bare waist. "I have. But not with anyone I cared about or . . . knew. One-time things. That's all." He raised his eyes to mine.

"That's all—ever?"

He smiled sadly, his fingers running just inside the perimeter of my loosened waistband. "It's not like there've been tons of them. There were more before, in high school, than there have been the past three years."

I didn't know how to reply to that. I couldn't focus on anything but the feel of his index fingers hooking into the belt loops at the side of my jeans.

"Lucas? I said yes and I meant it. I want *this*—as long as you have protection, I mean. I want this, with you. So this is okay." I was babbling, worried that it would end as it had six days before. I exhaled a breath and spoke just above a whisper. "Please don't ask me to say stop."

Staring down at me, he pulled and I lifted my hips. My jeans slid down my legs and he tossed them aside, shrugged out of his shirt and removed his jeans. "I want it to be better than okay. You deserve better than okay." After grabbing a condom from a box in the nightstand and tossing the small square on the bed, he settled between my legs. I was shivering like I had no experience whatsoever. "You're shaking, Jacqueline. Do you want to—"

"*No.*" I put my trembling fingers over his mouth. "I'm just a little cold." *And a whole lot nervous.*

He pushed the covers down beneath me and dragged them back up, over us. His weight pressing into me, he kissed me thoroughly before staring into my eyes, his fingers drifting over my face. "Better?"

I took a deep breath, my fears dissolving with his touch, the anticipation climbing faster than it had minutes ago in the kitchen. "Yes."

As his thumb caressed my temple, his fingertips teased into my hair. His eyes were so pale this close that I could see every fragmented facet. "You know you can say it." His voice notched lower, softer. "But I'm not asking you to, this time."

"Good," I answered, lifting my head to capture his mouth, my hands kneading up and over the hard muscles of his back before trailing my nails down the center from his shoulder blades to his hips.

His earlier hesitation gone, he removed the last scraps of fabric we were wearing, fixed the condom in place, kissed me fiercely, and rocked into me.

Had this been Kennedy, it would have been over in a few minutes.

My last coherent thought, as Lucas took his time kissing and touching every part of me he could reach and my body arched into his, was *Oh . . . so this is what all the fuss is about.*

• • • • • • • • • •

We lay facing each other, snuggled under the covers, shoulders peeking out. I watched his gaze drift over me, stopping on each feature as if he was memorizing it: ear, jaw, mouth . . . chin, throat, curve of shoulder.

He came back to my eyes then, lifting his hand and tracing over the individual attributes while watching my response. When his fingers trailed over my lips, they edged the border before rubbing across the lower one, and I swallowed and concentrated on breathing. His eyes fell there and he stared for a long moment before cupping the back of my neck, moving closer, and kissing me so softly I hardly felt it, until the thin connection caught and ricocheted through me, shooting to my toes like a current.

I sighed and our breath mingled. Pushing the covers to my waist, he urged me onto my back before propping his face on his hand and continuing his perusal. My exposed skin should have been cold, but I warmed under his examination. "I want to sketch you like this." His voice was as gentle as his touch—now skirting across my collarbone, back and forth, before moving lower.

"Can I assume it won't end up on the wall?"

He smirked down at me. "Er, no, this one wouldn't go on the wall, as tempting a thought as that is. I've done several sketches of you that aren't on the wall."

"You have?"

"Mmm-hmm."

"Can I see them?"

He gnawed his lower lip, fingers tracing along the curves of my breast and then following the bumps of each rib. "Now?" His warm hand curved around my waist and he pulled me closer.

I looked into his eyes as he lay over me. "Maybe in a little while . . ."

He scooted lower. "Good. 'Cause I've got a couple things I'd like to do first."

••••••••••

He pulled on his dark boxer briefs before padding out to the kitchen. I heard the front door open and close a moment later, his voice a low murmur mixed with Francis's insistent meows. He came back with a tall glass of milk and a plate of brownie squares.

Handing me the plate, he took a sip of the milk before setting it on the bedside table. I sat with the sheet held over my breasts and watched him move across the darkening room. He flicked on the desk light and picked up the sketchbook. Stacked in a corner of the desk, there were several just like the one he held.

In the center of his upper back was a gothic-looking cross, not quite high enough to peek out of a T-shirt neckline. The remaining tats were tiny scripted lines surrounding the cross, not meant to be read from a distance, just like the poem on his left side. His skin was clear from his shoulder blades down. Turning, he caught me studying him—I couldn't look away, so there was no hiding my appraisal.

He crawled onto the bed, propping the pillows and sitting behind me, his legs on either side of my hips under the covers. While I lay back against his chest and nibbled a brownie, he opened the sketchbook and flipped through pages, some containing little more than shapes, lines, and vague forms, others detailed portrayals of people, objects, or scenes. A few were finished and dated, but most were partially complete.

Finally, he opened to his first sketch of me—which he must have done during class, when I sat next to Kennedy. My chin was propped in my hand, elbow on the desktop. I took the book from him and browsed page by page from there, slowly, amazed at his skill. He'd sketched two of the oldest buildings on university grounds, a guy skateboarding down the drag, and a panhandler on the outskirts of campus talking to a couple of students. Interspersed with these were meticulous illustrations of mechanical things.

I turned the page to another sketch of me, this one very close-up—facial features and the suggestion of hair, but little else. Scrawled in the bottom corner was a date, two or three weeks before Kennedy dumped me.

"Does it bother you . . . that I was watching you before you knew me at all?" His tone was guarded.

I found it impossible to be bothered by anything at the moment, wrapped up in him as I was. I shook my head. "You're just observant, and for some reason you found me an interesting subject. Besides, you've sketched a lot of people who didn't know you were scrutinizing them so closely, I assume."

He chuckled and sighed. "I don't know if that makes me feel better or worse."

Leaning to the side, propping my head against his inked bicep, I looked up at him. Still clutching the sheet to my chest in a belated show of modesty, or insecurity, I watched his heated gaze flick there before rising to my face. "I'm not mad anymore that you didn't tell me you were Landon. The only reason I was angry was because I thought you were playing me, but it was the opposite of that." I let the sheet drop, and his searing gaze dropped with it. Lifting my fingers, I brushed them over the smooth skin along his jaw. He must have shaved just before I came over. "I could never be afraid of you."

Without a word, he took the plate from my lap and the sketchbook from my hand before lifting and turning me onto his lap. Arms surrounding me, his mouth moved over my breasts as my hands tangled in his hair. I ignored the reproach in my mind—the one insisting that I was the one withholding information now, and while I might not fear Lucas directly, I feared his desertion if I told him what I knew and how I knew it.

Inhaling the now-familiar smell of him, I dragged my fingers across the words and designs on his skin as he kissed me, banishing my shrill pang of conscience to a distant drone.

chapter Twenty-Three

"So where's . . ." Benji's voice trailed off when I glanced at him, and he finished his sentence with a quick head angle toward Lucas's unoccupied seat and a characteristic eyebrow waggle.

"It's final review day, so he doesn't have to be here."

"Ah." He smiled, leaning over the arm of his desk and lowering his voice. "So . . . since you know that bit of inside info, and you two left class together the last couple of days . . . can I assume that somebody's getting a little private tutoring now?" When I pinned my lips together, he snorted a laugh, held up a fist, and singsonged, "Nailed it!"

Rolling my eyes, I bumped his knuckles with mine, knowing he'd hold his fist aloft between us until I did. "God, Benji. You're such a bro-it-all."

He grinned, eyes wide. "Woman, if I was straight, I would steal you from him *so hard*."

We laughed and prepared to take macroeconomics notes for the last time.

"Hey, Jacqueline." Kennedy slid into the empty seat next to me and Benji gave him a narrow-eyed stare that he didn't deign to notice. "I wanted to give you a heads-up." He sat sideways in the desk, facing me, keeping his voice low. "The disciplinary committee decided to let him stay on campus for the next week, as long as he abides by the restrictions of the restraining orders—because he's pled not guilty, and because there's only a week left in the semester. He has to vacate the premises as soon as finals are over, though."

I already knew Buck was out on bail, and that he'd been served the temporary restraining order on Thursday afternoon—Chaz had called Erin to tell her, and she'd passed the information to me, as well as to Mindi and her parents.

"Awesome. So he's staying in the house?" We'd all hoped he would be kicked off campus, but administration was embracing an innocent-until-proven-guilty stance.

"Yeah, for the next week, but then he's gone. The frat doesn't have to be as impartial as university officials do." He smiled. "Apparently D.J. saw the light after Katie told him off. Dean finally agreed. Letting Buck stay for finals week was the only compromise they made—and he's only allowed to go to his scheduled finals and back." Laying his warm hand over mine, he stared into my eyes. "Is there . . . is there anything I can do?"

I knew my ex well enough to know what he was actually asking, but there was no second chance for him in my heart. That place was filled, but even if it hadn't been, I was sure that I'd rather be alone than be with someone who could desert me as he'd done. Twice. I withdrew my hand into my lap. "No, Kennedy. There isn't. I'm fine."

He sighed and shifted his gaze from my face to his knees. Nodding, he looked at me one last time, and I was both gratified and saddened to see the full realization of what we'd lost in his familiar green eyes. Standing to go to his seat, he excused himself to edge past my late-arriving neighbor who, for once, had nothing to say about her weekend plans.

• • • • • • • • • • •

Freshman year weeded out musicians who'd ruled their high school orchestra, band, or choir without a lot of practice—the ones who came to college believing themselves to be above mundane technical proficiencies like scales and internals, let alone music theory. Most music majors were devoted to perfecting our skills, so we spent hours a week practicing—often hours a day. Nothing was ever perfect enough to risk slacking off.

I'd come to campus a little spoiled. At home, I'd practiced whenever I wanted to; Mom and Dad had never limited me, though admittedly, I was reasonable in my practice times. Unable to keep my furniture-sized bass in my dorm room, I had to procure a locker for it in the music building and schedule booth times to play. I quickly learned that evening spots went fast, and though the building was open nearly 24/7, I didn't want to trudge across campus at two a.m. to practice.

Scheduling jazz ensemble rehearsals was even more of a pain. Beginning freshman year, we met two or three times a week. Recently, it had become obvious why Sunday morning studio reservations were easy to get: Sunday was hangover day for much of the student body, and fine arts majors weren't immune. By halfway through the fall semester, most of us had skipped Sunday morning rehearsal once or twice. What worked freshman year wouldn't work at all by the time we were juniors.

Just before the peer recital began on Friday night, I reiterated to one of our horn players why I couldn't make the hastily assembled last-minute rehearsal on Saturday morning, even though our performance was that evening. "I have a class tomorrow—"

"Yeah, yeah, I know. Your *self-defense* class. Fine. If we suck tomorrow night, it's on you." Henry was undeniably gifted, as if he'd been born with a saxophone in his long-fingered hands. His pompous attitude backed by genuine skill, he usually intimidated the hell out of all of us. In that moment, though, I was tired of him being an ass.

"That's bullshit, Henry." I glowered at him as he slouched smugly on the other side of Kelly, our pianist, who'd opted to stay out of the argument. "I only missed *one* rehearsal the entire semester."

He shrugged. "But it's about to be two, isn't it?"

Before I could reply, the recital began. I sat back in my seat, gritting my teeth. I was as much of a serious musician as anyone else in our group, but Saturday was the last self-defense class, the culmination of everything we'd learned. It was important.

Erin was stoked about the one-on-one matches Ralph had planned between each of the class members and either Don or Lucas. "I'll try to get Don," she'd promised while she got dressed for work and I got ready for the last mandatory peer recital of the semester. Squinting one eye into the mirror while applying a layer of mascara to the other, she'd teased,

"I don't wanna wreck your boy-toy's vital parts before you're done playing with him!"

I hadn't heard from Lucas all day, though we were both so busy that I almost didn't have time to dwell on the absence of communication and what it meant. Almost.

A year ago, I hadn't thought I would ever sleep with anyone but Kennedy. He'd been with other girls before me—if nothing else, his experience during my first time made that clear. That fact hadn't bothered me, much, though we'd never actually spoken about it. Lucas, too, was obviously experienced, though he told me none of those previous girls had been significant. If Kennedy had ever confessed something like that, I'd have been relieved, if not thrilled. Lucas's encumbered history made his revelation heartbreaking instead, and I was uncertain what it meant for him, for me, and for us.

• • • • • • • • • •

At the beginning of class, we reviewed every move we'd learned while Ralph circulated the room, giving tips and encouragement. Don and Lucas were absent for the first portion. Ralph wanted us to remain emotionally separated from them, so we wouldn't feel awkward inflicting violence on them in the last hour. I wondered, though, how many of us wasted precious seconds worrying that we were overreacting—tiny, valuable ticks of time spent not defending ourselves, thinking, *But I know this guy*.

My heart in my throat, I watched as each of my classmates used their newfound defense techniques on a fully padded Lucas or Don. As we took our turns on the mats, each of us benefitted from a bloodthirsty eleven-person cheering section, while the guys took turns so they could rest up from being pummeled, kicked, and verbally reviled. Since the padding cushioned our blows, they had to do a bit of acting—adjusting their reactions as though each landed punch or kick had done its job. So when Erin saw an opening and swung a perfect sweep kick to the groin, Don crumpled to the ground as if incapacitated.

Eleven voices screamed, "*Run! Run!*" But Don's big, padded body blocked a straight escape to the designated "safe zone" by the door, and Erin hesitated for a split second. He rolled toward her and we screamed even louder. Roused, she leapt onto his chest like it was a springboard and launched herself, turning when she landed and kicking him two more times before running away.

When she reached the far door, she pumped both fists in the air and bounced up and down while everyone cheered. Ralph clapped her on the shoulder as she rejoined us, and I glanced at Lucas. Wearing his ghost smile, he watched her. One more woman, empowered. One more given the ability to defend herself against attack. One more who might not meet his mother's fate. His eyes found mine, and I wondered if these single, hopeful moments would ever be enough to alleviate the ache that haunted him. The ache about which I was presumed to be unaware.

Pulling his gaze from me, he went to wait for the next potential victim to walk onto the mats. There were two of us remaining—a very soft-spoken secretary named Gail from the student health center, and me.

Ralph eyed the two of us. "Who's next?"

Gail stepped forward, trembling visibly. While Ralph murmured subtle tips—something he hadn't done for anyone else—Lucas went easy on her. Our booklet said that having the confidence to fight back was a critical part of self-defense training, and I knew they were giving her that. The more punches and kicks she landed, the louder we cheered her on and the harder she fought. When she returned to the group and accepted our emphatic praise, there were tears on her face and she was still wobbly—but she wore a mile-wide smile.

I went last, against Don. My adrenaline spiked the moment I stepped onto the mat, and I wondered if the tiny shockwaves running through me were visible to everyone, like Gail's unsteady hands had been as she held her small body in defense mode. I knew Lucas and Erin were watching me closely; they were the only ones who knew exactly what had brought me there.

The entire thing was over in a minute, maybe two.

Don circled me once, mumbling *hey, baby* comments—part of the scenario. I kept my eyes on him, my whole body taut, waiting. Suddenly, he swerved toward me and tried to grab my arm. I did a wrist block, then screwed up a snapkick and ended up in a front bear hug. I wasn't sure if it was in my head or actually shouted—because everything seemed slow-motion and muted, like we were under water—but I heard Erin's voice yell, "*NUTSACK!*"

I brought my knee straight up, tearing from Don's grasp when he grunted and released me. Running to the door, I heard Erin's cheerleader voice rising over everyone else's. She bounded across the room to hug me when I reached the safety zone, and over her shoulder, I watched Lucas's expression. He'd removed his headgear and combed his sweaty hair back, so I could clearly see his face, and the familiar barely there smile.

• • • • • • • • • • •

Lucas: You did well this morning.
Me: Yeah?
Lucas: Yeah
Me: Thanks
Lucas: Coffee sunday? Pick you up around 3?
Me: Sure :)

• • • • • • • • • • •

Saturday night's performance demanded my full attention, distracting me until I was in my room. Erin hadn't returned from yet another sorority gathering, but was due back soon. The entire dorm was wide awake, studying for—or freaking out about—finals, enjoying the last full weekend before break, or well past ready to go home. The voices in the hall alternated between pre-finals tension and pre-holiday excitement.

A deep-toned bass line seeped through the wall opposite my bed, and my fingers moved with it. Occasionally, the fact that I played the bass would come up with strangers, who typically imagined an electric instrument and a garage band. Lucas looked more suited to that part than I did—dark hair falling into his eyes, small silver ring following the full curve of his bottom lip, not to mention the tattoos and lean, defined muscle that would look so hot onstage, peeking from a thin T-shirt. Or no T-shirt.

Oh, God. Never. Getting. To. Sleep.

My phone beeped and displayed a message from Erin.

Erin: Talking to Chaz. May be late. You ok?
Me: I'm good. YOU ok?
Erin: Confused. Maybe I'd feel better if I just kicked him.
Me: NUTSACK!!!!!!!!!
Erin: Exactly.

• • • • • • • • • • •

"Those people are crazy." Knees pulled to my chest, I cuddled close to Lucas as he sketched a couple of kayaks out on the lake. "It's got to be even colder out there on the water than it is sitting here."

He smiled and reached behind me to pull my coat's hood up over the wool and cashmere scarf and hat I was wearing. "You think this is cold?" He crooked an eyebrow at me.

I scowled and touched my gloved fingers to my nose, which had the anesthetized feeling that comes from a shot at the dentist, right before they drill a tooth. "My nose is numb! How dare you scoff at my sensitivity to ice-age temperatures. And I thought you were from the coast. Isn't it warmer there?"

Chuckling, he stuck his pencil above his ear, under his cap, closed the sketchpad, and laid it on the bench. "Yeah, it's definitely warmer on the coast, but that's not where I grew up. I'm not sure you could survive a winter in Alexandria if you're this much of a candyass."

I gasped in pretend outrage, punching him in the shoulder while he feigned being unable to block the blow.

"Ow, jeez—I take it back! You're tough as nails." He turned and slid his arm around me, rewarding me with that full smile. "Total badass."

Between his proximity in the physical sense and his embrace in the emotional sense, I hummed happily and cuddled closer, closing my eyes. "I throw a mean hammer-fist," I mumbled into his hoodie. His leather jacket lay folded on the bench next to the sketchbook. He'd insisted it wasn't cold enough to need it, except on the motorcycle.

He echoed my hum, tipping my head back with an ungloved, curiously unfrozen finger. "You do. I'm actually a little scared of you."

Our faces were inches apart, his breath mingling with mine in one evaporative cloud between us. "I don't want you to be scared of me." The words I couldn't bring myself to add swirled through my mind: *Talk to me, talk to me*. Barring that, I wanted him to kiss me so I wouldn't feel the guilt escalate, threatening to spill out in one irrevocable confession. As if I'd made that request aloud, he lowered his head and kissed me softly.

chapter Twenty-Four

Most people would take off as soon as they handed in the last final. Erin was leaving on Saturday, but I was staying because my favorite middle school student had invited me to his concert Monday night—he'd made first chair and wanted to show off. We were required to vacate the dorms for winter break by Tuesday, so I would be going home that day, whether I wanted to or not.

Maggie, Erin, and I met in the library to study for our last astronomy exam of the semester. Around two a.m., Maggie flopped facedown onto her open textbook with a dramatic sigh. "Uuuuugh . . . If we don't take a break from this shit, my *brain* is going to be a black hole."

Erin said nothing, and when I looked at her, she was checking her phone, scrolling through a text, and then replying. She hit Send and noticed I was looking at her.

"Huh?" Her brown eyes were a little wide. "Um, Chaz was just letting me know the guys are taking turns keeping an eye on Buck. Making sure he doesn't leave the house."

"I thought we weren't talking to Chaz," Maggie mumbled sleepily—eyes closed, cheek pressed to the page we were reviewing.

Erin's eyes landed anywhere but mine, and I knew she'd

abandoned that plan. I decided to let her fidget a little longer before I let her off the hook. I'd always liked Chaz and could fault him only so much. I wouldn't want to believe my best friend was a monster either.

Checking my phone, I reread the texts I'd sent Lucas earlier, and his replies.

Me: Econ final: PWNED
Lucas: All because of me, right?
Me: No, because of that Landon guy.
Lucas: ;)
Me: My brain hurts. I have three more exams.
Lucas: One more for me, friday. Then work. See you saturday.

"Mindi's last final is tomorrow." Erin doodled a design around an equation in her notebook.

"I heard her dad is sitting in the hall during all of her finals," Maggie said.

I'd heard the same rumor. "I can't blame him, if that's true."

We watched Erin, who knew the truth between fact and campus gossip. She nodded. "He is. And she's not coming back, except to testify. She's transferring to some small community college back home." The regret in her eyes was bottomless. "Her mom said she's still having nightmares every night. I can't believe I just left her at the party."

Maggie sat up. "Hey. We left a *lot* of people at the party, and nothing happened to any of them. What he did to her wasn't our fault, Erin."

"I know, but—"

"She's right." I made Erin look at me. "Put the fault where it goes. On *him*."

• • • • • • • • • •

I finally told my parents about Buck. I hadn't talked to them since before Thanksgiving. Due to something left out of order in the pantry, Mom figured out that I'd been home and called me. I guess she wanted to make sure a stranger hadn't broken into the house and unalphabetized her grains and condiments, so I had to fess up.

"But . . . you told me you were going to Erin's?"

Instead of telling her that she'd come to that conclusion by herself—that I'd only mentioned Erin once, that she'd never bothered to verify what I was *actually* doing over Thanksgiving break—I lied. It was easier for both of us that way.

"Coming home was a last-minute decision. No big deal."

She started jabbering about the things we needed to do over the break—I was due for a dental appointment, and my truck's registration would expire in January. "Do you need an appointment with Kevin, or have you found a stylist there?" she asked.

Instead of answering her question, I blurted it all out—Buck's assault in the parking lot, Lucas saving me, Buck raping another girl, the charges we were pressing, the upcoming criminal case. There was no stopping it, once it started.

At first I thought she hadn't heard me, and I gripped my phone, thinking *I'm not repeating all of that, if she's too damned busy decorating for her party to listen to me for ten seconds.*

And then she choked out, "Why didn't you tell me?"

She knew why, I think. I didn't need to say it. They hadn't been the best parents; they hadn't been the worst, either.

I sighed. "I'm telling you now."

She was silent for another strained moment, but I heard her moving through the house. They were hosting their annual catered holiday party on Saturday, and I knew how control-freak and anal Mom was about the house being perfect for that. Growing up, I'd learned to make myself scarce during the entire week leading up to that party.

"I'm calling Marty right now to tell him I'm not coming in tomorrow." Marty was Mom's boss at her software consulting firm. "I can be there by eleven." I recognized the sound of her dragging her wheeled suitcase out from the closet under the stairs.

I gaped into the phone for a moment before sputtering to life. "No—no, Mom, I'm fine. I'll be home in less than a week."

Her voice shook when she answered, shocking me further. "I'm so sorry, Jacqueline." She said my name as though she was trying to find some way to touch me through the phone. "I'm so sorry this happened to you." *My God*, I thought, *she's crying?* My mother wasn't a crier. "And I'm sorry I wasn't here for you when you came home. You needed me and I wasn't here."

Alone in my room, I sat on my bed, dazed. "It's okay, Mom.

It's not like you knew." She'd known about my breakup with Kennedy . . . but I was ready to let that go, too. "You raised me to be strong, right? I'm good." I realized as I said it that it was true.

"Can I—can I set up an appointment for you with my therapist? Or one of her partners, if you'd rather?"

I'd forgotten Mom's occasional therapy sessions. She'd been diagnosed with an eating disorder when I was really young. I didn't even know what it was—bulimia, anorexia? We'd never really talked about it.

"Sure. That would be good."

She sighed, and I thought I heard relief. I'd given her something to do.

• • • • • • • • • • •

After we finished several cartons of Chinese takeout and a conversation about how we chose our respective majors, Lucas fished his iPod from his front pocket and handed me the earbuds. "I want you to hear this band I just found. You might like them." We were sitting on the floor with our backs to my bed. Once I was plugged in, he pushed Play, watching me as I listened.

His eyes locked with mine as the music swelled in my ears. I couldn't hear anything outside of it, couldn't see anything but his eyes on me. He leaned closer and I inhaled the soothing scent of him. Cupping my face in his hand, he moved his mouth to mine, kissing me at a leisurely pace that somehow matched the rhythm of the song. He tasted like the wintergreen Tic Tacs he'd been sucking on.

Handing me the iPod, he picked me up, deposited me on the bed, and lay next to me, drawing me into his arms and kissing me until the first song bled into the next, and the next. When he pulled back to trace a finger over the edge of my ear, I removed an earbud and handed it to him. We lay side-by-side on my narrow dorm bed—the length of which only just accommodated his body comfortably—listening together, immersed. He opened a new playlist, and I knew that the song he chose was something for me—beyond a band he wanted to share, or something for us to discuss musically.

My heart reached for him as we listened, staring at each other, and I felt the threads of connection between us—fragile filaments, so easily snapped. Like the poem etched into his side, we were each curving to fit inside the other, and this melting and reshaping could be deeper, more resilient. I wondered if he felt it, and when I listened to the lyrics of this song that he chose, I thought maybe he did. *Now don't laugh 'cause I just might be . . . the soft curve in your hardline.*

The hallway outside my door was mostly silent, finally, after a day of people packing up and moving out that had begun early. We talked—recent history only—and Lucas relayed the story of how Francis came to be his roommate. "He showed up at the door one night, demanding to be let in. Napped on the sofa for an hour, then demanded to be let out. It turned into a nightly ritual, with him staying longer and longer, until at some point I realized he'd moved in. He's basically the most brazen squatter ever."

I laughed and he kissed me, laughing, too. Still smiling, he kissed me again, hands wandering over my waist and hip. As we started to make out, I panted out the fact that Erin wasn't leaving campus until tomorrow—and therefore could walk in any moment.

"I thought you said she was leaving today."

I nodded. "She was. But her ex-boyfriend is charting a relentless campaign to get her back, and he wanted to see her tonight."

His hand wandered under my shirt, exploring. "So what happened with them? Why did they break up?"

My lips parted when his hand cupped one breast, molding it to his palm as though it was meant to fit there.

"Over me."

His eyes widened slightly and I smiled.

"No—not like that. Chaz was . . . Buck's best friend." I hated how my body constricted when I thought of Buck, how my teeth grated when I said his name. Without even being present, he triggered responses I couldn't quell, and that infuriated me.

"He's gone now, right?" he asked. "He's left campus?" Transferring his arm to my back, Lucas pressed me closer, his hand at the back of my neck.

Closing my eyes, I burrowed my head beneath his chin, nodding.

"I doubt he'll be allowed to come back next semester, even before the trial," he said.

I breathed him in, closing my mouth tight and inhaling the scent of him through my nose. I felt sheltered by him. Safe. "I'm always looking over my shoulder. He's like one of those jack-in-the-box clowns . . . I never told you about the stairwell, did I?"

I wasn't the only one incapable of suppressing physical reactions. His body stiffened, and his grip on me was suddenly less gentle, more charged. "No."

Mumbling the story into his chest, trying to stick to facts and nothing else so I could temper my own response, I ended with, "He made it look like we'd done it in the stairwell. And from the looks on everyone's faces in the hall . . . from the stories that circulated after . . . they believed him." I forced the tears back. I didn't want to cry over Buck anymore. "But at least he didn't get into my room."

Quiet for so long that I thought he wasn't going to comment, he finally pushed me onto my back, wedging one knee between mine and kissing me roughly. His hair tickled the side of my face, and I wrenched my hands—trapped between us—free, plunging them into his hair as though I could pull him closer.

The way he kissed me felt like a brand. Like he was tattooing himself under my skin.

He knew all of my secrets, and I knew his.

But that seeming reciprocity was a lie—because he hadn't been the one to reveal his own. I'd excavated them, and worse, he was unaware of it.

My guilt mushroomed between us, along with my longing for him to share that part of himself. To trust me with it. I was going home in three days. I couldn't bring this up with miles and hours between us, or keep it to myself for weeks longer.

When we slowed again, wrapped up in each other and allowing our libidos and heart rates time to decelerate, I saw an opening.

"So you sort of live with the Hellers, and they're family friends?"

He watched me and nodded.

"How did your parents meet them?"

Turning onto his back, his teeth slid over the ring in his lip and he sucked it into his mouth. I recognized this as his stress-disclosing equivalent of Kennedy's neck-rubbing.

"They went to college together."

The earbuds had been dislodged sometime during the last half hour. He turned the iPod off and wound the wires around it tightly.

"So you've known them *all* of your life."

He pushed the iPod into his front pocket. "Yeah."

Images of what I'd read, and what Dr. Heller had revealed, flashed in front of my eyes. Lucas needed comforting—I'd never known anyone who needed it more—but I couldn't console him over something he hadn't shared.

"What was your mother like?"

He stared up at the ceiling, and then closed his eyes, unmoving. "Jacqueline—"

The scrape of a key in the door startled both of us. The room was unlit, except for a low-watt desk lamp. When the door opened, a block of light, filled with Erin's silhouette, fell across the floor in the center of the room.

"J, are you already asleep?" she whispered, her eyes still adjusting from the bright hallway, or she'd have seen that I wasn't alone on the bed.

"Um, no . . ."

Lucas sat up and swung his feet to the floor, and I followed. *Timing is everything*, I thought.

After tossing her purse on her bed and kicking off her shoes,

Erin turned back toward us. "Oh! Hey . . . er. I think I might have some laundry I need to do . . ." She shrugged out of her coat and grabbed her nearly empty laundry basket.

"I was just leaving." Lucas bent to pull on his black boots and lace them up.

Mouthing, *Oh my God I'm so sorry!* over his head, Erin was the picture of contrition.

I shrugged and mouthed back, *It's okay*.

Following Lucas into the hall, I gripped my opposite arms, cold after the warmth of lying next to him. "Tomorrow?"

He zipped his leather jacket before turning to me, his lips set firm. His eyes slid from mine and I felt the wall between us then, too late. Our gazes connecting, he sighed. "It's officially winter break. We should probably use it to take a break from each other as well."

I tried to form an intelligible protest, but wasn't sure what to say. I'd just pushed him to this, after all. "Why?"The word rasped from me.

"You're leaving town. I will be, too, for at least a week. You need to pack up, and I'll be helping Charles get final grades posted over the next day or so." His justification was so logical; there was no concealed thread of emotion I could wrench free. "Let me know when you're back in town." He bent to kiss me quickly. "Bye, Jacqueline."

chapter *Twenty-Five*

As I drove to Lucas's apartment Sunday night, I reviewed the numerous reasons why popping up unannounced and uninvited was a bad idea: *he might not be there, he might be busy, he thinks he scared me away, he thinks we said good-bye*. On the other hand, I was only going to be in town until Tuesday morning, and I couldn't let him dismiss me without a fight.

After I knocked, I heard the bolt turn and then Lucas's harsh voice through the door. "Who is it, Carlie? Don't just open the door—"

"It's a girl." The door swung open and a pretty, blonde, dark-eyed girl was framed in the doorway. She blinked at me, clearly waiting for an explanation of who I was and what I wanted. I couldn't speak. I was sure my heart had lodged itself in my esophagus and stopped beating.

Lucas came up next to her, scowling. When he saw me, his brows rose into the hair hanging over his forehead. "Jacqueline? What are you doing here?"

My heart revved to life and I turned to tear down the stairs. Suddenly I was airborne, my bicep caught in his grip, swinging me from the top step as he brought me against his chest and I almost, *almost* stomped on his instep.

"She's Carlie Heller," he said into my ear, and I stilled. "Her brother Caleb is inside, too. We're playing video games."

My heart still pounded *fight-or-flight* as his words sunk in and I slumped against him, feeling like a jealous idiot. I dropped my forehead to his chest. His heart was pounding as hard as mine. "I'm sorry," I mumbled against his soft T-shirt. "I shouldn't have come."

"Maybe you shouldn't have come without telling me, but I can't be sorry to see you."

I looked up. "But you said . . ."

His eyes were silver under the porch light. "I'm trying to protect you. From myself. I don't do"—he swung a finger back and forth between us—"this."

My teeth chattered when I spoke. "That doesn't make any sense. Just because you haven't before doesn't mean you can't." Too late, I apprehended a different, more likely reason for his words. "Unless . . . you don't want to."

He sighed and released his grip on my arm to run both hands through his hair. "It's not . . . that . . ."

"Brrr! Are y'all coming in, or what? 'Cause I'm closing this door." I peeked around Lucas. Carlie Heller looked young, but she didn't look *that* young. She didn't seem resentful, though. And she appeared to be curious.

"Well, you asked for it." Threading his fingers through mine, Lucas turned toward the door and pushed it wider. "We're coming in."

Carlie darted to a corner of the sofa where Francis lay across a blanket. Scooping him up, she flopped him over her shoulder like he was an inanimate object. After climbing under the blanket, she rearranged the cat on her lap and picked up the controller. Next to her sat a scowling boy with the same dark eyes, a bit younger than (but just as sullen as) my middle school boys.

"Take all day," he mumbled in Lucas's direction.

"*Rude*." Carlie elbowed him and he rolled his eyes.

Lucas took his controller from the sofa cushion, gesturing for me to sit in the corner opposite Carlie. "Guys, this is my friend, Jacqueline. Jacqueline, these monkeys are Caleb and Carlie Heller." Carlie and I exchanged hellos and Caleb mumbled something in my direction. I pulled my feet beneath me and watched the game over Lucas's head.

When Carlie ushered Caleb out fifteen minutes later, his sulking hadn't decreased. He glanced back at me. "I can't have girls alone in *my* room."

She swatted the back of his head. "Shut it. Lucas is a *grown-up*, and you are just a horny *preadolescent*."

I tried to disguise my laugh as a cough as Caleb's face flushed red, and he shot through the door and pounded down the steps.

Carlie turned to hug Lucas and beam at me. "Y'all have a good night," she chirped, disappearing through the door.

He watched her walk across the yard and into the house, calling good night before shutting and bolting the door. He turned, leaning back against it, and stared at me. "So. I thought we said we were taking a break?" He didn't seem angry, but he wasn't happy, either.

"*You* said we were taking a break."

His lips flattened. "Don't you have to check out of the dorm for several weeks?"

I remained in my spot on the sofa, curled up into the corner. "Yes. I'm only here for two more days."

He stared at the ground, his palms flat on the door behind him.

I tried to swallow but couldn't, my speech turning shaky. "There's something I need to tell—"

"It's not that I don't want you." His voice was soft, and he didn't look at me when he spoke. "I lied, earlier, when I said I was protecting you." His chin came up and we stared at each other across the room. "I'm protecting myself." He took a visible breath, his chest rising and falling. "I don't want to be your rebound, Jacqueline."

The memory of Operation Bad Boy Phase crashed into me. Erin and Maggie had hatched the plan for me to use Lucas to get over Kennedy, as though he had no feelings of his own, and I'd gone along with it. I had no idea then that he'd been watching me the whole semester. That once we began talking, his interest would grow stronger. That finally, he would feel the need to turn away from me because of the depth of those feelings, not because he felt nothing.

"Then why are you assuming that role?" I unfolded myself from the tight little ball I'd become in the corner of his sofa and walked across the room slowly. "It's not what I want, either." As I approached, he remained frozen in place, sucking the ring on his lower lip into his mouth.

Straightening, he stared down at me as though he thought I

might disappear in front of his eyes. His hands came up to cup my face. "What am I gonna do with you?"

I smirked up at him. "I can think of a couple of things."

• • • • • • • • • •

"My mother's name was Rosemary. She went by Rose."

His disclosure brought me back to earth. Lying pressed to his side, I'd been distractedly tracing the dark red petals over his heart, wondering how to tell him what I knew. Or if. "You did this in memory of her?" A lump stuck in my throat as my finger outlined the stem.

"Yes." His voice was low and weighty in the dark room. He was so heavy with secrets that I couldn't imagine how he survived it day after day, never sharing the burden with anyone. "And the poem on my left side. She wrote it. For my dad."

My eyes stung. No wonder his father had shut down. From what Dr. Heller told me, Ray Maxfield was a logical, analytical person. His only emotional exception must have been his wife. "She was a poet?"

"Sometimes."

My head on his arm, I watched his ghost smile appear in profile, and it looked different from that angle. His face was scruffy, unshaved, and several places on my body boasted the slightly chafed evidence of it.

"Usually, she was a painter."

I fought to ignore my conscience, which wouldn't quit babbling that I should tell him what I knew. That I owed him the truth. "So she's responsible for those artist genes all mixed up with your engineering parts, eh?"

Turning onto his side, he echoed, "Engineering *parts*? Which parts might that be?" A mischievous smile tugged at his mouth.

I arched a brow and he kissed me.

"Do you have any of her paintings?" My fingers followed an orbit around the rose, and the hard muscle beneath it flexed with my touch. Pressing my hand to his skin, I absorbed the measured *thump-thump* of his heart.

"Yeah . . . but they're either in storage or displayed in the Hellers' place, since they were close friends of my parents."

"Your dad isn't still friends with them?"

He nodded, watching my face. "He is. They were my ride home at Thanksgiving. They can't get him to come here, so every other year, they all go there."

I thought about my parents and the friends and neighbors with whom they socialized. "My parents don't have any friends close enough to be incorporated into actual holidays."

He stared up at the ceiling. "They were all *really* close—before."

His grief was so tangible. I knew in that moment that he hadn't worked through it—not at all in the eight years it had been. His protective wall had become a fortress holding him hostage rather than giving sanctuary. He might never fully recover from the horror of what happened that night, but there had to be a point where it wouldn't consume him.

"Lucas, I need to tell you something." His heart drummed under my hand, slow and steady.

Other than shifting his gaze to me, he didn't move, but I felt his withdrawal as he waited. I assured myself that the disconnection was all in my mind—a product of my guilt and nothing more.

"I wanted to know how you lost your mother, and I could tell it upset you to talk about it. So . . . I looked online for her obituary." My breathing went shallow as the seconds ticked by and he said nothing.

Finally, he spoke, and his voice was undeniably flat and cold. "Did you find your answer?"

I swallowed, but my voice was a whisper. "Yes." I couldn't hear myself over the rapid thud of my heartbeat.

He shifted his eyes from me and lay back, biting his lip, hard.

"There's one more thing."

He inhaled and exhaled, staring at the ceiling, waiting for my next confession.

I closed my eyes and blurted it out. "I talked to Dr. Heller about it—"

"*What?*" His body was like rock against mine.

"Lucas, I'm sorry if I invaded your privacy—"

"*If?*" He shot up, unable to look at me, and I sat, pulling the covers up with me. "Why would you go talk to him? Weren't the gory details in the news reports sickening enough for you? Or personal enough?" He pulled on his boxers and jeans, his movements rough. "Did you want to know how she looked when they found her? How she'd bled out? How even when my dad ripped out the carpet with his bare hands"—he exhaled harshly—"there was a yard-wide circle of bloodstained flooring underneath that couldn't be sanded deep enough to get it all?" His voice broke and he stopped talking.

In shock and out of words, I could hardly breathe. He sat on the edge of the bed, silent, his head in his hands. He was so close that I could have reached out to stroke the cross that ran along his spine, but I didn't dare. I scooted carefully from the bed and got dressed. I pulled on my UGGs and walked to stand at the foot of the bed.

His elbows pressed into his thighs, his hands obscuring his face like blinders. I stared at the dark hair grazing his shoulders, the flexed muscles of his arm and the ink circling his bicep and flowing down his forearm, his beautiful, lean torso, and the words etched into his side like a brand.

"Do you want me to leave?" I surprised myself, uttering the words with a steady voice.

I don't know why I thought he would say no, or say nothing. I was wrong either way.

"Yes."

The tears started flowing then, but he couldn't see them. He didn't move from his position on the bed. I couldn't even be angry, because I'd crossed a line and I knew it, and meaning well wasn't good enough. I grabbed my purse and keys from the kitchen table and my coat from the sofa, ears pricked for the sound of him coming after me, telling me to stay. There was nothing but silence from his room.

When I opened the door, Francis shot inside, along with a burst of cold air. I pulled the door shut behind me before a sob broke free. Gulping the frigid air and wondering how I'd managed to screw this up so thoroughly, I was determined not to cry until I was in my truck. I slid my hand along the railing as I rushed clumsily down the steps, because I couldn't see through the combination of a moonless night and my tears. A splinter pierced my hand two steps from the bottom.

"Ow! *Dammit*." The physical pain provided the ideal excuse for the sobbing to start. I sprinted down the long, curved driveway, unsuccessful in my attempt to curb my tears long enough to get into the truck. "Damn. Damn. Damn. *Fuck*." I jammed my key into the lock by feel.

Déjà vu. That was the first thing I thought when I felt myself propelled across the bench seat. That was where the resemblance ended, though.

Buck shut the door behind him and slapped the automatic lock. His weight immobilized my lower legs and he had my left wrist in his hand before I could make out who he was, though I knew. "Good enough to spread your legs for anybody but me, huh Jackie?"

chapter *Twenty-Six*

On my back, with my head at an awkward angle against the passenger door, I jerked at my arm and struggled without success to move my legs. "Get off!" I yelled the words, knowing they would be meaningless to him. I was parked in the street—too far for anyone else to hear me. "Get out of my truck!" I'd dropped my keys onto the truck floor when he'd shoved me into the truck, and I searched the floor with my right hand, intending to use them as a weapon.

"I don't think so." He grabbed my right wrist and shook his head like he could read my mind. "You're not going anywhere until we're done talking. You and your lying cunt friend have *ruined* my fucking *life*."

And then, I heard Ralph's voice in my head. *Your body is already a weapon. You just need to know how to use it.* Abruptly, I stopped struggling and took stock: I couldn't kick. I could possibly get my wrists free by rotating and jerking them straight down, but then what? He would just grab me again, immobilize me further.

I needed him closer—the last thing I would naturally seek. I turned my eyes away.

"*Listen* to me when I'm talking to you, goddammit!" He

grabbed my chin roughly, his fingers digging in as he leaned over me and forced me to face him.

Right hand free.

While shoving my hand between us, grabbing and twisting his balls and yanking up as hard as I could, I slammed my forehead into his nose with as much force as I could manage in a straight upward trajectory.

The night in the frat parking lot, everything had happened so quickly that getting my bearings was impossible until it was over. This time, everything was in slow motion—so for an impossibly stretched space of time, I was positive that nothing I'd just done had worked.

And then he screamed, and his nose started gushing. I had never seen so much blood so close-up. It poured out of him as though I'd opened a faucet full-blast.

Left hand free.

He was listing to the side. Still yanking up on his balls, I raised my left knee and turned into him, shoving his shoulder with my left hand. He fell sideways into the cramped crevice in front of my truck's bench seat. The feeling rushed back into my legs, tremors wracking through me, and I went for the door, shoving it open so violently that it almost bounced all the way back.

Just before I cleared the door, his right hand shot out and grabbed my wrist, like the never-quite-dead psycho in a horror movie. I spun and smashed my fist down on the sensitive spot on his upper forearm, inches down from his the crook of his arm, and he released me, bellowing angrily and attempting to flail himself into an upright position.

I didn't wait to see if he succeeded. I vaulted from my truck and ran.

This would have been an ideal time to scream, but I could barely gasp breaths. I heard his footsteps pounding unevenly behind me and I focused on Lucas's door at the top of those steps. I was halfway down the driveway when Buck lunged from behind and grabbed at my hair, yanking me to a stop painfully. I yelped as we went down, immediately turning onto my side as Lucas had taught me, dislodging him.

Suddenly, Lucas was there. Like a dark avenging angel, he yanked Buck away from me and *threw* him, and then installed himself between us. I scrambled backward, crablike. He spared me one glance, his colorless eyes flaring in the dim light cast by the flood lights at the side of the house, before he turned back to Buck, who'd rolled to his feet. Blood coated the space between his nose and mouth and was smeared on his chin, but there was little on him aside from that.

A second floodlight at the corner of the house popped on, illuminating the scene.

Panting, I glanced down at my chest and started. My pink and white knit shirt was stained dark from the neckline to the top of my belly. Because of our positions when I'd slammed Buck's nose, my chest had caught the majority of blood that gushed from his face.

I battled the urge to rip my shirt off in the Hellers' front yard.

Crouching, he tried to circle Lucas. Rather than turn with him, Lucas moved sideways, remaining with his back to me, blocking Buck from getting any closer to me.

Buck's voice was a gruff snarl. "I'm gonna bust that lip wide open, emo-boy. I'm not fucked up this time. I'm stone-cold sober, and I'm gonna kick your ass before I fuck your little whore nine ways from Sunday—again."

Lying bastard.

Lucas didn't rush him, and he didn't respond at first, and then I heard his very controlled voice. "You're mistaken, *Buck*." Never shifting his eyes from him, Lucas unzipped his leather jacket, shrugged it off and tossed it aside. As he shoved the sleeves of the dark long-sleeved T-shirt above his elbows, I noted the worn jeans he'd pulled on earlier and the shit-kicker cowboy boots he grabbed when he was in a hurry, because they didn't require the time-suck that lacing his black combat boots involved.

Buck threw a wide punch and Lucas blocked it. He tried again with the same result, and then rushed forward to pin Lucas in a hold. One kidney punch and left ear cuff later, and Buck staggered to the side, pointing at me. "Bitch. Think you're too good for me—but you're nothing but a *whore*."

Lucas tracked him, staying between us. When Buck jabbed, Lucas grabbed his forearm and turned, wrenching Buck's arm in a direction arms aren't meant to go before turning him to deliver a quick uppercut to the jaw. Buck's head rotated so far he was almost looking backward over his shoulder. He turned back and Lucas snapped another blow straight into his lip. Holding his defensive stance and cocking his head once to each side, Lucas's ghost smile took on a menace it didn't imply when he turned it on me.

Buck roared and lunged forward, and they went down.

Height-wise, they were evenly matched. Weight-wise, Buck had a clear forty- or fifty-pound advantage, and he used it to pin Lucas, punching him in the side of the head twice before Lucas twisted, tossing Buck onto the top of his skull. Flopping onto his back, Buck shook his head twice, like he was trying to clear it.

Lucas tackled him, held him down, and slugged him four times in quick succession. The sound made me think of Dad texturing steaks, and my stomach turned. Buck's face was quickly becoming unrecognizable, and though I couldn't feel sorry for it, I was afraid Lucas was crossing into what might be construed as deadly force.

"Landon! Stop!"

Dr. Heller was tearing down the driveway.

He pulled Lucas off Buck, who wasn't moving. For a split second, Lucas fought back, and I was afraid Dr. Heller was toast, but I'd underestimated my professor and his Special Forces background. His arms a band around Lucas's chest and arms, he barked, "*Stop*. She's safe. She's safe, son." When Lucas sagged, Dr. Heller loosened his hold.

Lucas's eyes found me instantly and he lurched in my direction. Sirens sounded in the distance, closing in quickly. I heard them turn down the far end of the street at the same time Lucas dropped to the grass beside me. He was shaking violently, the adrenaline still pumping through him with nowhere to go. Breathing heavily, he stared at me, lifting a hand cautiously, like he was afraid I might recoil.

My jaw throbbed, and I deduced from his expression that it must have looked bad. His fingers grazed over it and I flinched. He snatched his hand back and I came up on my knees.

"Please touch me. I need you to touch me."

I didn't have to ask twice. His arms came around me, pulling me onto his lap and cradling me against his chest. "His blood? From his nose?" He pulled the shirt away from my chest, and it stuck, the blood already drying, to the bra underneath, and my skin.

I nodded, disgusted.

"Good girl." His arms slid around me again. "God, you're so fucking amazing."

I thought of Buck's blood on my skin and I pulled at the shirt as my stomach heaved again. "I want it off. *I want it off.*"

He swallowed. "Yes. Soon." His fingers moved gently over my face. "I'm so sorry, Jacqueline. Jesus Christ, I can't believe I sent you out the door like that." He choked up, his chest rising and falling. "Please forgive me."

As he caressed me, I turned my head under his chin, folding into him as small as I could get. "I'm sorry for looking her up. I didn't know—"

"Shh, baby . . . not now. Just let me hold you." He pulled me tighter still after grabbing his jacket from the grass nearby and draping it over me, and we stopped speaking.

An ambulance arrived, and the EMTs roused Buck, who at least wasn't dead. Arms crossed dispassionately, one of the officers monitored his care as he was transferred onto a stretcher while his partner conferred with Dr. Heller over the altercation.

"Lan—Lucas," he called. "You and Jacqueline need to give your statements now, son." Lucas stood carefully, pulling me up with him, supporting me fully. Dr. Heller reached a hand to his shoulder. "This young man is the son of my closest friend. He rents the apartment over the garage." He glanced at us with an odd look before continuing. "As I said, that fella"—he pointed at Buck, who was being loaded into the ambulance—"has a restraining order filed against him on behalf of this young lady, which he violated by coming to her boyfriend's home." Ah, there was the reason for the look.

The officers' eyes widened when they took in my bloody shirt. "It's his blood," I said, pointing toward the ambulance.

One of them smiled and echoed Lucas. "Good girl."

I leaned into Lucas, and he tightened his arms around me. The officers, already softened by Dr. Heller, couldn't have been more sympathetic. Twenty minutes and all of our statements later, they, and Buck, were gone, and Lucas and I were gathering my things from my truck and the road after assuring Dr. Heller and his family that we would see to each other's injuries.

Without speaking, Lucas led me up the stairs, into his apartment, and straight into the bathroom. He turned on the shower and lifted me onto the counter to pull off my boots and socks. Without pausing, he removed my shirt and bra and tossed them in the trash. His shirt, speckled with droplets of blood—both his and Buck's—followed.

Standing between my knees, he turned my face toward the light and inspected my jaw. "You're going to bruise. We'll put some ice on it to get the swelling down, after you shower." His jaw clenched tight. "Did he . . . hit you?"

I shook my head, which made it throb a bit. "Just grabbed it really hard. It's sore, but actually the spot where I headbutted him hurts more."

"Does it?" He brushed the hair back from my face and kissed my forehead so gently I couldn't feel it. "I'm so proud of you. I want you to tell me about it, when you can . . . and when I can stand to hear it. I'm still too angry right now."

I nodded. "Okay."

He ran his fingers over the back of my neck. "I knew I'd fucked up. I was getting on my bike, coming after you—and then you were running up the driveway." His jaw compressed and flexed. "When he tackled you . . . I wanted to kill him. If Charles hadn't stopped me, I would have killed him this time."

I didn't move from the counter until he'd undressed. He pulled me down, slid my jeans and underwear off, and led me to the shower, where he washed and inspected every part of me. We were both bruised and abraded in unexpected places, and I could barely lift my arms.

"That's normal," he said, wrapping a towel around his waist and folding another around me. "During a fight, you don't realize all the places you catch a punch, land wrong, or slam into something. The adrenaline deadens it—temporarily."

His dark hair grazed his shoulders, dripping lines of water down his back and chest. He sat me down to dry my hair, and I watched as thin rivulets snaked over his inked skin, flowing over the rose, cutting through the scripted words, and moving into the line of hair on his abdomen before finally soaking into the towel.

I closed my eyes. "The last time anyone dried my hair for me was in sixth grade, when I broke my arm."

He lifted each strand gently, pressing the towel around it to absorb the water without tangling it. "How did you break it?"

I smiled. "I fell out of a tree."

He laughed, and the sound reduced the pain of every sore place on my body to the dullest ache. "You fell out of a *tree*?"

I squinted up at him. "I think there was a boy and a dare involved."

His eyes burned. "Ah."

He squatted in front of me. "Stay here tonight, Jacqueline. I need to keep you here, at least tonight. Please." He took one of my hands in his, and I brought the other to his face, wondering how his eyes could look like chipped ice and still warm me to my core. A bruise was forming near one eye, and the skin was scuffed and split high on his cheekbone, but his face was otherwise unhurt.

His next words were a whisper. "The last thing my father said to me, before he left, was, 'You're the man of the house while I'm gone. Take care of your mother.'" My eyes filled with tears and so did his. He swallowed heavily. "I didn't protect her. I couldn't save her."

I pulled his head to my heart and folded my arms over him. On his knees, his arms slid around me while he cried. As I stroked his hair and held him tight, I knew this night had struck a chord at the heart of his pain. What tormented Lucas went further than the horror of that night eight years ago. What haunted him was guilt, however insanely misplaced.

When he grew quiet, I said, "I'll stay tonight. Will you do something for me, too?"

He fought back his instinctive wariness—I'd seen him do

this before, but never from such close range. He inhaled a shaky breath, shoring up his courage. "Yes. Whatever you need." His voice was gritty and hoarse. When his tongue rolled over his lip ring, I wanted him so badly that it was difficult to waste time talking.

"Go with me to Harrison's concert tomorrow night? He's my favorite eighth-grader, and I promised him I'd go."

He arched a brow and blinked. "Um. Okay. Is that all?"

I nodded again.

He shook his head and stood, leveling the ghost smile on me. "I'm going to grab a couple of ice packs from the freezer. Why don't you go get in bed?"

I stood, laying my hand on his chest and staring up at him. "Is that a dare?"

He laid one hand over mine and pulled me closer with the other. Leaning down, he kissed me gently. "It absolutely is. No falling out of it allowed, though."

chapter *Twenty-Seven*

The middle-school auditorium was packed with camcorder-wielding parents, bored siblings, and a smattering of grandparents. Skirting around clusters of people standing in the aisle, Lucas and I took aisle seats halfway between the stage and the back exit doors. I glanced down at the photocopied holiday green program. Harrison was in the highest orchestra, which meant it would be a while before he was onstage. I gave lessons to two of the other boys in the lower orchestras, though, and I'd never had the chance to see any of them actually perform. I was nervous on all of their accounts.

I leaned close to Lucas so no parents would overhear. "I should probably warn you that many of these kids have only been playing a few months—especially in the first orchestra—so they might be a little . . . inexpert."

The corner of his mouth turned up, and I wanted to lean up and kiss him, but I didn't.

"Is that your polite way of saying to prepare for some nails-on-a-chalkboard sounds?" he asked.

I heard Harrison's voice then from a roped-off section on the right side of the auditorium. "Miss Wallace!" I searched for him among a sea of black-polyester-tuxedoed boys, and girls with ankle-length school-color purple dresses. I located his blond head about the same time he noticed Lucas sitting next to me. His wave froze and his eyes widened. When I smiled and lifted my hand, he waved back once, dolefully.

"I take it this is one of the ones crushing on you." Lucas stared down at the boot balanced on his knee, scratching at a worn seam and trying not to laugh.

"What? They *all* crush on me. I'm a hot college girl, remember?" I laughed and his eyes burned into mine.

He leaned in close and whispered into my ear. "*So* hot. Now you've got me thinking what you looked like this morning, when I woke up with you in my arms, in my bed. Would it be too greedy to ask you to stay tonight, too?"

My face warmed from his compliment as I met his gaze. "I was afraid you weren't going to ask."

He took my hand and held it, balanced on my thigh, as the orchestra director took the stage.

An hour and a half later, Harrison found me at the back of the auditorium. He was holding a cluster of long-stemmed red roses, the color of which were identical to the blotchy, embarrassed shade of his face.

"I wanted to give you these," he stammered, thrusting the flowers into my arms. His parents stood about fifteen feet away, allowing him to deliver his gift alone.

I took the roses and smelled them as he shifted a cursory look at Lucas. "Thank you, Harrison. These are beautiful. You made me so proud tonight—your vibrato was awesome."

He grinned and tried not to, which gave him a sort of manic appearance. "It's all 'cause of you, though."

I shook my head. "You did the work, and put in the practice."

He shifted from one foot to the other.

"You sounded great, man. I wish I could play an instrument," Lucas said.

Harrison eyed him. "Thanks," he mumbled, frowning. Even though my student was taller than me, he was lanky next to Lucas's filled-out frame. "Did that hurt? On your lip?"

Lucas shrugged. "Not too much. I said a few choice four-letter words, though."

Harrison smiled. "Cool."

• • • • • • • • • • •

As we lay in the semi-dark hours later, we faced each other, sharing his pillow. I took a deep breath and prayed I wasn't about to drive Lucas away again. I'd never felt more connected to anyone.

"What'd you think of Harrison?

He studied me closely. "He seems like a good kid."

I nodded. "He is." I trailed my fingers along the side of his face, and he pulled me closer.

"What's this about?" He smirked. "Are you leaving me for Harrison, Jacqueline?"

Watching his eyes, I asked, "If Harrison had been in that parking lot that night, instead of you, do you think he'd have wanted to help me?"

His eyes locked to mine. He didn't respond.

"If someone had told him to watch out for me, do you think

they would ever, ever blame him if he hadn't been able to stop what would have happened that night?"

He exhaled harshly. "I know what you're trying to say—"

"No, Lucas. You're hearing it, but you don't know it. There's no way your father actually expected that of you. There's no way he even remembers saying that to you. He blames himself, and you blame yourself, but neither of you is to blame."

His eyes filled and he swallowed heavily, his grip on me hard. "I'll never forget how she sounded that night." His voice was choked with tears. "How can I not blame myself?"

My tears spilled over onto the pillow between us. "Lucas, think about Harrison. See yourself for the boy you were, and quit blaming him for not stopping something a grown man might have been unable to stop. What have you told me, over and over? *It wasn't your fault*. You need to talk to someone, and figure out how to forgive yourself for responsibility your mother never would have wanted you to accept. Will you try? Please?"

He brushed my tears from my face. "How did I find you?"

I shook my head. "Maybe I'm exactly where I should be after all."

Epilogue

"I'm going to miss you so much. I can't believe you're leaving me." Erin plopped down next to me on the Hellers' sofa. Lucas's graduation party was a backyard cookout, and we were escaping the heat and humidity for a few precious, air-conditioned minutes.

I leaned my head on her tan shoulder. "Why don't you go with me?"

She laughed and leaned her head on top of mine. "That's as silly of an idea as you staying here. You have to go do your great things, and I have to stay here and do mine. That doesn't mean it doesn't *suck*, though."

I'd applied to three music conservatories for transfer in the fall. None of it felt real until after the audition that I nailed at Oberlin—my top choice—and the email I received a couple of weeks ago, notifying me that I'd been accepted.

"Yeah, I guess you need to stay here and keep an eye on Chaz, too."

Erin's opposition to Chaz's breakup-reversal efforts ended on Valentine's Day, when he'd shown up with reservations for "their" B&B, after having flowers delivered every day for two weeks, turning our dorm room into a hothouse. With Erin's help, Chaz had weathered his ex–best friend's impending rape trial—and the associated rumors and innuendoes. Buck's recent pretrial plea bargain for a lesser assault charge was a relief to everyone, though he probably wouldn't serve half of his two-year sentence.

Through the open French doors, we watched our boyfriends talking in the backyard. They'd never be best friends, but they got along well, as opposite as they appeared.

Lucas had been so sure, when he'd encouraged me to apply for transfer into music performance programs, that we would be fine. He was still sure, and I believed him, but that didn't mean I wanted a two-year long-distance relationship. Dead-set against me making an academic decision based on his plans, he wouldn't accept me staying, and he wouldn't tell me where he'd applied or interviewed for jobs.

"I won't ask you to give up what you want for me, Jacqueline."

"But I want *you*," I'd mumbled, knowing he was right; I had no logical defense. In some ways, he was his father's son.

Ray Maxfield had become one of my favorite people. Lucas had taken me home over spring break, and I'd never seen him more nervous. For some reason, though, his father and I hit it off. I could see Lucas's tutor persona in him—his dry sense of humor and intelligence. The night before we left, Ray rummaged through the beach house attic and brought down a trio of framed watercolors of a small boy playing on the seashore. His mother had signed the paintings of her only child in the corners of each—ROSEMARY LUCAS MAXFIELD. We'd hung them in Lucas's bedroom, over his desk.

Even stranger, Ray was sitting outside with Charles and Cindy.

He'd taken a break from the fishing boat for his son's graduation—his first since he'd left Alexandria.

• • • • • • • • • •

"I accepted a job on Friday."

This was it. After applying for dozens of jobs during his final semester, Lucas had had several interviews, and a few second interviews. A week ago, I'd overheard Charles telling Cindy that he'd received a solid offer from an engineering firm in town. I'd been waiting for him to tell me.

When I left for Oberlin in August, we would be twelve hundred miles apart.

"Oh?" I avoided looking at him, afraid I would burst into tears.

Stuffing the leftovers Cindy sent with us into his fridge, I made no further comment, and he leaned against the kitchen counter, watching me. Finally, everything was stored away, and I couldn't delay the inevitable any longer.

At the look on my face, he caught my hand. "C'mere."

As he led me to the sofa, I blinked back tears and gave myself a stern lecture that mostly consisted of *Stop crying stop crying stop crying*.

Leaning into the corner, he pulled me into his arms. I halfway listened as he relayed the technical aspects of the job, the size of the company, the impressive pay, and the start date—the second week in July. Mostly I was wondering how often I would have the time to fly home. Free weekends were almost unheard of as a music student. Mandatory recitals, performing or attending, were unremitting.

"So my only question is this—do I want to live in Oberlin and commute to Cleveland, or live near Cleveland and commute to you?" His head propped on one bent arm, he gazed at me, waiting.

I blinked. "What?"

He smiled innocently. "Oh—didn't I tell you that part? The company's located in Cleveland."

"Cleveland, Ohio? You accepted a job in Cleveland, Ohio?" Cleveland was just over half an hour away from the college.

"I did."

My eyes filled with tears. "But, why?"

Arching a brow, he brought his free arm down and hooked my hair behind my ear. "You heard the pay, right? And also, to be near you." Thumbing a tear from my cheek, he added, "Mostly, to be near you."

I considered everything I'd learned from following Kennedy, everything Lucas had sworn he'd never ask of me. "But all that stuff you said about me not giving up what I want to be or what I want to do to be with you—doesn't that apply to you, too?"

He cupped my face in his palm and stared into my eyes, sighing. "First, this is a great job, and I'm excited about it." When he tugged me closer and kissed me, I leaned across his chest, one hand slipping under his T-shirt. I forgot that he hadn't finished his explanation until he whispered into my mouth, "Second, I'm ambitious, but I can succeed almost anywhere." Standing, he continued kissing me as he carried me into his room. When he let me slide from his arms to the floor, I yanked my tank top off, scooting into the center of the bed and watching him pull his T-shirt over his head. I could put him on replay doing that and watch it all day . . . if I didn't know what was coming next.

Crawling up from the foot of the bed, he lay over me slowly, dragging both of my arms above my head, gently, as he had the very first time he sketched me. With one hand, he crossed and secured my wrists. He'd taught me every possible way to escape this hold, but there was no way I wanted to get away. He was in a slow-motion mood—one of my favorites, though it meant I'd be driven crazy before we were done. I chewed the edge of my lip in anticipation.

He stared down at me, and I examined his beautiful eyes up close, something I knew I'd never tire of doing. "What I can't do anywhere is be with you." Leaning closer, he ran his tongue over my lips and his fingertips over my skin until I arched up and captured his mouth with mine.

He released my wrists, and I wrapped my arms around his neck, feeling our hearts beat in sync as lips followed a meandering path from my ear down. "Choosing to be with you isn't a difficult decision, Jacqueline," he breathed, pulling back one final time to stare into my eyes. "It's easy. Incredibly easy."

Sexual Assault Survivor Resources

YOU ARE NOT ALONE.

Over 17 million American women have been victims of attempted or completed rape. Experts estimate that only 16 percent of all rapes are ever reported to the police.

YOU DESERVE UNDERSTANDING AND HELP.

RAINN (Rape, Abuse and Incest National Network):
www.rainn.org

National Sexual Assault Hotline:
800-656-HOPE

SOAR (Speaking Out Against Rape):
www.soar99.org

NSVRC (National Sexual Violence Resource Center):
www.nsvrc.org

Rape Treatment Center:
www.911rape.org

Statistics from studies by the Department of Justice and the Centers for Disease Control and Prevention—see www.911rape.org/facts-quotes/statistics.

Acknowledgments

The world an author creates and the characters that inhabit it may come from her imagination alone, but few authors can wrestle the story that emerges into shape without help. My critique partners, Abbi Gline and Elizabeth Reyes, and my beta readers: Liz Reinhardt, Colleen Hoover, Robin Deeslie, and Ami Keller, have been invaluable in that regard, especially with this book. Thank you for your unique insights, your nitpicking where needed, and your cheering the face of my worries.

I couldn't have written *Easy* without the help of my husband, Paul. The creation of good fiction begins with raw, honest emotions—whether the author is penning a story about a mouse who wants dessert or a sprawling epic of Tsarist Russia. The subjects touched on in *Easy* come with an even deeper obligation to remain true to those emotions. Paul encouraged me constantly to fearlessly portray my love of hidden connections, and my belief that our close relationships with family, friends, and lovers—any and all of these, if we're lucky—are capable of healing the trauma all of us experience in our lives.

Thank you to Hillary Tayler Green for your insight into sororities, fraternities, and Greek life on the campus of a state university. I'm so proud to have watched you from the sidelines these past several years. Thank you to Hope Seggalink for the in-depth information on surviving college as a music education major and the hours of dedication involved. (Note: Any mistakes on either of these subjects are wholly mine.)

Thanks to my friends and family for their love and support, even when I seem to drop off the face of the earth for extended periods of time. Believe me, I notice you—hovering at the edges of my time, waiting for my free moments so you can persuade me to interact like a normal human being. I'm eternally grateful for your understanding of what makes me who I am.

Thank you Stephanie Mooney for beautifying the cover I dreamed up. It's perfect. Thank you Stephanie Lott for your editing skill . . . so sorry about that eye tic you developed on that one thing.

To my agent, Jane Dystel—you are one smart cookie, and I'm so glad to have you in my corner. Thank you for believing in me and in this book.

A special thanks to my new Penguin editor, Jennifer Bonnell. I haven't known you for long, but I love you already. I can hardly wait to get started on our next project.

To the girls of FP: I could have never imagined such a thing. You are all miracles, individually and together, and I'm in awe of each and every one of you. Thank you for your strength, love, acceptance, and empathetic ears. Write on.

To those who relate to any part of this story—if you haven't told, tell. Even if it's been months, years, decades. Tell someone. We remain silent because we've taken on a responsibility and/or a shame that was never ours to carry. Forgive yourself for things that were not your fault. Bad decisions, mistaken trust, physical weakness, or too much fear to act do not make an assault on you or someone you care about your fault. Ever.

If at all possible, please find a professional to help you sort it all out. Every college campus has counselors available for students—usually free of charge, and always confidential. Communities often offer free or low-cost counseling for the victims of assault and those who love them. Hotlines and online support, local and national, are available as well.

Discussion Questions

1. Discuss the circumstances surrounding Buck's attack. Would you have gone to the party if you were Jacqueline? How do you think her breakup with Kennedy affected her decision to go?

2. Despite making what could be considered a regrettable decision to follow Kennedy to college instead of pursuing her own artistic dreams, are there ways in which you think Jacqueline heading to Kennedy's college, as opposed to going to music school, helped her grow in ways she otherwise may not have?

3. Do you think that Lucas had other reasons beyond the nonfraternization rule for keeping his identity a secret from Jacqueline following her attack?

4. Why do you think Kennedy decides he wants Jacqueline back? Did he really miss her, or does the root of their problems go deeper?

5. Discuss the ways in which the self-defense classes Jacqueline takes help her to get over the attack. Did reading *Easy* make you want to learn self-defense?

6. Why do you think Jacqueline didn't want to report Buck's attacks? Do you think she felt personally targeted by Buck's attempted rape because they knew each other? In what ways do you think Buck's subsequent attack on another student pushes Jacqueline to take action in regards to his attack on her?

7. "Love is not the absence of logic, but logic examined and recalculated, heated and curved to fit inside the contours of the heart" (p. 215). Discuss the significance of Lucas's tattoo. In what ways do you think it comes to represent some of the overarching themes of love throughout the story?

8. How do you think Jacqueline's relationship with her parents, particularly her mother, changes by the end of *Easy*?

9. Discuss the ways in which the tragedy that befell Lucas's family affects him and his relationship with Jacqueline. In what ways do his personal troubles manifest themselves in his daily life? Do you think he helps women learn self-defense out of a sense of duty, a sense of shame, or both?

Ami Keller.

tammara webber

is the author of *New York Times* and Amazon bestseller *Easy* and novels in the Between the Lines series. Reading was one of her earliest loves, and writing soon followed. In high school she wrote sad romantic poetry and penned her first half-novel when she was nineteen (and accidentally destroyed it when she stuffed it into the shredder at work). Before becoming a full-time writer, she was an undergraduate academic advisor. She's a hopeful romantic who adores novels with happy endings, because there are enough unhappy endings in real life.

Tammara lives in Texas with her husband and too many cats.

Visit Tammara Webber online at
TammaraWebber.com
Facebook.com/TammaraWebberAuthor
Twitter: @tammarawebber